PRAISE FOR

D0372374

"I have said it before and I will say it again. The Pendomus Chronicles is one of the best trilogies of all time. The characters are all just as amazing as the world building. I truly hate to see it come to an end."

— NANCY ALLEN, THE AVID READER ★★★★★

"This was a really good trilogy, it has real characters that are believable and have great relationships with each other. It's easy to read and understand. It's full of commitment, love and hope for a better time."

— AMAZON REVIEWER ★★★★★

"I absolutely loved this whole set of books. They make you think. If you're looking for an easy read, be aware that this book in particular needs some concentration. I gave this book 5 stars because of the excellent writing, story content, and the flow of one book to another. I would recommend this book to anyone with an interest in this genre."

— AMAZON REVIEWER ★★★★★

"As in the previous ones the action and the intricacy of the story is superb."

— JOANN G ★★★★★

Original Copyright © 2017 Carissa Andrews

Published in 2017 by Carissa Andrews

Revised in 2018

Cover Design © Carissa Andrews

All rights reserved.

ISBN: 099105584-5

ISBN-13: 978-0991055845

DEDICATION

Life isn't about getting everything you want, it's about making the most with what you have.
The rest is just small revolutions.

I dedicate this book to all of us who fight the daily battles so one day, lives will change for the better.

ACKNOWLEDGMENTS

Pendomus was a world that solely existed in my head for years. With the love and support of a handful of cheerleaders, I was able to push forward and finish the aspects of Runa's story I knew I had to tell. Now, I want to give a shout-out to those who were amazingly supportive; helping me by reviewing the books, giving me feedback, and editing the series.

These stellar peeps include, but are not limited to:

Sherry Dumpprope
Colin Andrews
Kelly Casey
Kristen Maas
Twila Belton
Shauna Swanson
Jeremy Sundquist
Marra Roscoe
Evan Elg

REVOLUTIONS

THE PENDOMUS CHRONICLES: BOOK 3

CARISSA ANDREWS

IN TIMES OF GREAT STRIFE, OUR SUCCESS IS NOT IN STANDING
STILL . . .

BUT IN BEGINNING REVOLUTIONS.

1

RUNA

*A*FTER EVERYTHING WE'VE BEEN THROUGH, it all comes full circle.

I fought hard to escape the reality of the Helix; to become a different person on a different path than they wanted me to be. Who would have thought everything would prepare me for the eminent reality of breaking back into the Crematorium? Yet, here I am.

At least this time, it's under different circumstances—and with friends by my side.

"How are you handling this plan, Runa?" Trae asks, placing his hand on my shoulder. "I know it's a little crazy, but—"

I shake my head. This is exactly what we needed.

"I'm good. We don't have much time, if Kani is inside. We have to get to her before she's tortured, exterminated—or converted. Videus needs to be stopped. Putting an end to the Crematorium—or the Vassalage—whatever it is, is the best chance we have at hitting him where it hurts. He's done all he can to ensure no one even knows he exists. It's time to make sure it stays that way," I say.

The remainder of the plan goes unspoken, but neither of us are taking it for granted. We know what needs to be done and who has to do it.

With every passing day, it feels as though the memories outside myself are getting stronger. I'm not sure where they come from—Adrian, the bloodlines, the Four Pillars. All I know is my calling—*my purpose* is getting stronger. More persistent. It's almost as if I have no control over it any more. Honestly, I'm not sure I mind.

I take a seat on the edge of the large wooden table inside the Archives. We've been studying the digital paper schematics we were able to find of the Helix, trying to suss out the best way back in for hours now. The ones Landry had were far too old to provide the level of detail we needed.

"Ammon, do you think you'd be able to use your powers on metals? Or are you limited to stone?" I ask, turning to him.

Ammon raises his head from the table, groggy and disoriented.

"Huh? Did you say something?" he asks.

I realize this is a bit much for a young kid like him to handle—even someone as smart as Ammon.

"Can you manipulate metal the same way you manipulate rock?" I repeat.

Ammon's small shoulders shrug, "Dunno. Never really had a chance to try."

"Maybe it's something worth trying. It would certainly come in handy if you can," I say.

Trae nods, "And all that comes second to what Landry's working on. If we can get the EMP ready, we can shut everything down. It should at least buy us enough time to get inside before the system's repair can kick in."

Tapping the table beneath me, I nod and bite my lip.

"I wish there were better guarantees, but I know we're well beyond that. We don't have the time or the resources to launch anything bigger than a small surprise. I hope it's enough to get Kani back, at the very least," I say.

"Runa, I know you don't think Baxten's alive—but I think we should still try to look for him when we're in there," Trae says, rubbing his temple.

"Adrian told me he's too far gone. I have no reason to believe otherwise." I say, shaking my head. "Besides, we'll only have time for one search and rescue."

Accepting this truth has been a hard one, but necessary.

Trae nods, his mouth flattening into a thin line as he sits with my decision.

I know he doesn't understand, but I've tried saving Baxten—and nothing I've done has ever led me to his rescue. Even if he is alive, I have a feeling his timeline is tied and can't be meddled with. For some reason, I understand that now, even if I don't understand why.

"How long do we have before Delaney and her team are ready?" I ask.

Trae raises his eyebrows and leans back in his chair, "Hopefully soon. But getting everyone on the same page takes time. We might be better off getting into the swing of things and letting them catch up."

"That might be a good idea," I say.

I feel agitated, like I need to be in motion soon or my insides will make an escape for the outside.

"Guys, we've been going over all of this forever. Are we ever going to eat?" Ammon asks, eyeing the food pack.

"If you're hungry, help yourself, Ammon," I laugh, forgetting how uncomplicated things are for someone his age.

Ammon may be my twin, but he's lost years by being pulled from his timeline and brought ahead into mine. He's also extremely intelligent for his age, but he isn't able to grasp all the nuances Trae and I have to consider. In some ways, it reminds me of the way I was before I left the Helix. It's only been a few short months, but it feels like I've added years into my life experience.

Ammon digs in, happily engaged with finding his latest snack.

I turn back to Trae. His eyes are on the virtual map, but I can tell his mind is elsewhere. He's been this way since I came back. I can't quite put my finger on it, but something isn't quite right with him. He seems unhappy, discontented— disconnected. Perhaps he's grieving still. Losing Fenton was a blow to all of us, but I think it was harder on Trae than he allowed himself to feel.

Landry still suffers, too, but his grief is more outward. Easier to understand. Trae seems to have gone in deep, pretending as though nothing has changed. With Kani missing, and feared captured, I'm afraid it's thrown Trae into a tailspin.

Every time I try to bring it up, he quickly changes the subject. There's also the headaches. From what I understand, they began after I left. I don't know what the correlation is, perhaps stress, but he's not the same Trae I left behind.

The haunted warning of Trae from the future timeline isn't far from the forefront of my mind, though.

"Keep a close eye on me."

That's what he told me before we were whisked away from him and found ourselves inside a crystalline version of the Tree of Burden. His warning makes sense because the longer I'm around my Trae, the more I worry about him.

Future Trae also warned me not to trust anyone. Kani, and Landry, in specific. For obvious reasons, I haven't been able to assess Kani, but Landry seems no different than before. He's as helpful as ever, even though the loss of his

4

brother is still palpable in the bubble around him. He's been putting together an EMP device to help us shut down the Helix's computerized system so we can find our way to the Crematorium. With Fenton gone, I don't know how we'd ever find someone else with the ability to do something like this.

"Runa—"

I look up, realizing I was as much in my head as Trae has been lately. He watches me closely, concern mapped across his features. The worn expression ages him beyond his years and his brown eyes look so tired. Dark circles cut groves beneath his eyelids and I reach out, touching his cheek with the palm of my hand.

"Sorry, I'm here," I say.

His eyebrows pull in, but I don't remove my hand. Instead, I allow my thumb to caress the place where his dimple usually shines.

"Are you okay?" he asks.

I smirk, "Funny, I was going to ask you the same thing. You look like you need some sleep."

His eyes drop to the table, then flit back up to me.

"I—yeah, I haven't been able to rest much lately. I guess I don't understand why I didn't try harder to stop her. Or remember what the hell was happening during all of it."

"Kani's a big girl, Trae. You both made the decision to go to the Helix together. Whatever happened during the lost time isn't your fault. She's good at taking care of herself."

"Then why are we launching a mission to get her back?" he chuckles.

"Because she's our friend. And it just so happens that where she went and where we need to be going coincide," I shrug. "Have any more of the memories come back to you from that time?"

Trae shakes his head and stands up.

"They're so goddamn fragmented. Like someone took the pieces and smashed them like glass. I catch glimpses and then they're gone," he says. "I remember Kani and I entering the Helix. I remember walking through the long hallways, but that's it. I don't remember seeing anything. Getting caught by anyone. I don't even know why we woulda just walked in like that. Seems reckless."

"Could it have been a trap?" I ask.

"Maybe? I dunno. Nothing else makes sense, does it? Then again, with these damn headaches, nothing is jiving the way it should," he says, pacing the way he does when he gets agitated.

"It's okay, one step at a time," I say, raising a hand and dismissing the conversation. The last thing I need is for his stress levels to rise and the headache to come on full strength. The last one put him out for days and as much as I hate to admit it, we don't have time for that now.

"Guys, seriously… This has been going on for *hours*. Can I do something different yet?" Ammon asks, his face full of crumbs.

"Any chance you can practice your mojo on some metal stuff?" Trae offers, pointing down the hall of the Archives. "But practice down there—away from anything important, okay?"

Ammon makes a face and catches my eye, "Do I have to?"

I bite my lip. Truthfully, I don't think practicing is wise in here. There's so much history and I'd hate for any of it to be broken.

"Why not try small?" I suggest. "Find an old knife or fork and see if you can bend those the way you can move the stones. If you can, then we at least have something more to go on. If you can't, well, it seems pretty unlikely then, right? I think I saw some down the hallway, a few meters that way." I point in the direction.

Ammon shrugs, wrinkles his nose at Trae as if he smells bad, and walks off in the direction I pointed.

"Cute kid," Trae says. "Are you sure you're related?"

I suppress a chuckle. In some weird ways, Ammon reminds me a lot of myself when I was his age. It would have been so amazing to have grown up together the way twins normally would.

I can totally see the resemblance, even if Trae can't. Granted, he never knew me as a child.

"Pretty sure," I say instead.

Trae shakes his head and flicks his eyebrows. Taking a deep breath, he crooks his neck—a sure sign his headache is attempting to return.

"Do you need anything?" I offer.

His eyes widen, and his body stiffens slightly. He hates that I notice when something's wrong.

"No, erm—I'm good. Thanks, though," he says, running a hand long his neck.

"You don't have to do that, you know," I say.

"Do what?"

"Pretend it doesn't bother you. Pretend that you're okay. Whichever. We'll figure out what's going on with your headaches, but in the meantime—you can trust me, Trae. I only want you to be okay."

His face hardens, and his irises go darker than normal. It's like he's not even the same person sometimes.

"You worry about your part of the plan, and let me worry about what's going on with me. Okay?" he says. The words come out harsh, a jagged edge taunting my pulse to pick up speed.

Before reacting—as I normally would have—I hold my breath and wait. I watch his movements. I listen to his breath. Then, something strange begins to happen.

A high pitched mechanical noise enters my perception—

almost like the sound of interference on a radio. For a moment, I hold completely still, trying to put a place on where it's coming from. The sound squeals, fluctuating in and out.

"What in the hell are you doing?" Trae asks, not even trying to hide his flare up of irritation.

"Shhhh—" I say, raising a finger and continuing to listen.

Just when I think I have a grasp on what it is, like water through a sieve, it slips away. As I try to hold onto it, Trae takes a step back, surveying our surroundings in an odd way. His eyes are wide, calculating. He doesn't say anything at all, but for a brief moment he looks disoriented.

"Guys—guys," Ammon shouts, bounding towards us. "I did it. I can't believe it, but I did it."

He comes to a halt between the two of us, a fork—or what's left of it, held high, the tip of it bent backward and kissing the back of his hand.

Trae's eyes narrow, his lips pressed tight.

Hopping off the table and grabbing Ammon by the elbow, I say, "That's amazing Ammon. Come, you'll have to tell me more about it. Trae, you'll stay here and do some more digging right?"

I watch his movements, his mannerisms. His eyes kiss the top of the table, but content in surveying the room, Then he nods without saying a word.

Tugging Ammon along, we walk for a distance before he pulls his arm back.

"Runa, what's—"

"It's—something's not right with Trae," I confide. "I don't know what it is, but he's not…he's not in his right mind."

"Well, he's been through a lot since you left. I know it's only been a few weeks for him, or whatever, but he's lost his best friend, then your other friend, whatsername. Couldn't that be kinda normal for him now?" Ammon asks, a fair reasoning coming from this ten year old.

"Yeah, you could be right," I nod. He's been through so much and maybe I'm just reading more into it than necessary.

I bite my lip, unable to shake this gnawing sensation in the pit of my stomach.

Ammon watches me the way I watched Trae. I feel the weight of his stare, but focus on my intuition until I come to a resolve.

"No," I say, shaking my head, "that's not it. I know it should be. I know that makes a certain amount of sense, but it doesn't feel right. If there's one thing I've learned, it's to trust myself when I feel something is off."

Ammon stands on his tip toes and leans to look over my shoulder.

"You know, I think you should go with your gut," he says.

I turn around, following his gaze to where Traeton is. Instead of continuing any kind of research in the books we'd been looking at, Trae stands beside the table with a shovel in his hand. Taking a long swing, he starts whacking the floor. The first reverberation clatters loudly, echoing against all the walls and ceiling.

"What is he doing?" I mutter.

"Digging, by the looks of it," Ammon says.

"We need to figure out what the hell is going on with him," I mutter, my head racing. "Whatever you do, don't confide in him. In fact, don't trust anyone. It's not wise to involve Trae with the rest. I think we'll handle this mission together—you and I. Okay?"

Ammon nods, "Fine by me. Can't say I overly liked the guy from the get-go anyway. Remember the way he was in the future? Dodgey."

Trae was a little strange, I'll give him that. Very hermit-like. But he was nothing like this.

"Give me a minute. I'll find a way to distract him so we can make our way to the Helix alone. I don't think any more digging, research, or preparation is going to help us anymore. The plan hinges on us anyway. What we have—I hope—is the element of surprise. I'd like to keep it that way."

"Do you really think you'll be able to keep him distracted?" Ammon asks.

"I don't know, but I have to try. Right?" I say. "Great work on the fork, by the way. That's awesome. Now, if only we can get you working on bigger things, we'll be in good shape and won't have to resort to Plan B."

"Yeah, I was surprised it didn't take that long. Took a few tries to concentrate on it, though. Manipulating the metal was different from moving rock,"

"How so?" I ask, starting to walk back toward Trae.

"Moving stone feels like a piece of me travels to the stone —or maybe through it—to make it shift. With the metal, it was like being outside myself, pushing on it from the outside with an invisible hand or something," he says, his eyes distant as he tries to put the experience into words.

"Interesting. Well, keep working on it. When it's time to go, I'll signal you. Keep an eye out, okay?"

"Oh man, is this going to be another one of your covert escapes? Remember last time we had to leave here?" Ammon says, rolling his eyes.

"I remember. And I don't know yet how it will play out. Just cut me some slack, would you?" I say, eyeing Trae again. "I'm doing the best I can."

Ammon flicks his hand, telling me to go and I turn back the way we came. I keep my eyes trained on Traeton, witnessing the efforts he puts in, trying to dig a hole in the floor. This isn't the first time something has completely short circuited in Trae's mind. I wish I knew who to ask, who I could trust. With Fenton gone—it feels like no one is truly safe any more.

No, these mental lapses of Trae's are something I definitely need to figure out on my own.

2

TRAETON

I HAVE NO IDEA WHY I am meant to be digging here. It is such a menial task. Could not the young offspring be doing this? My host's brain is the texture of dried paint, and pieces are beginning to flake away. I am meant to blend in. Keep the status quo. Field the intel. I am unsure how much longer I will be able to fully garnish the cooperation my master seeks.

"Thanks, Trae. You can stop digging now," Runa says, a curious smile caressing her face.

Somewhere deep inside me, I feel a strange stirring. It is as though I want to touch her. Or perhaps, be touched by her. A part of me is unsurprised, the other is oddly aroused by the desire. It is disconcerting, and I am unsure what to do with the sensation.

For a moment, we gaze at one another, each being unwilling to be the first to look away. Then she steps closer, taking one of my hands in hers. Radiant energy pulses between us at the place where her skin touches my host's. It is a strange sensation, yet also oddly welcomed.

A loud, gnawing rip tears at my consciousness, as pieces

of my own awareness shift aside for the host. I can't control it, I know that now. He will eventually push me out yet again. He is strong, this boy. But there is nothing either of us can do about the situation. We are bound now.

The energy from the Daughter of Five builds from the palm of my newly acquired hand and travels up my arm, into my shoulder, then neck. Eventually, it rises like a viscous, warm liquid pooling at the base of my host's spine where his neck and head connect.

The disorienting disconnect subsides, and the rough texture shifts to one of moldable clay.

I rest for a moment.

Closing my eyes, I cling to the things making sense in my brain. The touch of her hand. The way her energy feels. The way it makes me feel.

"Trae, you seem so tired," Runa says. "I think maybe you need to rest. Like Ammon said earlier, we've been at this for hours. I know things haven't been easy for you, especially with Kani missing. Why don't you take some time to get some sleep? We could all get some rest, then head out afterward."

Sleep does sound like a welcome change of pace. But there is something I should be doing—or paying attention to. I just cannot remember what.

Glancing around the room, I do not even know where we are. Or where I would find rest. Should I be this confused?

My gaze rests on the beautiful face of the girl in front of me. Her multicolored eyes and scarred cheek are mesmerizing, though I cannot place why. I could get lost in their depths, though. Her eyebrows pull in, but her face is open.

Runa, that is her name. *Runa.*

How could I forget?

"Come on, I'll lie down with you," Runa says, smiling softly.

Taking a firm grip on my hand, she leads me away from the tables of maps, away from the shelves full of artifacts and books, and down a narrow hallway ending in a small, circular room. Inside is only one bed large enough for the two of us if we huddle close.

Releasing my hand, she takes a seat and kicks off her boots. She scoots to the side of the bed and pats the space beside her. Everything inside me is screaming to lie down with her—except for the one irritating sensation twisting and writhing around in my temple.

"I do not know if—" I hear myself begin.

"You don't need to know anything or worry about it, either. This is where we're both meant to be. You know it, and I know it. After everything that's happened and the way we were separated, I don't ever want to be apart. If I have the opportunity to be close to you, I'll take every chance I'm given. I hope you feel the same," she says, her eyes drawing me to her.

Relinquishing all of my worries, I lie down beside her. As our bodies touch, the energy radiates like a wave rolling across my entire being—wrapping me in a warmth of security and peace. I cannot explain it any other way. She takes one hand, running her fingers through my hair and electrifying the nerve endings in my scalp.

I relax into the overwhelmingly peaceful sensations, and close my eyes. Even if I was not tired, it would be difficult not to fall asleep under these circumstances.

It reminds me of when she held me in the palm of her hands...

EVERYTHING *in this place is a goddamn maze. Shouldn't I be the one in control of my own damn mind? Why in the hell does it feel like I've lost the reigns completely and someone—or something else has taken command?*

My surroundings are a mixture of grey slab stones, and large steel bars. Or is this just a conjuring in my mind? I'm having trouble determining fact from fiction lately.

Whatever, I'll roll with it. What else is there to do?

The way out is blocked. A door with an interesting mixture of metal and electricity keeps me detained here. I've tried to break through a hundred times before—with no such luck. At least, not until whatever holds me captive gives itself up, or is needed else-where. I'm not sure if I'm meant to know, or hear them speaking, but I've caught snippets from time to time. It's the most bizarre sensation to be hearing conversations when no one else is around.

Is this what it was like for my sister Ava?

Once I was able to regain control—only for a moment or two before I was pushed back into this room. But it was something. Kinda gives me hope that I'm not completely done for. At least, not yet.

The last thing I overheard was the command from whoever's controlling the creep who's taken over my mind. It's strange—like my brain has been hacked and has a brand new, albeit temporary, resident. But that resident isn't even the one in control. It's someone else; someone more powerful. Even in this disjointed state, I'd know who it is anywhere. Who else could it be?

Of course, it's Videus.

He's up to plans and schemes. Behind closed doors and familiar faces. He's far more insidious than we even gave him credit for. I thought he was just some jerk who had a god complex. Now, I know he does.

I'm almost certain he doesn't realize I'm still here, though—that I've been catching glimpses into their plans. And that gives me hope that I can carry it with me and maybe reverse this situation. I hope I can. No goddamn way I'm staying trapped like this forever. I'd go outta my mind.

I'd snicker, if I had a body.

I'm already outta my goddamn mind.

It's strange, here in this place everything is fresh—seared into my memory and consciousness. I know what's happening and I know who's responsible. I understand my lack of control and that I need to find a way to get it back. But outside—once I'm released, I know I'll forget. Happens every time.

It's like a strange haze takes hold of me and as much as I try, I'm unable to hold onto the threads of this place. At first, I figured it was just a dream. But I know better now.

With everything that's happening to me—with what's happened to Kani—I know time is of the essence. My one problem is staying clear enough when I'm back in my body to either warn Runa, or find a cure for myself. So far, every attempt has been completely unsuccessful. It's excruciating.

One of these times, though, I know I'll be able to break through the barrier. I'll be able to uncover more—or get the help I need. Perhaps even now, Runa's looking for a cure. She's not stupid. She has to know something isn't right with me.

I take a breath, trying to uncover conversations elsewhere in the real world. Where my body is. Am I still with her? She wouldn't leave me, right?

Sucks that this joker is with Runa and I'm stuck in here. Sick joke, actually. It's been so long and all I want in this sick, sad, stupid world is to touch her. To hear her voice and stare into those amazing eyes.

But it's no use. I try for ages, but can't connect to the audio of my own life. My intruder has too strong of a hold right now. However, I catch glimpses of his actions. Digging for something. Why the hell is he digging in the Archives?

Then it happens—I slip into my body, right beside the intruder. It's a strange sensation. I can see and hear everything as myself, but I have no control whatsoever. I'm a casual observer of my body and its surroundings.

Runa is there—taking my hand and bringing me to a place alone.

"Runa—Runa, you have to hear me. I'm trapped—" I scream inside my prison, trying to do my best to break the bubble holding me captive.

My body lies down with her and I can feel the sick pleasure of my intruder radiate through my body.

He's happy to be with her like this. Happy to be beside her and have her warmth radiate through him.

It's sickening and the intense desire to rip him limb to limb emerges. I swear it—if he hurts her, I will come for him. Even if it means ending myself to do it.

She places her hand on my head, stroking my hair and the lines between the intruder and myself begin to blur. Warmth circulates from where she touches, and for the first time in forever, I feel something real. I have no description for it beyond magical. The bonds keeping me captive begin to break down, little by little, and I sense him struggling to hold on to my body. For whatever reason, her touch—or his happiness—maybe both, is causing him to lose his connection with me.

I take every advantage I can to push him out with my mind—trying to consume as much space again as possible.

Suddenly, the irritating disturbance in my mind I've caught glimpses of—almost like the eLink connecting, clicks into place.

~It's no use Traeton. It's taken me a while in this incarnation to find you. But I know what you are to the Daughter of Five. I know everything. You're going to be the reason Runa fails. You'll be her downfall and she'll never see it coming. Stop fighting it. There's no way you can break these chains, they've been prepared especially for you.

I AWAKEN to the faint hum of the lighting system inside the

place they call the Archives. I have never realized how loud electricity can be until now. How do they not hear it?

My host's mind is fuzzy again, and trying to gain clarity is difficult. I have never been here for this process with a human. Rest comes much differently for me when I am in my own body.

Rolling over, I find the bed empty—

The Daughter of Five has left the man she is endeared to. This is unexpected.

And not good. My master will not be pleased.

Swinging this body to a seated position, I blink away the disorientation. Everything in this human body is groggy, still tired. How do humans handle this? No wonder my master chose to eliminate sleep. It is cumbersome and odd.

My mouth—*his mouth*—why do I do that? I am not him. And this body is not mine.

His mouth is dry, like all the moisture has been sucked from inside. I must find some water. Then, I must find the others.

~*Where did you go, dear friend? I've been trying to reach you.*

Is this what awoke me? My master, calling?

~*I was told I needed sleep. I complied as to not draw attention to myself.*

My response sounds reasonable to me, but I know better of my master. He will want me to return.

~*We have the girl. Your job has ended. It's time for you to return. I need you here.*

~*As you wish.*

As my master leaves our connection, there is an emptiness left behind in my host's mind. Perhaps it is beginning to lose its integrity after all of the meddling we have done.

I almost feel sorry for him. This was not his fight, nor his struggle. It was not for any of us, I suppose. But this degradation—he is simply an unfortunate casualty.

I know my master will want me to return instantly, but my heart is inexplicably heavy about this news. As much as I know of my master's plan, there is a small part of me that wants to cheer for the Daughter of Five. If she is truly the girl of the prophecy, we could all be freed. No more cages, captures, mind games, or control. Free to live our lives as we had for eons before humans. Before my master.

I do so miss the grass, the trees in full bloom. The sweet smell of the Everblossoms.

Walking out into the main part of the Archives where the humans have spent the majority of their time, I take a final look around. I cannot place why—but this location has a familiarity to it, though I do not believe I have ever been here before. Perhaps it is simply residual feelings in here from my host's memories. It is hard to say.

A feeling of sadness arises in me—perhaps in us both. The man's mind has bled through a couple of times as I tried to restrain him. If he is able to understand the situation, I am sure he will not be happy. I rest my eyes on the long hallway and the ornate arches in the ceiling.

So very familiar—

Then it becomes all too obvious.

Instantly, I regret having stayed because what I see could get us all killed.

It has been so long since I have pushed my mind to the time before humans. I should never have pushed my thoughts back that far.

This place—the Archives—I thought it was simply an underground hideaway the humans had built to house these histories. But it is not. It is far older, with a very special purpose.

Deep conflict arises within my being—not my host's—mine. Clenching hold of my better senses, I struggle with what to do next. I wish I had the others to discuss this with, but to do that would put everyone at risk. It would be treason.

Perhaps the prophecy was right—perhaps the girl really is the Chosen. If this should be true, I cannot allow my master to learn of this place.

What I am saying is anarchy and I will likely pay with my life.

Turning to the only one I can, I open the floodgates on the man named Traeton. We will need to devise a plan together.

The wall between us drops like a curtain and anger rushes at me like a desperate wind. My consciousness is pushed to the back as the man regains control.

He drops to his knees, groping at his head.

"Stay out," he cries.

I try to hold on, try to keep control of some pieces of this information so I can relay what is so necessary, but he's much stronger this way. Stronger than I anticipated.

I'VE NEVER HAD my brain split apart in fragments, but I'm pretty damn sure it would be like this. The headaches I've had before are nothing compared to this.

The lights—they're so bright and so loud. How can the lights be so damn loud?

I shield my eyes, dropping to my knees to keep from being sick. Everything is overwhelming and disorienting. I'm not sure why. It's like I'm seeing things with two different sets of eyes and neither one are in focus.

I didn't think I'd ever be back where I belong. Back in my own mind, my own body. It's been so long since it was just me in here.

What caused my intruder to release me?

Like a tickle in my brain, I realize he hasn't. Not fully—he's still here with me.

Dammit.

"Phug you. You hear me. You're not going to spy on Runa and the others through me. You're not using me anymore. I'm done with being your damn slave—" I spit, looking for something—anything I can use to put an end to this.

I have control now, and only one choice. If he's still here, there's only one reason for it. Which is nothing good.

I hunt for Jayne—my sonic resonator—or any other way to end my own life. If I have control now, I need to act. I need to remove any more harm that can come to Runa through me.

Suddenly, my feet are solid weights, making it impossible to move forward. Slowly, the thoughts from my captor creep in, but they're nowhere near as strong as they were. I understand only pieces of what the intruder is trying to relay.

Protect. Daughter of Five.

I don't know why, but he feels scared shitless.

What in the hell would cause Videus' crony to be afraid? Doesn't that run in opposition to the rules they're used to enforcing?

My anger and bloodlust dissipate as curiosity takes its place.

On same side. Please.

The thought is clear, but does nothing to quell the skepticism coursing through every vein in my body.

"Same side? Oh, now we're on the same damn side? Give me a break. It's been months—months, dammit. You've wiggled your way into control, spying on Runa, gathering intel and sending it back to Videus. Why in the hell would I believe you now?" I spit. "Just because you're now the one who's scared? What did you do? Forget to call in?"

Silence.

"Come on, what happened chatty? Where are you now? What are you really up to? Talk to me—" I yell.

Suddenly, I look around the Archives and chuckle.

I really have lost my ever-loving mind.

Still, nothing. It's like whatever power he had over me has completely diminished, but he's still here for fun.

"Screw you," I sputter.

Until I can find a way to get this thing out of my head completely, I need to at least warn Runa and the rest of the team. I know she's planning to hit the Vassalage, and she needs to be aware I'm compromised.

"Runa—" I call out, "Where are you?"

Only silence greets me.

It's everywhere.

I walk over to the table flooded with maps. Beside a stack of books is a note.

Traeton,

Ammon and I have gone to take care of Videus. I'm sorry we left you behind, but it's best if you stay here. I don't know what's going on with you, but I feel as though you need to rest.

Trae, if the worst happens—if I get captured, and you are able —warn the others. We need to move on to phase II of the plan. We can't let Videus win.

We cannot let desperation and despair sweep us up and swallow us whole. We need to stand together and fight this until our dying breath. I know I will.

I wish we had more time. We never got the moments I'd hope to have with you, or the future I could envision. But I want you to know this—it's only you. You're the one I wanted to see forever with.

Stay safe,
Runa

DAMMIT.

Anxiety rips at my insides. She already knew I wasn't myself.

Her note is cryptic, but I have no doubt she'd never go unless she felt it was absolutely necessary to leave me behind.

One thing bothers me, though...it reads like a suicide letter. Like she doesn't think she's gonna be coming back, but I'll be dammed if I'm gonna let that happen. I throw the note down, slamming my hand into the stack of books. They clatter to the floor, spilling out their pages. Kicking them for good measure, I stop.

One of the books doesn't look familiar. It's locked front face is beautiful. Bound in some form of leather, with a large tree burned to the front of it. Etched within the side of the trunk is a large door, reminding me of the Tree of Burden Runa had gone into.

Interesting

I pick the books up and place them back on the table.

What's my next plan of action? What can I do with the least amount of casualties?

Then it comes to me. I know exactly what I need to do.

3

RUNA

*E*VEN THOUGH WE'VE ONLY just met a few weeks ago, I feel as though I've known Ammon my whole life. His blood runs through my veins, and mine through his. We're connected in a way no one else can truly claim. At this point, not even my brother Baxten—and definitely not my mother. Perhaps it's the similarities in our abilities. Or because we're twins. Maybe both. Whatever it is, I'm thankful I have him by my side.

Especially with Trae being compromised.

We've been apart for so long, and now, even though we're near each other—we're still in separate worlds. How did everything get so messed up?

"Are we going to get that EMP thing from Landry?" Ammon asks, ripping me from my internal anguish.

"No, there isn't time. If we're going to act, we need to act fast," I say, adjusting my pack.

"Alright, I hope you know what you're doing," he says, grabbing his supplies and following after me.

When we reach the end of the tunnel and ascend the ladder leading outside, Tethys is ready and waiting.

Ammon still hasn't gotten used to her without the ability to see her, but there's no other creature on the planet I trust more. Having both of them by my side fuels me with the energy I need to accomplish this dangerous mission.

Best case scenario, I'm able to gather information on the Vassalage and find a way to destroy it. Worst case...well, let's hope it doesn't come to that.

Grasping onto Tethys' fur, I pull myself to her back and reach for Ammon. He takes my hand and before I know it, the trees are a blur as we make our way to the Helix. My insides twist like serpents of excitement. It's all so irrational —heading there this way. No backup. No real plan. Yet, irrationally, I know it's how it needs to be.

"So, erm. What's your plan for getting in this thing?" Ammon asks, reading my mind.

I shake my head, "I'm not sure. I'm kinda hoping the pathway will reveal itself as we get closer."

Tethys snorts, clearly not as certain about my plan as I am.

I look over my shoulder as the trees become a blurred memory in the distance. The Helix rises before us, a monstrous structure full of ominous double meanings. When I lived inside, I had no idea how much I'd truly come to despise this place.

"Whoa," Ammon mutters. "I've never been this close. I— I've heard other kids talk about it, but...being here is kinda —whoa."

I nod, sympathizing with his shift in perspective as he sees the Helix for the first time. I'm sure, in a reverse kind of way, it was the same for me when I'd seen the Lateral for the first time. It's a whole different world hidden inside the one you're used to.

Tethys brings us as close as she dares, instinctively

veering toward the doorway she'd been waiting at when Trae and I had gone in before.

"How will we know which hallway we're in and where to go? Do you remember the layout of this place?" Ammon asks, his nerves suddenly getting the better of him.

"I remember this place like the back of my hand. I also have something Videus will wish I didn't—the visual schematics for how to get to the Crematorium, the passcode, and who's in charge," I say, finally putting to words what I had been holding onto.

"What?" Ammon says, his mouth dropping open. "How do you know all that? I thought the mainframe was destroyed? And why are you waiting to tell me this now?"

I bite my lip, unsure how much I should burden Ammon with.

"I kept it to myself because of what's happening with Trae. Future Trae warned us—"

"Warned you, ya mean," Ammon corrects.

"Warned me, then. I have to heed that warning," I say.

"So, how did you acquire all the information?" Ammon says, scratching his head.

Tethys comes to a halt, and I drop off her back. Ammon follows suit and his feet hit the floor. We remain safe and unseen inside her shield, and I walk around to face him.

"When I was still a part of the Helix, they offered me a professional appointment as a Cremator," I say, aware of the irony in it all.

"Wow. So, what—what the heck does that mean? They wanted you to what? Work there?"

I shake my head, "No—they were trying to dispose of me. But because they had to make me believe this was where I was meant to be, they had to follow protocol. I was automatically given all of the details when I was appointed."

"So, you've had all these details? Why the heck were we looking at the maps for *hours*?"

"Because I wanted to be sure. I can't trust everything I've gotten from the Helix. What if it was wrong? I needed to verify their authenticity. Well, if I could."

"So, they just handed you everything? Huh. Kinda dumb on their part," Ammon says. "What happened after you were told to be a Cremator, then? Wasn't that supposed to be, like a good thing? I remember a friend saying professional appointments are a big deal in here."

"They are," I shrug. "But I never went in. I couldn't believe Cremator was the role they'd assessed for me. I just—I wasn't about to do that for the rest of my life. So I left the Helix."

"Wow," he says, his mouth popping open. "I can't even stand up to my best friend, let alone walk away from something like that."

"It's not as dramatic as you make it sound. I just knew I wasn't meant to be there. Well, until now. We just need to hope things haven't changed. Otherwise, that's where my plan will fail us," I say, trying to smile as reassurance, knowing it's failing miserably.

Ammon's eyes widen.

"Don't worry," I say, "I'll keep you safe. I wouldn't have brought you if I didn't think we could protect ourselves. Unfortunately, I think we'll need your abilities at some point."

Ammon straightens his shoulders, "I know. This is just a lot to take in, ya know?"

"I do," I say, placing a hand on his shoulder. "But we got this."

I smile at him, and turn to Tethys. Her energy is peaceful, and calm. At least on some level, she agrees with what I'm doing. That gives me a boost of encouragement, because I know what I'm about to do won't be popular with anyone else. Delaney and the team won't be pleased. Landry will think it was completely reckless. When Trae finds out, he'll come looking for us—

Running my hands along the side of Tethys' neck, and to her shoulder, she leans into me. She's been through so much as well and she seeks a time of peace. For so long, Pendomus has been in complete disarray. The Four Pillars—AirGliders, TerraDwellers, Salamanders—and even my beautiful Water-bear—the last of her kind. None of them ever wanted any of this.

I may never understand Videus' motives, but I do know it's time to set things right.

"Come on," I say, taking Ammon's hand.

Tethys snorts, but releases her shield, leaving us exposed to the elements and in full view of the Helix. Moving quickly, we make it to the obscured doorway as it blends into the building.

Ammon puts his hand out in front of him, and gently pulls it back toward his body. The door unlatches of it's own accord and swings open from the wrong side.

"Whoops," he says, smiling sheepishly. "Still getting used to metals. Mechanisms are hard."

"We could have just opened the door. They aren't locked," I laugh.

"Oh," Ammon's face falters. "How was I meant to know that?"

"It's okay," I laugh, messing up his hair. "Just wait for my signal next time. You're in my territory now."

The sterile fumes of the hallway assault my senses—and for the first time, it reminds me of the stench of death and decay.

"Ugh," Ammon says, holding his nose. "Do you smell that?"

I nod.

"Why does it smell like rotten meat?" he asks, keeping his hand in place.

"I'd never noticed that before—but you're right."

My eyes search the quiet corridor as we enter slowly. The backlighting flickers softly, almost imperceptibly. Everything is silent, too quiet. If I wasn't aware of the time of day, I'd almost be worried they knew we were here. But this is top production time and everyone has to be *productive*.

The weirdest part of this trip is the lack of new information coming at me. Before I went into the Tree of Burden, my eLink connection would have been triggered walking into the Helix. But the passage into the portal destroyed its relay. In a strange sort of way, I feel like a ghost—able to walk these halls without a constant barrage of information streaming my way.

Luckily, I'm still able to access any of the downloads I'd been privy to before I left because they're stored in memory.

I walk quickly, with purpose, knowing Ammon is right behind me. I keep my mouth shut, but direct him instead with a hand gesture as we turn down a side corridor to the right. The long tunnels seem to go on forever and for someone who's never been inside, it would be so easy to get lost. They all look the same.

Meters away from the doorway leading to the lower level, the influx from a checkpoint flickers like waves across the entrance. In the past, I could roam these hallways fairly unabashed, thanks to the eLink in my brain. Whenever you get within a couple meters, it would log you in and allow you to pass. Shutting down all the security features and disabling the shield. But now—

Ammon must notice my hesitation, because he grabs hold of my hand and squeezes. As I turn to him, his eyebrows are knit together in worry.

I bend in, whispering, "This is a checkpoint. If we go

through without at least one of us actively connecting to the eLink, the forcefield will slice us into plaid chunks. The doorway we need to take is on the other side."

"Of course it is," he exhales. "Please tell me you have a plan."

"Of course I do," I breathe. It's a lie, kind of.

I know we have to act quickly, before any of the heat sensors or cameras trigger a warning of us. Seconds maybe.

"Why don't you use your Daughter of Five mental connection thingy to distract the system?" Ammon suggests.

I shake my head, "I don't think that's how it works. I've only ever connected to living things."

"Well, how do you know unless you try? Isn't that what you said to me about the metal bending?"

My eyebrows flick upward. He's right, I did say that.

"Let's give it a go," I say, nodding.

Ammon turns toward the checkpoint, his eyes wide and watchful.

I close my eyes, trying to envision the inner workings of the checkpoint. The electrical connections, the lines of communication that bring its signals to the main hub in security. Oddly enough, the sensations take hold and instinct takes over. Manipulating the electrical currents and information from the Helix's mainframe system isn't all that unlike digging around inside a mind.

The currents of it feel alive, as alive as any brain or creature I've connected with so far. Suddenly, the data breaks off, separating into strings of code. Though I've never looked at code in my life, I know I can mold it—shape the information to read what I want it to. See what I want it to see. And it's not just this checkpoint, either. They're all connected.

For a split second, I push the details I need into the code. Asking it to flip into routine maintenance, pulling down the shield, pausing the live feed cameras and sensors, and allowing us to pass unnoticed.

I hear a soft mechanical sound hum and come to a stop as the shield across the hallway dissipates.

Turning to Ammon, I grab his hand and without a word, we make for the doorway across the checkpoint. I don't know how long it will hold—seconds, minutes...but whatever it is, I know we need to cross before it flips back.

I hold my breath as we cross the threshold, half expecting something to give us away. When it doesn't, I race with Ammon to the Crematorium's stairwell door. It's unmarked, and barely noticeable if one wasn't aware of its existence. There's no label. No sign saying Crematorium. There's not even a handle.

Instead, there are small markings etched on the right hand side. I'm suddenly aware of how similar the etchings and unlocking mechanism are to the chains that shackled Ammon to the cavern.

I place my hand on the markings and push once on the bottom, once on the top, then twice in the middle. Before our eyes, the door dissolves and the stairway unfurls before us. It's an oddly ornate spiral staircase, leading straight down, rather than the typical forward descent. The lighting changes from the sterile, cool backlit light of the Helix hallways to a more warm, natural golden light. Under other circumstances, I would have loved it. But here, inside the Helix and where we're heading—it's ominous.

On the walls are strange etchings and framed body parts, with temperatures marked along side them.

"What's with all the creeptastic decorations?" Ammon asks, mirroring my sentiment.

"Pretty sure they're meant as a subtle reminder about how long it takes everything to burn," I say, taking a tentative step into the stairwell.

"Yeck," Ammon mutters, sticking out his tongue.

Behind us, the doorway seals itself with a soundless shift. Amber darkness falls upon us and turns my stomach as the cool light is extinguished.

We walk slowly, refusing to touch anything unnecessary, including the railings. The lights begin to switch from warm electrical to full-on wall torches. I can't tell if they're holograms meant to look that way—or if they really are fire. Either way, it doesn't bode well.

The descent takes us a couple of levels down—to an open landing. It's not very big—ten meters by ten meters, maybe.

The walls are thankfully blank, but remind me of the place we entered when we found the blood ice sculptures. I glance over at Ammon.

"I have a bad feeling about this," he says.

I nod, walking into the landing and trying to assess what to do next. There are three walls and the stairway where we came. It appears to be a dead end, but I know better. This is the way. But for some reason, there's more security protocols happening. Perhaps since I left. Maybe it's always been this way. I don't know.

I squint, trying to access the part of my memory that dealt with the direction of the Crematorium. Closing my eyes, I start on the left-hand side. I reach out with my left hand, running it along the blank walls as I walk in slow, deliberate steps.

"Runa, what are you doing? Shouldn't we be looking for a way outta here, not wiping your fingerprints all over the place?" Ammon says, getting nervous.

"Ammon, I need you to use your abilities. Sense which one of these walls is a holographic mirage."

"How do you mean?" he asks, stepping into the landing and walking forward.

"In order to move the rocks, you have to sense them,

right? Dig deep into their makeup? Well, one of these walls isn't real. We need to figure out which one so we can understand how to go through it," I say.

Ammon shakes his head, blowing out a puff of air.

"Well, I've never had to do something like this before, but I'll try."

"That's all I'm asking," I say, continuing to feel the stones with my hand as I walk along the walls.

I try to sense with my hands which is the fake one, but they all feel the same to me. Solid.

Ammon closes his eyes. For a moment, his expression going completely blank—almost peaceful. Then he tips his head to the side.

"Strange," he says.

"What is?" I ask, walking to him.

"All of them are fake."

"How do you know?" I ask, taking in the space around us.

He shakes his head, "None of them feel real. Like you said, when I go to move them, it's like I'm a part of the rocks. Like they're an extension of my hand or something. These, though —they feel like air. Tuffs of nothingness in the middle of long arms extending outward. Except that one."

He points to the wall directly in front of the stairway, "That one feels like it's close."

"I don't think I follow you. Long arms? Close? Shouldn't they all be close?" I ask.

"No, no. The two on the side feel like they're different. Unworldly. Long arms or tunnels reaching out in opposite directions. Like they burrow through the planet as far as I've ever reached out to, anyway. I can't tell you where they lead. But the one in front. That's the one connected to this place," he says, opening his eyes.

"Okay, well, we'll have to figure the 'arms' out later, if we can. For now, we need to stay focused on why we came here,"

I say stepping forward toward the wall Ammon believes is connected to the Helix.

Everything about it is the same. It looks like it's a solid wall made of concrete, or stone. To the touch, there's nothing that stands out. Nothing that makes me believe we should be able to go through it.

"What if we try to walk through it? Remember that wall in the Archives? You were able to go through that," Ammon suggests.

I shake my head, "That was different. It was a part of the trial. Besides, do you remember how you weren't allowed through? This feels solid to me. There, the wall didn't. I could tell I could go through it."

"Bummer. Well, I got nothin'. I can't move it aside because it's not there," he says, scratching his scalp. The dark hair is growing out to the point where his blonde roots are making more of an appearance. It's been weeks since I found him in that cave, and I'm amazed at how quickly he's filled out and his hair has grown. He looks so much healthier now. And a lot more like me.

"Maybe we need a key?" I say. "The Archives usually needs a key to move the wall aside. And there have been others. Maybe I'm missing something in my memory downloads."

Then it hits me.

The Crematorium badge they'd tried to hand me when they'd offered me the professional appointment. I'm so stupid. I left it behind. When I was told I'd be a Cremator, I walked out without a second thought. I can still recall the badge sitting on the counter as I left.

"Oh no—what have I done?"

"What?" Ammon asks. "Why are you 'oh noing'? C'mon, there's no time for 'oh noing'," he says, his voice cracking slightly.

"There's a badge. Everyone with professional appointments has one. I should have remembered—I should have..." I say, shaking my head. "Think Runa, think."

"Better think fast. I don't want to get stuck down here," Ammon says. "You *know* nothing good's gonna come from that."

"Maybe I can manipulate the inner workings again? If it's a badge, there's a mechanism, right? That means there has to be a connection to something."

Once again, I close my eyes and try to find a connection to the doorway—hoping the same principles will apply to this security feature.

Behind my eyelids, the code in the workings begins to stream—but nothing makes sense. It's all garbled nonsense. I'm not able to catch anything to focus on or stop it long enough to manipulate it. I sit with it for as long as it's comfortable.

Pulling back from the connection, I open my eyes. Before me is Ammon, his eyes brimming with tears.

"Told you nothing good," he says.

My eyes shift beyond him to the two Salamanders climbing the walls and heading toward us.

And the man beyond them, with the Ibis headdress.

4

RUNA

HY COULD I NOT HEAR AMMON calling to me? Was I really so focused on the inner workings of the doorway? I tug his arm, dragging him to me as I position myself in front.

"It appears we keep meeting in the most opportune ways," Videus says, drawing his words out slowly and deliberately.

"And so far, how's that worked out for you?" I spit.

I bite my lip, my mind racing through scenarios of how I could get us out of this mess. We're trapped like animals down here—with no perceivable way out—at least not yet. Not without some time.

Videus considers for a moment, walking silently forward, "This is true. I keep running into you, yet you keep managing to slip away. We'll have to remedy that."

"Let Ammon go. It's me you want," I say, trying to be reasonable.

It's true, though. Videus has always been after me. Everything he's done has been to track me down, or try to coerce me out.

A bubble of laughter erupts from Videus' throat.

"My dear Runa, always the sweet, docile saint, trying to protect others. But we've been over this before. Why would I let him go when I have you already? The two of you together is a far better prize than simply the Daughter of Five alone."

Roaming closer, Videus' dark cloak sways ominously, caressing the floor. I force myself to look up into the place where his face should be. I take a breath, reminding myself the pool of blood hiding his face is simply a hologram—just like the walls around us. It's not real. Beneath it, somewhere, is a real man. A sick, twisted man—but a man nonetheless.

I take a deep breath, unafraid of the creatures beside him. If there's one thing the trials I've passed changed, it was my perception of all of the creatures of Pendomus. They're held as captive as I am. Besides, if I can reach them—I may tip the scales.

Keeping my eyes open and centered on Videus, I extend my consciousness out to the Salamanders. Almost like sending out feelers, I touch the edges of their minds, trying to find a way in. Unfortunately, they're able to block me out. I turn my attention to Videus, attempting the same thing. His mind, however, is like an underground vault. Impenetrable.

"Don't bother, *Everblossom*. Do you think I wouldn't have taken precautions after all this time? After the many times we've been through this dance. I've been preparing for this for ages. Far longer than anyone has ever anticipated any confrontation throughout the dawn of time," he says, waving his hand and taking another step closer.

"Are you going to actually do something, or are you just going to talk us to death?" I say, defiance building in me.

This has gone on for far too long. I feel my powers rising, my abilities getting stronger. But more than that, I no longer question who I am. Or what I'm doing and why.

"Runa—I don't think it's wise to taunt the creepy guy in the cape. Do you?" Ammon says, tugging at my arm.

I feel his trepidation. I know what this looks like to him. But the feeling I had before we came hasn't left me. This is all part of the process somehow. This capture.

I need to lean into it and see where it leads.

Videus takes a step closer—his face inches from mine. As he leans in, I focus on the way the blood dripping from his Ibis headdress flows downward. As he bends in, the droplets fall, exploding into red splatters as they hit the floor.

Surprised, I suck in a breath.

"Oh, the things I plan to do to you, dear Everblossom. Dying is too easy. No, there are bigger plans for you and we're going to have to get started," he says, waving his hand out in front of him.

The walls around us vanish, unveiling the three pathways. Ammon was right—to the right and left, dark tunnels appear with no apparent end. Turning around, behind us are enormous metallic double doors with rivets the size of my fist. With the flick of Videus' wrist, the doors open wide.

Intense heat rolls toward us, thrusting against us like a wall all its own. It's not a wet heat, instead it's a dry, smoldering heat that immediately parches my lips and leaves me thirsty.

The Salamanders, edge forward, sliding off the walls and surrounding us. Their movement is intended to make us move, but both Ammon and I hold our ground.

"You've grown brave, Daughter of Five. It's almost a pity it won't last. Now, move," Videus says, his voice turning gruff.

Huffing loudly, the two Salamanders push forward. Electricity arches between them like an electrified blue rope. Videus takes a step back, letting them do his bidding.

Ammon and I stand immobile, but as the electrical arch gets close, it sears the air and the edge of my trouser leg. I stumble backward, pushing both of us toward the open doorway.

Between the heat of the tunnel and the blue electrical arcs of the Salamanders, the pressure is extremely oppressing. It's hard to breathe—and sweat instantly pools at the small of my back, only to dry out and start all over.

The Salamanders push us onward, and Ammon and I continue to stumble down the hallway. To the right, a large half-moon desk comes into view. The check-in station for those who work here. It's the entry point for the Crematorium. The desk is vacant and no one else is anywhere in sight.

Is this intentional?

How much advance warning did he have that Ammon and I would be here? Did Videus ensure he'd be alone?

To the left is a series of large loops with old-fashioned keys dangling nonchalantly. Almost as though they're decor for a place in a torture chamber…and I suppose they are.

The Salamanders continue herding us down the hallway —past the desk, past the keys, and on to a series of doors. Each door is like the others, large and see-through, with an electrical current pushing through them in a very similar way to the checkpoints in the Helix. With one difference—a large clear keyhole hovers in the middle of the open space.

"You won't be able to manipulate these doors, Everblossom. If you try to escape, you'll be incinerated down to your DNA. I kinda hope you try, but then again, where's the fun in that?" Videus says, his voice oddly cheerful for a place like this.

I try to slow us down, to take the time to peer into each cell as we pass by. Sunken faces, wide eyes peer out—but none are familiar from what I can tell. In one cell, a man sits crouched down, hands huddled in front of him as he cradles handfuls of his own hair.

I keep my eyes open wide, taking every nuance I can in. Videus has to be keeping Kani here somewhere.

"Keep moving it along," Videus says. "There's no need for stalling. This is the beginning of your new life."

I shiver away the thought. Any length of time in here would seem like an eternity.

We walk for a couple hundred meters and suddenly the series of doorways and cells branch off in a large honey-comb-like maze. No longer are the cells buried in rock, but divvied up into glass cells as far as the eye can see.

I stop short, looking at the sea of bodies as they meander aimlessly inside their confinements. The heat is unbearable, as if the source of the intensity is here—but all I see are people.

"What have you done to them?" I say, turning around to face Videus.

"What I've had to. You still don't get it. You don't under-stand how you've destroyed everything. How all the suffering leads back to you. All these people—you're the reason they're here. In my hunt for you, they've been the casualties. I've tried to make them useful. To turn them into something I can endure. But these ones—they're the ones who refused to break for one reason or another. So instead of regaining their freedom by working for me as a Labot, they're stuck here. They've been most useful in my studies toward understanding what makes the Daughter of Five so goddamn special."

My eyes widen and Ammon tugs at my arm. His finger-nails dig into my skin.

"They're not all here," I say, jutting my chin out.

"Of course they're not," Videus spits. "I'm not stupid. I know which are better suited elsewhere. Take your little pet, for instance."

Ammon whimpers, hiding completely behind my body. I feel his small frame begin to shake uncontrollably.

"What about him?" I prod, searching for my own information.

"Well, for starters, he was a *pet* project of mine. One of utmost importance—so I kept him elsewhere. Consider it a diversified investment of sorts. I had to be assured he'd be safe. Granted, I didn't know you'd go looking for him. But all's well that ends well," Videus sneers. "Synchronicity is a funny thing."

"Why keep him in the cavern like that? Why did you need to starve him, or beat him, and shackle him?"

"Oh, my dear, Everblossom, all will be clear in time."

"Comforting," I say, channeling Kani.

I glance around the space, looking for Kani's trademark long black hair and green streaks. She's no where to be found. At least, not anywhere I can see in the sea of bodies in front of me.

"Now, this is how things are going to work," Videus says.

His Salamanders take their queue, circling around us and penning us together.

"I'm going to take the boy and return him to where he came from."

"No—" Ammon screams. "No, I can't go back there. Please, please Runa—don't let him put me back in there. I—I can't go back to the cave. Please."

My mind races, trying to find a way out of this. A way to keep Ammon here.

"Why would you need to do that? You said it yourself. You have what you really wanted—me. What difference would some small little boy make to you now? Look at him, he can barely stand and you're scaring him senseless," I say, trying to tug at some threads of reason, hoping one might lead to something.

"Nice try, Daughter of Five. But this little boy, as you put it, has some very interesting capabilities. In fact, if I didn't know better, I would say he's more dangerous than you are. It's just a pity the prophecy was about a girl—a daughter. Otherwise I would have pegged it on him to be the one to try and stop me."

"Maybe you're right," I say, "Maybe Ammon is more special than I am. But he wouldn't hurt anyone. And he's no threat to you. Let him go."

"Because you say so? Oh, Everblossom, I've been through this so many times in my head. I know exactly what I'm doing. And why I'm doing it."

I snicker.

"Enlighten us then—you're just going to kill us anyway."

Videus chuckles and raises a hand, pointing to the sea of people beyond.

"Do you see them? Really see them? Mothers, fathers, daughters, sons. Some as old as ninety. Some as young as two. Take a good, long look for me," Videus says.

Giving a backward glance at Videus, I turn around and look again. Not a single person has glanced our way. Not a single one has offered acknowledgement in Videus' direction. They continue on their strange, broken patterns. Some shuffle from side to side. Others walk in circles inside their cells. A few are on the floor, hands in their heads or holding their ears. He's right, too. Young, old. They're all here and separated by thick sheets of glass. Not a single one of them is trying to get out. None are yelling, screaming, hitting the glass. It's like they've all given up.

In one of the cells a few rows back, a small child, no more than three lies on the ground. Such an odd thing, because they're so active at that age. At first, I can't tell if she's still alive, except when you watch her for a few moments, you can see her arms move. They flop suddenly, almost as if she's seizing. Then stop again.

"Help her—that little girl needs help," I cry, pointing her direction.

"She'll be gone soon enough," Videus says, a hint of amusement in his voice.

I swallow down the bile that arises. This man is so sick. He's torturing people here. He's killed those in my bloodline just to get to me. Crafting his blood snow statues from their dead corpses. The blood mask he wears is simply another symbol of his obsession.

I turn back to him.

"What happened to you? What could possibly make a person do this?" I say, suddenly overcome with a fierce sense of sorrow.

Videus snickers.

"We've already had this little chat, Everblossom, dear. It's time to stop stalling."

With a flick of his finger, five of the cells ignite into a set of searing hot blue flames. I know the intensity of the heat instantly because it hits us where we stand. The screams of pain that escape those in the cells lasts no more than seconds before they're snuffed out completely. When the flames cease, nothing remains in the cells except for a thin layer of gray on the floor—ash.

A silent scream erupts and I cup my mouth. The little girl —the three year old girl is gone.

"Let's make something perfectly clear. You will be going into one of these cells made especially for you. Once I have the information I require, you will greet the blue flame. If I don't get what I require, five more of these—" Videus stops, his blank bloody face staring out over the room, "*people* will be incinerated."

43

Distain drips from his voice and a shiver creeps up my spine, coiling like a snake.

If I give him what he wants, I'm dead. If I don't, innocent people will die.

I take a deep breath, turning to Videus, "And if I give you what you want. What will become of them?"

Videus laughs, "Why would that be your concern?"

"Well, there isn't much incentive in your offer," I say, trying to be more brave than I feel.

Ammon whimpers, sinking to the floor at my feet.

"You're not overly in a position to bargain for anything," Videus says, still laughing.

"If you want me to cooperate—I need your word. You need to promise me that everyone will be let go. Give them new NanoTech clothing and set them off on their own. If they make it in the woods, at least they aren't here. If they don't—then the onus is on them," I say.

"And why would I do that? What difference would that make?" Videus says, distain dripping in his voice.

"Because if I don't get what I want, you won't. I already know when you do—you'll kill me. Then you'll kill all of them. So what difference would it matter to me that you're taking them out five at a time? At least those are the lucky ones. They have less time to endure this hellish place," I spit, my loathing for this man bubbling to the surface.

Videus paces, hopefully considering what I've said.

The Salamanders huff menacingly, waiting for an order from their master.

"Very well. You have my word. Once I have what I'm looking for, I will release them all," Videus says slowly.

"And how do I know you'll keep up your end of the bargain. I'll be gone, after all. I need assurances," I say, jutting my chin out.

"Runa—" Ammon warns. I know he doesn't want me to

push Videus too far, but I have a plan now and I need to see it through.

I'm met with silence, and just as I start to think Videus will simply kill us—he grunts. Walking to me slowly, he places his forefinger and middle finger between my eyebrows, touching the center of my forehead. It's not what I expected, but the results are almost the same.

Suddenly overwhelmed with images given to me from Videus, I see everyone being released. I sense his admission and promise to follow through. There's no hidden agenda in it. The people here simply don't matter more than the information he seeks. I see them being released, to fend for themselves—but still free of their confinement. I see Ammon being let go to find his way back to where he belongs. Before he removes his fingers, I get a flash of something else— perhaps something he didn't meant to transmit, but something important just the same.

I see a flash of a boy. No more than ten years old, laughing, and playing. His golden hair dancing in the sunlight as he runs and hides behind a snow covered tree. The feelings connected to it are so overwhelming, they bring tears to my eyes, and a heaviness to my heart. This is why—what it's all been for. On some level or another, Videus once loved this golden haired boy, full of light and laughter.

He removes his fingers, taking a step back.

"I assume that's sufficient," Videus says, clearly unaware of the additional details he's passed along.

Swallowing hard, I nod.

"It is," I say, my mouth suddenly dry.

"Runa—you can't possibly trust this guy," Ammon says, groping at my arm, his voice a higher octave than before.

I bend down, looking Ammon in the eye. I understand now, why I was meant to find this brother of mine. Ammon is tied to Videus' desire for vengeance and the deep seeded

45

pain he feels. He's searching for recourse—and a ghost that's all. After witnessing the memory, Ammon has a similar build and is of similar age to the boy in Videus' mind. Of course, this is who he'd use against me, he's an archetype in this sick man's mind.

It's also why I know he'll be safest if I cooperate now—at least in some form.

"Ammon, everything is going to be alright. Nothing bad is ever going to happen to you," I say, trying to reassure him.

Shaking his head, he keeps repeating, "No, no, no…"

I stand up.

"I want him to be the first let go. If you release him, I'll cooperate fully. Right now," I say.

Videus takes a deep inhalation, and begins pacing again.

After a moment, he turns to me and says, "Done."

Immediately, the Salamanders surrounding us shift around, herding Ammon away from my grasp and back the way we came.

"No—Runa, no! You can't possibly trust him. Please, don't do this—" Ammon screams as he's pushed further and further away. "I need to stay with you. I need—"

Videus grabs hold of my wrist and drags me along the corridor. A squeal of surprise erupts from my lips, as I'm forced to leave Ammon and follow along. I claw at his hand, trying to pry away from his grasp.

"Let me go—I'll follow you," I say.

Videus drops my hand and stops moving. Swooping his hand out in front of his body, he motions for me to take the lead.

"Your new home is up ahead," he says, jabbing me in the side to continue on.

Lamenting not getting a proper goodbye, I realize I can use it to fuel my cause. I need to get out of this—to get back to him and be a part of his life. To make sure he's safely gotten away from all of this.

Passing by glass cage after glass cage, the people inside are devoid of their innate spark. I don't know what Videus has done to them, but it's as if no one is taking up residence inside their own bodies anymore. None of them look our way, nor show any kind of sign they are afraid for their own lives. It's like they simply—exist.

"What have you done to everyone?" I ask, unable to help myself.

"When you play with people's minds in order to search for something you seek—this is what you get. Now, it seems they're nothing more than flesh and bones...and *blood*," Videus says.

It occurs to me, a sudden flash of insight, this is why he agreed. This is why they mean nothing to him. They're no longer here—no longer inside their own minds. They've vacated and who knows if they'll be able to be brought back.

Oh—what have I done?

I take a deep breath, suddenly overcome with a mixture of anxiety and despair.

"Welcome to your new home," Videus says as we come to a final glass cube.

Raised up higher than the others, the cage of glass is vacant. As we near, a set of three glass steps appear, granting us access to the space.

"Get in," Videus says, jabbing his finger into my side.

I take a final glance at the people surrounding me.

It's all my fault they're here, just as Videus said.

My mind starts spinning in all various directions, and I feel the ancestral blood coursing through my veins begin to ignite. With a simple glance, I can distinguish those here who are blood tied to me, and those who are not.

47

Videus was so close—more than not are somehow tied directly to my bloodline.

I step into my glass cage and Videus follows.

Once we're both inside, the cube seals itself, then the glass frosts over—an opaque white.

A glass chair rises from the floor, along with several tables covered in metallic tools of various shapes and sizes.

"Shall we get started?"

5

TRAETON

*I*F I GOTTA DEAL with this damn intruder in my head, I'm gonna at least make the most of it. Let's just see how Videus likes me knocking at his door. Gathering up the tools I need to back Runa up, I start by stuffing everything into a pack. I'm well aware there are a ridiculous number of ways this could go sideways. How could it not? But that's not really the point. I need to do something while I'm still me. If Videus gets close enough, I'll need something to take him out. Something small and discreet.

I walk the aisles of weapons and grab an electric blade. It's god knows how old, but I've got no doubt it's effective. Plus, it's different in that it only becomes a blade when you grip it tight. Hell, it could even come in handy if I need to throw a wrench into the Helix's electrical system. Nothing like a good power overload—as long as I'm not attached to the damn thing.

The intruder continues attempting to break back into my mind. Desperation fills his pleas and I stop for a moment in the spirit of gloating.

"Yeah, how does it feel? Knowing you want to say something, affect change, and you're trapped in there?" I say, my own pain bleeding through my words.

There's one difference between the two of us. Curiosity is stronger than any direct order. At least for me. Always been that way—just ask Delaney.

I take a seat for a moment, closing my eyes, and resting my head on the table. As much as I hate it, I need my own intel.

"What can I expect when I get into the Helix? Has Videus amassed his army of Labots?" I ask, quietly trying to hear the answer that comes.

It comes like static, bits of words at first.

Better...stay...torture...

"Torture? Torture who?" I growl.

If he's hurting her—so help me, I'll kill Videus the moment I lay eyes on the bastard.

The separation between the intruder and I is ironically cumbersome. If I can't get rid of him, I wish I could at least interrogate him properly. This is bullshit.

"Come on—answer me, dammit," I yell, standing up and pushing the chair out from beneath me. "If you're gonna hide in there, the least you can do is be useful."

"Who are you talking to?"

I spin around to find Runa's brother, Ammon—at least I think that's his name—entering the Archives. I've gathered snippets here and there during my time being trapped, but at least I caught that much.

Tears stream down his face, and his face is darkened with ash and snow.

"Nothing—never mind," I say.

But I warn you, you better find a way to get your damn messages clear, or get the hell outta my head. You're not welcome here.

"Ammon, what's happened to you? Where's Runa?" I say, dropping to my knees and grabbing onto his arms.

His little body releases, and he crumples into a ball on the floor.

"He has her—the man with no face," he says, his little ten year old body quivering.

"Dammit. Are you hurt? How'd you get away?" I say, my mind racing.

Was the intruder telling the truth? Trying to warn me of what Videus was doing?

"Runa—she promised to give him whatever he wanted. But he had to let me go," Ammon sobs, his shoulders sagging. "Why? Why would she do that? She has to know he can't be trusted. He'll play the part—be whoever works so he can get close enough to break her. I should know."

My eyes widen.

"What do you mean, Ammon? Play the part? Can he take on different faces?"

"I don't know, maybe. I just know one minute he's calm and understanding. The next minute, he's hitting your face so you can't see. He's insane."

"When he had you, what information did he try to get from you?" I ask.

"It was all about blood and siblings. I didn't even know I had a sister until—well, until recently. Oh, god—I can't lose her now, too. I just found her," he sobs.

Taking him in my arms, I hold him close. I can't imagine the kind of psychological pressure this would put on an adult, let alone a child.

"Ammon, it's okay. We won't lose her. We have to find a way to get her outta there. I have a plan, but I need your help," I say.

"Runa already has a plan," Ammon says simply, pushing back and wiping his face.

"She does? Why didn't you say that sooner? What—what's her plan?"

Ammon's face goes stone cold. He wipes the tears from his face and he places his calculating eyes on me.

"I—I don't know if I can trust you," he finally says.

I sigh, knowing he has no real reason to. Hell, I don't even know if he should.

I nod.

"You're right. I don't know if you can either," I say honestly.

Surprised, Ammon twists around, looking deep into my eyes.

"Do you know? Is it the real you again?" he asks.

I hold my breath. *He knows.*

"Yeah, for now," I nod, "but I don't know for how long. Dammit, maybe it's best to trust Runa's plan and don't involve me in it. I have a plan of my own, but I can follow through alone."

In all honesty, who knows how long I'll have control of myself. For now though, I feel better than I have in ages—since well before Runa and I went to the Helix. But if Videus could hack my brain once, I wouldn't put it past him to do it again. Especially when he realizes his crony isn't responding to him.

Ammon nods quickly.

"Okay, that's okay," he mutters.

Suddenly, from the pile of books on the table, bright white light radiates out, filling the room. Ammon gasps, walking away from me and toward the source. Grabbing the book with the tree on the cover, he clutches it to his chest. His eyebrows drag downward, as do his lips.

"What is it?" I say, walking toward him, and shielding my eyes.

Backing away from me, the light streams out of the large tome like a beacon.

"I—I was supposed to check on this and take it someplace safe. But I don't know now," he says.

I step toward him, and he takes another step back.

I hold my hands up, trying to will to him that I'm not going to attempt anything.

"What is this book? Why does it matter where it is?" I ask.

"Runa needs this," Ammon says. "It's important."

"How do you know?" I ask, confused.

The book is hers? Where did she get it? How is it important?

"I need to go back," Ammon says, stiffening. "I need to get this to her."

His little body begins to quiver again, but he doesn't move, and he doesn't set the book down.

"Look kid, you're very brave. You really are. But this isn't your burden to carry. I'm on my way to the Helix to help bust her out. If it's as important as you say, let me take it to her," I say.

Ammon shakes his head, his eyes wide.

"Walk me through this. If you go—you take the book to her, right? How do you plan on getting it to her? What's your strategy?" I say, trying to reason with him.

He blinks rapidly, searching his mind for a remedy to this issue.

"I—I'd have to go back in. Use the same door as before," he mutters.

"And then what? How did you get past the checkpoints?" I say, trying to draw out the conclusions for him.

He sighs, "Runa."

"Have you ever been in the Helix before? It's pretty easy to get turned around in that place," I say.

Ammon slowly shakes his head, and bites his lip, "Just the once."

"I spent most of my childhood there. I know my way around. Let me help. I'll get it to her, I promise," I say.

I'll get it to her, or die trying. Either way, I'm good.

Ammon takes a deep breath, his eyes cast to the floor. Slowly, he extends his arms, holding the book out for me.

I take the book, running my hand over its cover.

"The Caudex is sorta her compass. It gives her important information now that her connection to—I don't know who —her guide I guess, has been severed. If it's glowing, it means there's something new she has to be aware of," Ammon says, eyeing me closely.

"Would it be safer to open it and relay the information to her directly?" I ask.

"So you can steal the secrets of the book?" Ammon says, skepticism and distain edging into his voice.

"No, look, it makes more sense is all. What's more conspicuous? A large, glowing book? Or information stored in some guy's head?"

"What does conspicuous mean?" Ammon says.

I laugh. I almost forgot he's just a kid.

"What would call more attention? That's what it means," I say.

Ammon's face flickers and he rolls his eyes.

"Well, obviously, the book would be more conspicuous," he says, "but there's one problem."

"And what's that?" I ask.

"The Caudex can't be opened without the key. And I don't have it—Runa does," Ammon says.

"The key?" I say.

Of course.

I look down at the large book. The leather binding, the burned tree into its cover.

"This is the Tree of Burden's latest incarnation, isn't it?" I say with wide eyes. "Her stone—it's what opens it. Am I right?"

Ammon's eyes widen, but he nods once.

"Okay, I guess there's only one way forward then. I'll have to find a way to hide the book from view—or camouflage it. I might have to get it close to the Helix, then hide it," I say, my brain going off on various courses of action trying to come to the best conclusion.

"No—no hiding it. If you're taking it, you bring it straight to her," Ammon says, his eyebrows pulled in and his lips tight.

"Alright, kid. Straight to her," I nod.

"Maybe I should come along—" he says, concern hidden in his tone.

"Believe me kid, this isn't my first time breaking into the Helix. Probably won't be my last. If the hardest thing I have to do is smuggle in a glowing book, I think I'll be alright," I say.

Somewhere in the back of my mind, the intruder is flailing about—frantically trying to get my attention. Everything's so damn important with him. Too bad he can't just spit it out and communicate properly. I ignore him for now, not wanting to call any more attention to my compromised mind.

Ammon eyes me closely, but nods.

"I'm going to pack up the rest of the supplies I need and I'll get going. Are you going to be okay? What's your game plan?" I ask.

"Need to know, remember?" Ammon says. "And you don't need to know. Runa and me worked out our own plan. I know what to do from here on out."

"Alright then, let's get to work," I say, nodding back to him.

I gotta hand it to the little guy, he's tougher than he looks.

I set the Caudex down, the light still shining brightly from its edges. Digging into my pack to make room, there's no chance in hell of fitting it in there. The pack is too damn small.

Carrying it is my only option, but I'll need to figure out what to do with it before I head inside. I can't risk bringing it into the Helix. I know the kid wants it to go straight to her, but I gotta make an executive decision and nix that one right now. It'll be way too noticeable and I have a pretty good chance of getting caught—

"Be careful with the Caudex, Trae. It's very special to Runa. She protected it wherever she went," Ammon says. "She didn't want the man to get it."

"I will, kid," I promise. "I'll do my best to make sure nothing goes wrong, and Runa's able to get whatever she needs from her book."

"Okay, good," Ammon says. "I'm gonna head out now. There's more I need to do. Good luck, okay?"

Walking over to him, I place my hands on his tiny shoulders. They fit easily into the palms of my hands, but they're sturdy and sure of themselves—even with the extra weight of both my hands, and his new task.

"You're a good kid, Ammon. Runa's lucky not only to have you on her team, but as a brother. You need to know that," I say.

Tears threaten to well up in his eyes, as they glass over. He puffs up his chest and nods.

"Now, get outta here and get that next phase initiated," I say, turning him around and walking him toward the Archives door.

When we reach the entry to the hallway, Ammon stops and turns back to me.

"You be careful, too," Ammon says. "Runa—she doesn't quite know how to say it, but she loves you."

I inhale quickly, my heart tripping over a beat.

"Why would you say that?" I say.

"We—she's been through a lot. But her trials, and everything she's gone through—you were a big part of them. She worries a lot about you. She didn't say so, but I know it's why we went into the Helix so soon. She wants to cure you, or find a way to fix whatever was going on. But she knew she couldn't do it from in here," he says. "Don't you dare let her down."

My eyes widen with surprise, and I lick my lower lip.

"I won't," I say.

"Good," he says, walking out, and entering the long tunnel to the surface. "Then, I'll catch ya soon."

He holds up his right hand and waves without turning back.

The corner of my mouth quirks upward. He reminds me so much of Fenton when we were younger, it's uncanny.

"Bye, kid," I mutter under my breath.

Turning around, I head back to my pack, and the insanely bright glowing book.

"What in the hell am I going to do with you?" I say.

A grin slowly spreads across my face. I know exactly what I need to do, and its genius. Well, as long as I can hold onto my body, anyway. If I can't—well, things could go sideways in the worst way. But it's a risk I'm willing to take to get to Runa and give her the tools she needs to defeat Videus once and for all.

I look around for anything I could use to wrap the Caudex in.

~Do not bring the sacred Caudex anywhere near the Helix. It would be the worst mistake of your life.

The intruder's voice rings out in my head as if he's

standing right beside me. Or as if an eLink connection opened up and I wasn't aware I gave my permission.

My footing falters for a split second, but I regain my balance. I pat my chest—so far, still me. Too bad my heart's outside my body now.

"Why would bringing the Caudex be such a bad gig?" I ask. "If it helps Runa, I need to get it to her."

~Throughout the centuries, Videus has been searching for the secrets held in the sacred text. He has tortured and enslaved many of us, desperate for the details buried in there. If you walk in with it, you will be handing those secrets directly into his hands.

"Aren't you here because of him? What difference is it to you? Isn't this what you both want, then?" I ask, playing devils advocate.

~Nothing could be further from the truth. Being inside of your mind—the longer I was away, the more control over myself I found I could exert. I do his bidding, but not of my own volition.

"Oh, come on. You're trying to sell to me that you're the victim here? Kani—we—I—she's gone now because of us. You were here to bring Runa down. To spy on her intentions, and find a way to break her—use her—or deliver her to Videus. I was in there. I could hear what you two planned from time to time."

~For many centuries, my kind has been enslaved to do his bidding. The control he has, it extends far and should not be over-looked. It is very unfortunate I was consumed in such a way. As hard as you try to fight him, eventually, you succumb.

I walk to the nearest set of shelves holding garments, bags, and other objects possibly capable of carrying a big, glowing book.

"Let's say I believe you. Sure, why the hell not? Why are you willing to break ranks now?" I say, scratching the back of my neck. "And don't tell me you had a change of heart."

~As I said, the longer I was inside your mind, the more capable

I have been at taking back my own volition. It was not until I realized where we are, than I knew what I must do.

"Where we are? We've been in and out of the Archives multiple times since you took me over—what's different this time?" I say.

My head's spinning. I honestly don't know what the hell to believe. Then, the memories of my intruder's final moments in control of me start to filter in. As if they bleed together, I'm aware of not only the juxtaposition of my body and mind's position, but also his mind—but more than that. I actually experience his memories, as well.

They flood in backward order from the moment before he gave me back control—then extending as far back as we have time for. Centuries, maybe.

I know exactly who I'm dealing with now.

"Whoa," I say. "Shit—this, this changes things."

Wetting my lips I realize just how far this goes. How far everything with Runa, the planet, the birds—Videus. It's ingrained in the entire fabric of reality. We're all pawns in the game Videus has been playing to get what he wants—but only he knows what that is.

This place, the Archives, is a beacon of hope for the planet. It's not even meant to be underground.

"Alright—if you're serious about keeping this information from Videus, we'll need to work together. Because, like it or not, I have to get it into the Helix to help Runa. I owe her that much," I say.

Hell, I owe her so much more.

~But the sacred Caudex—

"Don't get your trousers in a bunch. We'll keep it safe somehow. We have to.

~And if we fail?

"Then it won't overly matter one way or the other, will it?" I say.

~I suppose it would not.

This place—I knew it was unique, and held so much of the treasures of Earth. But I had no idea it was here before humans colonized. That something else built it with such magnificence. I look around at the artwork and craftsmanship with new eyes.

"This place is part of the prophecy?" I say. "Are you sure?"

~I have never been more certain. In the battle to come, it must be preserved so it may rise again.

"Battle? Who said anything of a battle?" I say, walking back to the pack I plan on still taking with me.

~It has been foretold. Long before your kind came here, a prophet of the Four Pillars described the impending darkness. Unfortunately, his teachings went largely unnoticed. We lived in utopia, it was a hard seed to swallow.

I grab the Caudex and place it inside a small child's blanket. Folding it around the book, the light dims, but still glows faintly.

"Dammit," I mutter, grabbing a second blanket to wrap it in.

"Four Pillars? What are those?" I ask.

~We were—are the guardians of Pendomus. Without us, the planet cannot revolve the way it should. The world will find no seasons of change. No peace in growth. No leaves, no grass, no Everblossoms.

"How did Videus take control of you? Why would you follow him?"

~It is in our nature to help. We were a peaceful planet. No hate, no evil. We had not experienced these emotions before. It was not even a consideration.

"So you got duped?" I say, tying the dimmed Caudex to the outside of my pack.

~Yes, I suppose you could say so.

I nod. It's how it always happens. You trust someone you

shouldn't have given a second thought about and—bam! You're in shit. Seen it a hundred times before.

"How's he controlling you?" I say, trying to find a way to help Runa on her path, but protecting us both on this mission.

~His mind control is beyond anything I have ever dealt with. The creatures of Pendomus have always communicated telepathically. Somehow, he found the path of our connections, and used them to control our will—we could hear his voice, and no longer each other's. As our connection faded, we also began to lose our own voice, our own volition. I do not know how he does it, only that he does.

"Alright, I have a plan, and I'll need you on board. So buckle up. We're gonna phug up his plans," I say, grabbing my pack and walking out the door.

6

RUNA

I STAND IN HORROR, unsure which direction to go, or how to avoid any of this. Words wash off Videus like water, and my abilities don't have any effect on him directly.

"Take a seat, Everblossom," Videus says, a scowl hidden in his words.

I step backward awkwardly, taking a seat in the glass chair. Watching every move Videus makes, I focus on the dark color of his blood mask, and the contrast of him to the white light in this glass cube.

"Alright, shall we get started then?" Videus says, his words taking an odd cadence as he holds his a's slightly longer than he should.

Swallowing my fear, I sit up straighter.

"Not that you have a choice, mind you," he laughs. "I will get what I need, one way or the other. So, please, test me. It'll be so much more fun."

Out of nowhere, clear straps of energy arch over my wrists and ankles, binding me to the chair.

I clench my jaw, and tighten my fists. I refuse to give Videus any satisfaction.

"This is such important, and delicate work. Not meant for a man's hands," Videus begins, running his fingertips over the series of instruments and knives on the table. "I have important questions I need answered and I need assurances I'll get the truth."

I lower my eyebrows, assessing every move.

"I already said I'd cooperate. Now, let's get on with it," I spit.

My anger to the injustice of it all runs in the undercurrent of my emotions. Anger Videus will torture me for whatever end, only he really knows. Anger he feels I'm somehow responsible for his suffering. Anger before I even knew who, or what I was, he was hunting me. Anger everything I thought was true has a ring of fantasy.

My thoughts land briefly on Traeton. Will I ever be able to help him? To restore his mind? Was this plan to come here too half-cocked to be successful?

Videus nods, the Ibis on top of his head bobbing slightly, "I know, but this is so much more fun."

He chuckles. It's oddly comforting, and completely mortifying as it twists into something menacing. Suddenly, the door behind him opens.

"Ah, just in time," Videus says.

Waving a hand, a Labot enters the enclosure. Her face is wiped—as they always are. Dressed in standard NanoTech, down to the boots on her feet. Her long black hair drapes down her back, with hints of green peeking through.

"Kani—Kani, is that you?" I scream, without thinking.

Videus chuckles, "I suppose to you she would be, yes. You should realize, she can't hear you. The woman inside now is merely an instrument."

I glare at him, grinding my teeth and wishing I could

make them both understand. But how would you ever help someone this insane understand? Or someone who's mind is being controlled? Logic no longer applies.

I close my eyes, trying to reach out to Kani—break into her mind, and sever the connection. But I'm met with static and disrupted, erratic energy.

When I open my eyes, Videus tick-tocks his pointer finger from side to side.

Something oozes from my nose, and there's nothing I can do to wipe it away.

"See, we picked this cage especially for you, Everblossom. We knew you'd try some of your...mental acuities," he says, snickering.

"We?" I spit, keeping my eyes locked on both of them.

"Why, yes. We," Videus says, pacing, "See, before Kani became a faithful servant, she was most helpful. She explained a lot of details I hadn't fully understood before. She helped me pick this one out so we could keep you focused."

My heart sinks. I know Kani and I were never *best* friends, but I considered her a friend, nonetheless. Would she really have done this to me? To the rest of the planet? Surely she knows there's more at stake than just her own pain or dislike of me?

Maybe she did and it didn't matter.

Kani steps forward mechanically, choosing an instrument from the table. Even in her Labot state, old habits die hard. She chooses a knife, similar to the one she's always had strapped to her leg.

However, without her signature snarky expressions, my blood runs cold. This, cold, calculated machine is absolutely terrifying.

"Why don't you ask your question already?" I say, ripping my eyes off of her, and placing them back with Videus.

"Haven't you gotten more brave? Good for you, what fun would it be trying to get this out of a sniveling, crying Daughter of Five?" he says, smirking. "Though, I have to admit, I've fantasized it that way a number of times. I cannot tell a lie."

I keep my eyes fixed on him, refusing to look away.

"Alright, you want to begin, let's begin," Videus says, peering over his shoulder at Kani.

A silent command passes between them, and within seconds, she's at my side, knife drawn and ready. Then, she slowly kneels down, keeping her facelessness pointed at me. She grabs hold of my right hand, and deliberately digs the tip of the knife beneath the fingernail on my pinkie.

Biting down hard, I refuse to scream—though the pain is unbelievable. Lightening sparks through my whole body, recognizing the point of entry as a source of intense agony.

"Now that I've got your attention, I need you to know I'm not unwilling to go here. I want you to remember this moment. Remember the feeling of your friend's blade twisting into your body. There are thousands of spots like this all over the human body. We don't need to cut huge gashes to be effective. Just know next time, it won't be so pleasant. And if you lie, consider an eyeball to be next. Perhaps that pretty blue one," he says, stepping forward. "Now then, how do you do it?"

"Do what?" I spit, trying not to focus on the blood escaping through my fingertip and the sound it makes as it hits the floor.

"Move through time," he says, simply.

"I—I'm not," I begin.

Stinging discomfort lashes out as Kani twists the knife slightly.

"I mean, I'm here. This is my time now," I say, back-tracking to the truth.

"Are you so certain?" Videus says, bending in.

The bloody mask looks so real—and perhaps it is. All this time I thought it was another elaborate hologram, but now I'm not so sure.

"I—I—" I stumble for words, unsure where he's going.

"When I came back, everything made sense again. I could tell I wasn't in the loop any longer," I say.

"Loop? Is that what you're calling it. Interesting," he tips his head to the side, "Not quite what I'd call it, but alright. I can go with that. How did you get into it?" Videus demands.

My mind races, there's information I don't want to give over to him—but will he know if I don't? Where is this all leading? And how long can I stall him until I have a plan?

"The Tree of Burden. When I entered, it took me through and dumped me into an alternate timeline," I say.

Not a total lie.

"And where exactly did it start? Were you in control of it?" he asks, leaning in closer.

"No, at least, I don't think so," I say, my finger throbbing. "At first I wasn't even aware I was out of my timeline. I was sheltered from anything that would have given it away."

"Peculiar," Videus says, scratching his chin. Blood leaks from his mask to his gloves, but he takes no notice or care.

Kani's Labot form hovers in wait, her knife centimeters from my finger. The tip pulsates, but I can already feel my blood coagulating, wanting to make me whole again.

From somewhere nearby, an alarm blares, and the lights dim, then red lights blink furiously.

"Sort that out," Videus commands to Kani.

She nods, spinning the knife in her hand as she stands up. Then she flings it to the table as she heads out the way she came. The knife lands with a soft thud beside the others like it as its tip digs into the table, swaying goodbye to its wielder.

"Happen often?" I ask, quirking an eyebrow.

Videus snorts, "It's none of your concern."

His demeanor doesn't change at all. It's hard to determine if he's rattled, or simply feels unconcerned about the change in ambiance.

"The Tree of Burden," Videus begins again, as he meanders toward the table of knives and other instruments, "what was it like? Inside it?"

My eyes narrow as I try to follow his direction to a final conclusion.

"Answer me," he snaps.

"It was like a tree—any other tree on Pendomus," I say.

"Except?" Videus prods.

"Except for when I left my friends behind. It held the gateway to the time loop," I say.

"How did you know what to do?" he continues.

I'm unsure how much I want to explain about Adrian and the voices. Or the others I assume are out there, helping me in some way. I've never really met them, I've only felt their presence.

"I didn't," I say. "I followed my intuition, mostly. I did whatever I felt was the right thing to do at the time."

"So, you went into the Tree of Burden on a hunch?" Videus snickers.

"I guess I did," I say, pressing my thumb to my pulsating pinky.

"What about the information?" he says.

I narrow my eyes, "What information?"

"Don't play coy with me, Everblossom," Videus says, suddenly inches from my face. His breath is stale—like a room closed off for centuries.

"I—I—" I stumble for words, "I don't know what you're referring to. What information? You need to be more specific."

Videus' ibis twitches almost imperceptibly.

He's closer than I thought to exploding. Unrest—or hatred—maybe both, is running under the surface of this calmer demeanor.

"Videus, I went in on a hunch because what choice did I have? The information I received was minimal, but you'd backed us into a corner. I didn't have time to extrapolate anything else. I trusted in my ability to figure things out, that's all," I say.

Clenching a hand in front of him, Videus' fingers tighten —as do the electrical restraints around my wrists and ankles. I'm thrust into a blinding pain as electricity courses through my veins without him ever lifting a finger to the knives. I close my eyes, trying to wield the energy—to subdue it.

Suddenly, I hear screaming—it starts low and grows louder and louder. Red and white light blinds me behind my eyelids until everything abruptly stops.

I close my mouth—cutting off the scream.

Silence falls, and I open my eyes.

Videus is gone.

Darkness consumes everything.

WHAT MUST BE HOURS LATER, I open my eyes feeling groggy and disoriented. I'm still attached to the glass chair—the restraints still intact, digging into my skin, but without sending their electricity through me. The table full of instruments has vanished, but I know without a doubt, Videus will be back for more. Perhaps when he's more restrained, himself.

My head lolls to the side, unable to hold itself just yet.

Come on, Runa. Get control.

I have to work quickly. I don't know how much time I

have until Videus comes back for more—and I don't plan to waste this opportunity.

I take a deep breath, and allow my eyes to close again. If anyone is watching me—it will simply appear like I've passed out again.

Taking slow, deliberate inhalations, I center myself, and call upon the energies in the bloodlines. Alone, I may not be strong enough to do this—but together—embracing the energies of those who came before me—I hope I have a chance to succeed. Kani didn't know anything about the bloodlines, so there's a chance Videus doesn't fully understand either.

The energy builds slowly, awakening inside like a sleeping cat stretching. My body shudders, and clarity strikes my consciousness without any effort on my part. Connected to the source of all—my ancestors and those who made me possible—I lean on their leverage to push my mind out toward those in cages alongside me. I hope like hell their connection to the bloodlines—to me—will allow me the access I need—even in this place.

At first, my consciousness creeps slowly, hunting for a way out of the glass enclosure Videus put me in. It's true, his efforts would certainly keep me in check—if I hadn't had my bloodlines backing me up. It's funny—all this is possible because Videus kept trophies of his victims. I still don't completely understand why. I guess I don't overly have to. His sick fascination with the bloodlines will be his downfall, I swear it will.

My mission now is about protecting the rest of us, and getting everyone out. With a little luck, I'll find something to help Trae.

Reaching out further, pushing my mind to find a way, the energy of it melds with the glass box. I push through it, rather than find a place of least resistance. As my consciousness passes through the glass, it scatters, disorients. What-ever this is, it's no ordinary glass—it's something more.

It's still not capable of containing me, though. Once my consciousness pushes past the box, I see everything. I'm connected to each and every one of the people here in a way I've never imagined being connected to anyone. Not only can I see them as my consciousness hovers overhead, but I can *feel* them all. As though each one of them are simply an extension of myself.

Casting out a distress call, of sorts, I wait to see if anyone responds. To see if they're still there, trapped inside their own heads—or if they've been released through the suffering they've endured.

At first, nothing happens. But then, like a slow tickle across my brain, I sense the awakening of…*something.*

What is it?

I focus on it, sending out the message that I'm here. That they aren't alone.

Then it comes to me, what the something is.

Hope.

For the first time in a long time for most of them, the inklings of hope arises. It's small—the energy of it overall. But it's there. And it gives me something to latch onto. Hope means they're still alive—Videus hasn't broken all of them. And that alone gives me something worth fighting for.

~Hello?

One voice calls out in my head.

~Hello? Is someone there?

Another.

~It's been so long. Am I dead?

~Please, please—I'm trapped.

~Hello?

The flood gates of voices in my head begin to open. The awareness of their minds, their souls all awakening to my presence fills me with such relief. I'd half expected them to be as broken as they appear from the outside.

~*I'm here. I need you to know you're not alone. Not anymore.* I respond.

~*Who are you? How are you doing this? That—that man. He's tortured me. I didn't think I'd ever hear anyone again.*

~*How can I hear all of you?*

Another voice.

~*Can everyone hear each other?*

I ask the question. I need to know if this connection pushes the limits of what I've ever done before.

~*I can, yes.*

~*Me, too.*

~*Yes.*

Good. This is good.

~*Listen everyone, I don't know how yet, but we will find a way out of here. I have friends on the outside—and I'm working on a plan.*

~*Who are you?*

~*My name is Runa. Runa Cophem.*

~*Runa?*

One voice calls out, desperation clinging to my mental projection.

~*Right, Runa.*

~*Oh my g—Runa. It's so good to hear you. I—I thought you were dead.*

I push my consciousness further, pinpointing the source of this voice. Like zooming above the sea of bodies, it finally rests on the body of a man, crumpled in the corner of his glass cell. His dark hair has grown out and shaggy, extending over his ears. The skin on his hands have taken on a grayish quality.

~*Baxten? Baxten, is that you?*

71

My heart skips a beat. I'd been told he was lost. But here he is.

Suddenly, my resolve falters slightly.

How can he be here?

~Yes! Runa, yes! It's me. I don't know where I am. Or what the hell is going on. A man—he has a—I don't know what's wrong with his face. I've never seen—

Someone else chimes in.

~I've seen it too. What is that?

~Me, too. Oh, god, what is he?

The voices start flooding in, and they're hard to control—hard to piece each one out so I can make sense of them all. But the sentiment is the same. They're scared as hell and they've seen Videus personally.

~Baxten, did he do anything to you? What has he done?

I ask, needing to understand more about the nature of everyone's capture.

~When I first got here, I was so disoriented. I—I remember looking for you, but then, I swear Runa—I swear on all my life, a giant creature came out of nowhere. It wrapped itself around my legs and burst into flames. I thought I was gonna die. The next thing I know, I'm here. Alone, strapped to a slab of glass. What is this place?

~We're in the Crematorium—all of us are.

~The Crematorium? Why are we here—?

~Crematorium?

Panic builds in those connected to the conversation and I know I need to dampen it quickly or it will get us all killed.

~Yes, but it's not just the Crematorium. It's used as something else. A holding cell for all of us. Videus—this man—he wants information from us. More from me. So, if you want to stay alive, do as he asks. Do you all understand? It will keep you alive until I can get us out.

They each begin talking at once, some making sounds of acknowledgement, others of protest.

Suddenly, a searing pain rips me from the connection and my consciousness promptly returns where it should be—a girl in a room, bound to a chair.

My eyes pop open.

Beside me, Kani's disturbing faceless form hovers just to the right, in my periphery. Suddenly, pain floods my consciousness. Buried in the back of my right hand is a long knife. My fingers are splayed open, without my conscious effort to do so.

Videus stands before me, a little bird resting on his shoulder—*Caelum*. His mask of blood and the headdress look oddly appropriate beside that traitorous bird.

"Ah, there she is," Videus says. "I have a surprise for you."

7

TRAETON

*H*IDING THIS BOOK should really be priority. Not only is it getting damn heavy, but the Caudex seems to glow brighter, the longer it's ignored. Pretty soon, it's gonna be a mini-sun bursting from my arms. There's no way I'll be able to bring it directly to Runa without setting off some major alarms and I'm pretty sure getting caught with it will be worse than hiding it now.

Trudging through the deep snow, I play out what will happen next. What my plans will be, heading into the Helix. I need to get to Runa—if I can convince Videus I'm still being controlled by—*whoever this is*—then maybe I stand a chance. He might just let me in, or allow me to stay. Whichever. At least, that's the plan.

Of course, the opposite could always happen, too. Could be a stupid plan. So, I can't rely on any of Videus' generosity to get me through this. I need a backup as well.

~We could wait for the Daughter of Five to escape on her own.

The intruder is back.

"You're kidding, right? Who knows how long that could

be. And what could be done to her in the meantime. No thanks, I'll pass," I say aloud.

~If my master gets even a hint you are not me, things will not end well for either of you.

"They're not ending well now. We can't just sit and wait for things to happen. Or let Runa do all the heavy lifting. She needs help, and I'm not about to sit here. We need to go in," I say. "You got a better idea?"

Silence greets me.

Of course he doesn't have a better plan. His plan is to stand back and see what happens. Some plan. No, we have no choice but to head in and hope for the best.

~Where will you hide the Caudex? It's power will not be contained for long.

"Hell if I know. You gotta bunch of clever hiding spots here on Pendomus, oh great Pillar?"

~All of my hiding spots are now dead.

My footing falters slightly, "Well, that's morbid. So, you're pretty much no goddamn help."

~It would appear not.

I scan the surrounding area. Without heading all the way back the Lateral, there's really nothing but trees, and more trees.

"Come on. You've been on Pendomus for how long? You have to know some better spots to hide this than me. Any dead trees? Another small cave? Anything?" I say.

Maybe this isn't a good idea.

~There is one spot which may work. However, it is more open than I would like. It could still be found, if someone were to look close enough.

"Well, it's better than what I got. Where do we find this mystery spot?" I say.

~Turn right and follow the sun's halo. I will let you know when we get close.

It occurs to me I'm putting an awful lot of faith in someone who, just days ago, had been taking over my body upon Videus' command. I hope like hell I'm not misplacing this trust in the name of saving Runa.

~I will not betray the Daughter of Five. She is our last hope to restore the balance to our planet. I realize this now.

"Don't read my mind and then answer my thought. It's creepy. And you better damn well keep Runa safe. So help me, if you turn on me I will hunt you down," I say.

~You would not have to look far. I am stuck here with you.

"You know what I mean," I spit.

~I do not.

"I mean, I'll figure out who you really are and how to end you. Hell, I'll end myself, too, if I have to. Just to get rid of you," I say.

~That does not make much sense. You would die.

"Yeah, that's the general consensus," I say.

It should probably phase me, but it doesn't. If it meant saving Runa, or eliminating a threat that I could harbor, I'd do it in a heartbeat.

~You are an odd man, Traeton Revasco.

I snicker.

"From you, I'll take that as a compliment."

~Take it as you will.

I scan the trees around us. It's eerily quiet out here today, and I can't help but feel an ominous forboding about this adventure. Where'd all the damn birds end up? They're usually so damn cheerful as they flutter about.

~They are most likely congregating about my disappearance. I have missed my check-in point. We will need to deal with this if we are to be welcomed inside the Helix.

"One issue at a time. We can suss out how to handle that on the way in."

~If you would like.

"I would. Alright, where's this hidden spot you speak of?" I say. "I'd like to get a move on."

~Not much further. Continue toward the sun.

After what still feels like forever, it occurs to me where we're headed.

"Wait, wait," I say. "We're not going back to the Tree of Burden are we?"

~It is the only place I know where Videus will not be able to find it.

"There isn't even a goddamn tree anymore. It's burned to the ground. Your pal made sure of that. How in the hell are we going to hide the book in a bunch of ash?" I say.

Anger wells up inside me. I should have known better. Talk about a gigantic waste of my time. Every minute wasted is another minute Runa has had to endure inside the Helix.

~You may be surprised at what you encounter when we arrive. Please, it's not much further.

I shake my head. I must be insane, or stupid. Hell, maybe both.

Damned if he isn't right, though. As we get closer, instead of the pile of ash I expect, a crystalline tree stands in its place. I approach slowly, taking in the sight. The branches extend upward, touching the blue sky and reflecting the sun's light in fractals across the snowy ground.

My mouth drops open as I walk in full circumference. It's breathtaking.

"How—how did you know it would be here?" I ask.

~I knew if Runa was truly the Daughter of Five, the Tree was not lost to us. It must reemerge in order to bring us her light.

"Yeah, okay. Don't get all spacey on me. You're starting to sound a lot like the guys in the Lateral who've been smoking too many leaves."

~I am not sure what that means.

"Forget it," I say, shaking my head. "What now? Where am I supposed to put this thing? I don't see the opening from before."

~You will have to rest it upon its roots.

"Are you kidding me? Out in the open?" I gasp.

~The Tree will protect its own, masking its energy. Very few on Pendomus will be able to see it.

"Well, that's very reassuring. Who are those few? Others like you?" I say.

~Technically, yes. But they would have to be looking for it.

"And you don't think Videus will be looking for it?" I say, rolling my eyes.

~Good point.

I wipe my hand across my face. How in the hell do I get into these messes?

As if sensing the Caudex, the Tree begins to pulse light and hum softly. It's a soft, low energy at first—but grows louder the longer we're near. Suddenly, the beautiful crystalline branches bend down, snatching the Caudex from my grasp.

Bending back up to the sky, the book is cradled in its embrace, nearly hidden in broad daylight, thanks to the reflective light of the Tree.

"Well, I guess that's that."

~It would appear so.

"I sure as hell hope Runa knows how to get it back from the Tree," I mutter.

~I am sure the Tree will deliver it to her when it is time.

"Oh, now you're sure about something. Figures. C'mon. Let's get our asses over to the Helix and get this over with. I have to know Runa's alright," I say, turning around.

I throw a final glance at the Tree. It truly is magnificent.

The crunching of the snow drones on for a few moments,

as I lose myself in my thoughts. There's so much at stake here —and I can't let anything go sideways.

"Alright—if I'm going into this, you need to tell me who the hell you are. I can't expect to pretend being you if I don't even have a name," I say, unsure I really want to know.

~I am Caelum.

My heart drops and I stop walking.

"You've gotta be kidding me. *The* Caelum. As in, Videus' right-hand—er, *shoulder*—bird?" I say, gasping.

~Is there another?

God, I hope so, but I'm not that lucky.

I should have guessed he'd only send his most trusted on a mission like this. Of course, it's him.

My jaw and fists clench.

Caelum. Shit.

~I will not betray you.

"Yeah, okay. I'm sure you said that to Videus, too. No offense, but I'm not all that convinced at this particular moment in time."

And he knows exactly where the Caudex is. How stupid— how goddamn stupid.

I run my hand through my hair, curbing the impulse to pull it out.

Well, we've come this far—no real chance of turning back now. I can't escape him, even if I wanted to. He knows too much now, anyway. The Caudex's location, the Archives and what it is—I have to follow this through to the end and hope it all turns out well.

~I would feel the same, if I were in your position.

"Well, gee, that's really comforting."

~I simply mean it is okay to be leery. But we will need to work together if we are going to make a passable impression upon my master.

"Yeah, okay. Whatever," I say, swiping my hand in the air.

"Let's get on with this. How do I pass as you without drawing attention to myself?"

~For starters, you must not let your emotions show. You are much too controlled by them and it will be an immediate warning.

"Emotions, check. What else?"

~Do not speak until spoken to. When you enter the Helix, the safeguards will automatically give way. Enter like you belong there, and you will be accepted.

"That's good news, I guess," I say.

~Once approached, tell them the connection was compromised and you were unable to rendezvous. That will explain the need to come back in person. I have been able to block all communication from the others, so this will seem believable to them.

"If you've been able to do that, why didn't you do it sooner?" I say, making a face.

~It was not until I was in your Archives that I realized what was going on. It was as if being in a trance. I may have had the ability, but it never occurred to me to use it. Does this make sense?

"Yeah, I suppose. Kinda like an indoctrination. Or maybe you were just asleep at the wheel," I say.

~The wheel?

"It's an old expression. Not even sure what it was meant to mean. I just like the way it sounds."

~Odd.

"I suppose. Okay, what else?" I say.

~Whatever happens, it is imperative you go with it. Your natural instinct will likely be to fight it, but do not. You will give yourself away and everything will be lost.

"Can you explain? What will I want to fight? Any advance warning will help me prepare."

~Keep your face still as stone when you see Runa—or any other who you may know. Do not let your expression flicker, or it will give you away. If my master asks something of you, go with it until you have succeeded.

"What if he asks me to kill someone?" I say, anger coursing through my veins.

~*In all my time with him, there has never been a need for such one-on-one violence. He has other methods in place to handle those necessities.*

"Reassuring," I lament.

~*It may not seem it, but it should be. Do you think you will be able to manage this?*

"We'll find out," I say, tipping my head to the side and shrugging.

It doesn't take long until the Helix' structure looms in front of me. I pause momentarily to take it in. It's a beautiful building, if only it didn't symbolize everything that's wrong with the world right now.

~*Do not linger. You are being watched. My master has eyes on every square inch of this building.*

My eyes widen. Runa and I didn't know that last time.

I take a deep breath, flatten my facial expression, and square my shoulders. Walking with purpose to the door on the side of the building, I enter in like I own the place. It's an odd feeling—being the imposter for a change.

As I walk in, the sights and smells of the Helix make me want to gag. Everything so forced, and artificial. How in the hell do people not realize this?

~*It's all they know. How would they expect something different?*

Stop doing that.

I roll my eyes, keeping my mouth clamped shut.

Yeah, okay, I suppose stopping isn't gonna happen. It's still odd to have someone talk to you in your own mind. Especially when they're responding to something you think —and not something you say. Not sure I'm gonna be able to get used to that.

~*Continue down this hallway for a meter or so. When you*

come to the checkpoint, you will need to allow the retinal scan. It will recognize you—and will also alert my master you are here.

I take a deep breath.

Swell.

My footsteps echo off the boring gray walls. The hallway is devoid of anyone else—an oddity, but not completely unheard of. My best guess on time is the middle of the day. Most everyone will be at their professional appointment stations.

As I reach the checkpoint, I deliberately keep my face stone cold, and my arms at my side. I envision Caelum moving like a robot, so it helps me alter my innate mannerisms. I step forward to the retinal scanner and allow it to verify my identity.

As promised, the safety features release and I'm allowed to continue on.

I never thought about it before—but it's strange that the Helix needed so many safety features. Was there ever a problem with safety or order? In all my time here I can't say there ever was. Maybe it was in anticipation of these moments.

~My master has an obsession with invulnerability. These checkpoints also allow for the flow of data—keeping track of the comings and goings of his flock.

I snort. Is that what we're calling people now? A flock?

~It seems a fitting description.

Struggling to keep my face flat, I can't help but snicker. I suppose to a bird, that would be an apt descriptor.

~You will take the door to the right.

I follow Caelum's direction, making my way to the door. As I approach, it swings open for me.

~This is a sensored door. It will recognize those with authorization.

I keep my gaze focused straight ahead of me, but it's damn hard not to stare at my surroundings. The decor of the place shifts entirely from the cold, sterile environment I'm used to and into a warmer, darker light. Walking down an ornate staircase, I keep my movements almost mechanical. Flames—or at least sconces with the appearance of flames—flicker on the walls. They cast deep shadows, giving an intensely ominous vibe.

Creepy decor, Caelum.

~*I must admit, this is the first time I've come from this direction. It is the first time I would have used your human form to enter.*

Not even when we—I mean when you helped Kani be taken captive?

~*No, I had no need. Videus took her and I was told to return to my post.*

Oh.

The thought that it was my *being*, even if not technically me, that allowed Kani to return to the Helix—to be taken captive—it's not something I overly want to think about.

I enter an open square, with no apparent doorway, but as we approach, the wall directly in front of us dissolves. Beyond, Videus stands in waiting.

~*Do not move. Simply wait for instruction.*

I stand like a statue, arms at my sides, and my gaze softly focused in front of me. Videus walks forward, an odd mask covering his face with a strange looking bird atop his head. It takes everything I have not to laugh at the ridiculousness of it. I mean, what does he think he is, part of a cliche horror movie from back on earth? He even has a damn cape.

Circling me like a predator, Videus moves wordlessly. His hands are clasped behind his back, making his cape float outward at the floor.

"Tell me, where have you been?" Videus asks.

Without turning to him, I slowly blink and say, "My connection was severed. When it became apparent, I made my way back to you."

Standing just off to the side, not directly in front of my gaze, I feel the weight of his faceless stare. His assessment is clinical in the way he watches me. Any wrong move, and I may as well kiss this whole thing goodbye.

~Do not move at all. Do not look at him. It's what he's waiting for.

I cast my gaze in the distance, seeing the long tunnel of stone with doorways on either side. Trying not to dwell on what they are—or who may be in them—I soften my gaze, clear my mind, and wait.

After what seems like forever, Videus says, "Very well. I had wondered. You were meant to check in two hours ago. Thank you for returning to me."

I tip my head, in lieu of words.

"Do you have any news for me?" Videus asks.

~Tell him the Daughter of Five left while you were asleep. He knows that already and wants you to verify.

"Yes. R—The Daughter of Five left while we were asleep. I am unsure where she went," I say.

"I am aware of this," he says, moving to the other side of me.

I keep my gaze straight ahead.

"She and the boy were looking for ways inside the Helix. It is possible they were going to attempt to break in."

~Tell him that is all you remember from this last round. End with the word, omega. It is his secret code word, for instances such as this. It is meant to assure him it is I talking, and not someone else.

"That is everything I remember from this last round," I say. Tipping my head slightly, I end with, "Omega."

Videus' shoulders straighten perceivably. Confidence of some sort restored to him with the final word.

"Very good, Caelum. Now, I need you to do something for me," Videus says. "Come, follow me."

As I turn to follow, the last thing I see is the blunt instrument in his hand as it comes down on my face.

8

RUNA

*B*EING ABRUPTLY PULLED from the connection with everyone else is disorienting enough, but the knife buried in my hand sends tendrils of agony throughout my limb. An intense urge to vomit surfaces, and I struggle to hold it back.

"You doing okay, there, Everblossom? You're looking a bit green," Videus says, chuckling slightly.

I clench my teeth and make myself look into the space where his eyes should be.

"I'm fine," I say.

"Wonderful," he says nonchalantly. "Now, where was I? Oh, right—*surprise.*"

Videus steps to the side, revealing the crumpled form of Traeton. His blue hair, matted to his head with blood. The side of his face is swollen and bruised.

"Rise," Videus commands.

Trae doesn't move, instead, he takes a deep breath and flashes his tongue across his lips.

"I said rise," Videus says, using his left hand to create a quick hand gesture.

Whatever the gesture was, Trae's hands fly to his head and he crumples over in agony.

"Stop—stop! Why are you doing this?" I scream.

"Well, for starters, because I can. Don't ever forget that," Videus says, turning his empty face toward me.

Taking a few deep breaths to regain my calm, I say, "You don't need to torture him. He's not going anywhere."

"Hmmm," Videus says. "You have that part right. The rest is just a perk."

He closes his fist, and Traeton cries out in pain.

"Now then, I'm sure you know why I've returned. Well, beyond the obvious gift," he laughs.

"I've been cooperating with you. You promised me—you told me everyone would be let go if I cooperated. Just let Trae and the others go. You can have me," I say.

"Runa—no," Trae says, his speech garbled and disjointed. He looks up through one good eye. The other is completely swollen shut. His nose bends at an awkward angle, clearly broken.

Anger builds from the base of my spine, coursing through my veins. Everything in the room rumbles, as I focus on Videus and ending him.

Trae's hands fly out, seeking balance, despite being so close to the ground. Videus, merely laughs.

"Ah, I knew you had more buried in there," he says.

Surprised, the anger dissipates as curiosity replaces it temporarily.

Was that me? Did I actually do that?

"See, I've been tracking people like you, Runa. People with special...*abilities*...to do things no one else can do. There's something special about Pendomus. It's done some-thing special to humanity that we never anticipated," Videus says.

"If humanity is so special, why are you trying to cage and kill us all?" I spit.

"No, no my dear. You misunderstand. Humanity isn't special. No, humanity is incredibly unremarkable. I said Pendomus has *done something* special to humanity," Videus annunciates the words slowly. "I merely need to harness it."

"Look around you, Videus. You already have. What more could you want?" I say, the anger beginning to mount again.

Videus rushes forward, his blank, bloody face inches from mine. Caelum grips his shoulder tightly, and chirps in surprise at the sudden movement.

"I want to end this all," Videus says slowly.

My pulse throbs behind my ears, and I try desperately not to take in the stench of his presence.

"End this? I don't understand," I say.

"Runa—don't listen—" Trae starts, but Videus abruptly cuts him off with another hand gesture. Trae's battered form drops to the ground completely.

"Traeton—" I cry. "What have you done to him?"

"Don't get your wires in a twist. He's alive," Videus says, "for now."

"You're sick. You need serious help, you know that? If anything needs to end—it's you," I spit.

Videus begins to back away, perhaps out of anger with my words. But he returns, his face once again close to mine. He takes the hilt of the knife digging into my hand, and twists.

I can't hold back the scream erupting from my lips.

"Don't you think I've tried? You're a fool. You've always been a fool," Videus says. "This place, Pendomus, it's like a maze. Only those who know the game can enter and leave. Some of us are stuck. Others, ripped from us. So you either play the game, or you become part of it."

"You've started the game," I say, confused. "All of this—all the pain and suffering. This is all you. Don't you understand that? You could hop off at any time, you could do whatever you wanted and no one would be the wiser. Why do you stay here? Why continue with this loop?"

A deep, maniacal laugh bubbles from deep inside Videus' chest.

"*Loop*. There it is again. Such a fine word, and so fitting," he says. "Which brings us back to you. Let's stop playing coy, shall we?"

I narrow my eyes, wishing I could look into his.

"Where is the book?" he says, slowly.

My heart skips a beat. I know exactly what book he's referring to.

"What book?" I say, innocently.

Videus twists the knife again, sending blinding pain through my whole body, short circuiting all of my thoughts momentarily with the agony.

"I'll ask you one more time," Videus says calmly, "Where's the bloody book?"

The calm demeanor he's taken on is far more chilling than the absurd, angry man. It's like his humanity slips from his grasp and something else takes over completely.

What could he possibly gain from finding the Caudex? What secrets does it hold that he shouldn't be privy to? For the life of me, I can't think of any. However, the book still has pages yet to be revealed to me. There's no knowing what could still be concealed. Adrian told me to keep it safe...

"Times up," Videus says, flicking his hand toward Trae.

Instantly, Trae wakes up, a high-pitched scream escaping his lips.

In reflex, my body tries to stand, despite the restraints.

"Stop," I beg, "please, just leave him alone. I'll tell you how to find it, I promise."

"Good girl. I knew you could be persuaded," Videus says, returning his empty gaze to me.

Helping him find the Caudex would jeopardize more than the book. I know this. Adrian and my trials—they've drilled into me the importance of it not getting in Videus' hands. But perhaps if I can lead him differently...maybe I can at least protect Trae from being further tortured.

"The Caudex is near the Tree of Burden," I say, slowly.

It's not a complete lie. Technically, the Archives is out that way. But if I steer him toward the Tree of Burden, at least I know he'll need my help.

"Release Trae and I'll take you to it," I say quickly.

Maybe, just maybe I can lure Videus from here and save Trae.

"The Tree of Burden is ash," Videus says, his words slow and deliberate. He raises his hand again toward Trae, but it hovers there, waiting for more information.

I rest my eyes on Trae—his broken and beaten body. Even after all the strangeness with him since my return, the bizarre outbursts and odd behaviors—the true him, the true man...he has my heart. I can't get around it, and I need to find a way to protect him, so I can get him back.

"It's not in the Tree, only near it. Please, let me show you," I say.

If I can get Videus away from all of this, perhaps I have a chance at getting the upper hand somehow. Tethys is out there. And if Ammon was released, as promised, he should be on his way to alert Delaney and the rest of the team at the Lateral. Who knows, maybe they'll—

Videus laughs, but it's not a convincing one. Instead, it's more like a condescending chuckle meant to intimidate.

"There's nothing you could possibly do to get me near that tree again, dear Everblossom. Whether resurrected or not. No, we'll just have to do this the hard way."

He stands near me, his bloody face undulating. I can't tell if he's thinking, or frozen when there's no eyes to gauge expressions.

Then I feel the odd tingling sensation creep over the back of my skull. It starts at the base of my spine, spreading out over the top of my head, like tendrils. Goosebumps rise over my body as I wait. As quickly as it started, the sensation dissipates.

"Then you'll never get the book. You won't be able to see the Tree to gauge where I hid it. It might look destroyed to you, but it doesn't to me. My vision allows me to see it as it truly is. Perhaps it's the Tree that once was—maybe it's resurrected, I don't know how it works. I just know it's hidden from you for a reason. Just as it was before," I say.

"Then going out there would be futile for me, would it not?"

"Not if you take me with you. I can bring you to the Tree," I lie.

I have no interest whatsoever in helping him open the Caudex. I'd die first. But if I can gain his trust—

Videus springs to life again, "Tell me, what do you know about the planet, Everblossom? In all your adventures as the Daughter of Five, what have you uncovered. I'm truly intrigued. Tell me everything—"

His change of subject is unnerving.

"What difference would any of that make? It won't bring back your brother—isn't that what everything's been about?" I say, trying to understand.

How can everything be linked? The past, the future, the present? How can Videus be so heartless and cold? How could the planet be put in peril thanks to a man who didn't exist when humanity first arrived on Pendomus? Instead, his time travel escapades have caused all of this.

My mind can't wrap around the technicalities and subtleties of what he's done.

It's all so confusing.

"It has everything to do with my brother—everything to do with bringing him back," Videus says, his teeth grinding.

Trae mumbles, grabbing hold of his side as he tries to sit up.

Videus flattens his hand, and Trae drops to the floor like an empty vessel. His eyes closed, his breathing slow and unfettered.

"The Caudex won't bring him back, it's not that kind of book—" I bite my lip.

Instantly, Videus is millimeters from my face.

"Don't you dare tell me what it will or will not do. If it were under my control, I'd erase you and your friends before you were all born. Keep that in mind. My brother's death is on *your* hands. If that book can't help me, there's no point in keeping any of you around. I simply don't understand why I can't—" he says, pulling the knife from my hand to hold it at my throat. Then he takes a deep breath, dropping the knife to his side and standing up straighter. "The Caudex is the key to making things right."

"His death is on my hands? Has it ever occurred to you it was simply your bother's time to go? For whatever reason, the wheels set in motion, both future and past—demanded his sacrifice?" I say, through gritted teeth.

Energy in my fingertips starts to bleed from my hands, rising up my arms. As if tapping into something beyond myself, I embrace the shift, allowing it to occur. My hand throbs, gently closing itself up before my eyes.

"If it weren't for you, he'd still be here," Videus spews.

"If it weren't for *you*—there would have been no need for a Daughter of Five in the first place. I'd just be some girl living on Pendomus. Maybe everyone else would be normal, too. Your brother may even still be here, if it wasn't for *you*," I say, power rising with each word of truth uttered his direction.

"Lies. I've tried thousands of ways to ensure his safety. Each time, I fail. I can't keep doing it without the book—every time I reset time, I lose memories—making it much more difficult to try again," he says. "I need a more direct path now."

I narrow my eyes, wondering if this really is what it's all about. Just a man, trying to save his brother from death—and failing over and over. It's driven him completely mad.

"What I want to know is how you were able to affect change in the continuum when you were in the past. Don't try to say you didn't, I felt the ripples of time shift," he says, clutching the knife tight.

I blink at him. I honestly have no idea what he's even referring to. What was I able to change?

"Why wouldn't you just ask for help dealing with your brother's death? There had to have been people you could turn to," I say, oddly empathetic. I know I shouldn't be—but a piece of me can't help it.

"You don't understand. You know nothing," he says. "Just a child, playing at grown up games."

"Then help me to understand. I know this can't really be you. This man you've become—you can't make me believe deep down, you're not still a man in there. I'm sure your brother would never have wanted—"

Searing hot pain flashes across my left eye, as my scars burn. My head rocks to the side from the brunt force of his punch. The knife in his hand, is unforgiving in its resistance.

"Enough. You have no right to assume you know what was in my brother's mind," Videus says, taking a calming inhalation. He adjusts his robes, and squares his shoulders.

A Labot man with enormous muscles opens the glass

door. He takes a wide stance and rests his arms behind his back. No words necessary.

"Take him to lockup. I need some time *alone* with him. It's pretty clear I won't get the information I want from the Daughter of Five—at least, not yet. Let's see what I can glean from her lover. Maybe then it will encourage her to be more cooperative."

With that, the Labot grabs hold of Trae's limp body and removes him from the room.

"What are you going to do with him?" I ask, panic seeping into my resolve.

Would he kill Trae? Or does he have some kind of torture planned? Trae doesn't know anything—at least, not enough to satiate Videus even if he did talk. He's never seen me with the Caudex, let alone know how to find it—even though it's right there with him in the Archives. At the time, I felt badly for not sharing that side of me. But he wasn't himself and I knew it. Now—now, I don't know whether to be relieved he knows nothing—or worried.

"Please—please don't hurt him," I plead.

Videus doesn't even look back or answer me. He simply follows after the Labot and Trae.

The door closes behind them, frosting over and sealing itself, with me still trapped inside.

I need to find a way out of here. Now.

Closing my eyes, I focus the energy I felt rising earlier and directing it at the restraints of the chair. I may not be able to dig into the inner workings of wiring, or coding—but perhaps I can overload the energetic hub.

~Are you still there?

~Will you help us?

~What has he done?

The voices come flooding in as I tap into the bloodlines for help. It's hard to tune them out—allowing my own energies to focus to the level of precision I need. The barrage of data intruding my brain is overwhelming.

~Everyone—everyone, please. You have to stop.

I say in between comments.

~I can't help anyone locked in this room. I need to focus—find a way to get out of this chair. Either give me your ideas, or stay silent for a few minutes so I can think. Please.

After a moment, the voices settle down. Although I can still feel them all as they stand by.

I try again, focusing my mind and energy on the chair, trying to break free from my restraints. As I do, the restraints tighten further—cutting off circulation to my wrists and ankles. Whatever Videus used to bind me, it's worked like a charm to keep me as contained as possible.

Damn. How am I going to get out of this before he comes back?

~I have a suggestion to try. I think it may be of help.

One of the voices says. His voice and his mannerisms, even here in my mind are so familiar. It's like I've talked to him before.

~Be my guest. I don't think I can muster enough strength.

~I do not believe it is about strength. I have been here a while. If there is one thing I have learned, it is that the Ibis man wants compliance. That is all. Perhaps if you did not fight against them at all—they may release?

~It's worth a try, I guess.

Closing my eyes, I turn my focus to relaxing. Allowing non-confrontation to well up inside me, and letting go of as much inner struggle as I can muster. I'm able to hold onto the sensation for a fleeting second or two, but it's so hard. Anger continues to bubble up unexpectedly. How do I relax and comply with everything I've been put here to fight against?

It's infuriating.

In fact, the more it infuriates me, the more the restraints are fueled, burning brighter and more intact.

~You need to let go. Forget who you are. Forget where you come from and where you have been. Try to erase it all from your mind and just...be.

~How? How do I let go of all that I am?

~You simply do.

His words of wisdom resonate with me on a core level. There's more to his words than meet the eye and I'm not sure why.

~Who are you? What's your name?

~I am no one.

I nod to myself. It reminds me of the man who would come to me in my mind when I was going through the trials. Perhaps the same man? Or is he simply leading by example?

~Okay, no one. Let me try this again.

I blow out a deep breath, feeling the air pass through my lips. Closing my eyes, I free my mind of everything. My path. The time loops. Videus. Fenton. Trae— I let it all go until all that's left is darkness. I sit with it, allowing the darkness to simply be.

I feel its weight, only I don't recognize it as such. Instead, it feels more like floating. Or being in the birthing chamber with fluids supporting my body all around.

I release all of my troubles. My birth right. The bloodlines.

Suddenly, I feel my face flicker—like a large feather flitted over it. The sensation brings me quickly back to my body— but it was enough. The restraints are gone and I'm free within the confines of the glass cage.

~Thank you, no one. It worked. Now I just have to figure a way out of here.

~You better do it quickly. It's almost time for the raining fire again. Now that you're out, you're fair game.

With that, he's gone, the connection severed between us.

9

TRAETON

*A*S MUCH AS I'D HOPED Videus would greet me —*us*—with open arms, I hadn't expected to endure such a beating in the name of shock. He's a sick, twisted man.

"Alright, what now?" I whisper.

I should probably simply ask the questions in my head, but I feel like if I keep doing it—I'll lose all sense of myself. I need to keep whatever grasp on reality I can find in this hell.

~Videus will expect a more detailed report of what happened while we were away. We were lucky he had not the time when we first arrived.

My hand rises to my swollen cheek, "Yeah, lucky."

~The beating was unfortunate. I am sorry you had to be aware for it. My master cares not for the face. It is always the first thing he will go for when he needs information, regardless from whom.

"Well, isn't that super?" I say, spitting the last dregs of blood from my mouth. "What's he got against faces?"

~I am not sure. It has always been this way.

"Maybe he can't stand seeing the humanity in their eyes?" I offer, standing up.

It's been five minutes since we were ushered out of the

cage where Runa's being held. Other than being restrained, she looked mostly okay. Which, truthfully, is both as much a relief as it is surprising.

"Why's Runa still okay? I mean, not that I'm not grateful, but why hasn't he hurt her?" I continue to whisper.

~My master is oddly superstitious for a man of science. Now that he knows he has the Daughter of Five, it is my belief, he will tread very lightly until he acquires what he needs.

"Which is?"

~He is hunting for the true prophecy before he proceeds. He wants to ensure his steps forward will be most effective.

"Effective for what? He already has world domination," I say. "I mean, what more could a guy really need?"

~I do not believe that was ever the core of his motivations. It is far more difficult to parse out than this. He is a complicated creature and I feel at his very core, many of his insights may be compromised.

"Well, that's a no brainer. He's out of his goddamn mind," I say more softly than before.

I really need to keep my voice down. The walls could have ears for all I know. With my good eye, I try to gander at the walls and ceilings to get a better look—but it's hard to tell if there could be any listening devices. If he really wanted, Videus could hide cameras or mics just about anywhere and I'd be none the wiser.

~When my master arrives, I will need to take the forefront. He is most concerned about many things I have had in the works. If for some reason you falter with the dialogue, he will become extremely suspicious. It is the last thing we need at this moment. He will not hesitate to kill us both.

I nod—sounds like a good idea anyway. At this point, any civil dealings with Videus and I'll likely find myself squeezing his throat closed—or die trying. That was my favorite way to dispose of him outta all of my daydreams, anyway.

The door to the vassalage cell opens, and in steps Videus —his mask made of blood and the idiotic looking bird headdress. I want to point out how ridiculous he looks, but mentally take a step back—allowing Caelum to do his thing before I make a mess outta everything.

"Caelum?" Videus asks, stepping inside the room. His dark cloak drags on the floor ominously—like it's meant to sweep along the dark aura around him. It does a good job of it.

"Yes, my master," I hear myself say.

So weird being in here, but deferring to someone else.

"Explain to me something. Why did you not come back to your body when I called upon you? Even without hearing me, I would have thought you'd have sensed the calling," Videus says, taking another step inward.

"I did not hear the call at all. There is something wrong with the man's mind, perhaps his nervous system is compromised. I am not sure why, but I was unable to be released at all," Caelum says. "It may be due to the brain degradation we have spoken about. I fear that it may become increasingly more difficult to evacuate."

There are truths mixed in his words that I feel resonate, but definite falsehoods as well. I'll hand it to him, he's a convincing liar.

Walking on by, Videus takes his headdress off and places it on a counter behind us. For a moment, his back is to us and it's hard to tell what he's doing. His bald head drops slightly and a slow sigh escapes him. Perhaps he's more of a man than I gave him credit for.

"We'll have to get you on the diagnostic table if this continues to become a problem, Caelum," he says. "I can't afford having you—"

"Would it be so bad if I were in this body instead of my own?" Caelum asks.

"I would hate to lose your ability to see from above. With the new weather controls I've been working on—you're the only one I trust with some of my most sensitive missions," Videus says, turning his head to the side and speaking over his shoulder.

I'm not sure why—but his silhouette looks so familiar. Could I have seen him before?

"I understand, master. I shall continue to try. I will let you know if I am unsuccessful. Have you perfected the white elephant technology?" Caelum says, continuing to stand as still as a statue.

Weather controls? White elephants. What on Pendomus are we talking about? And is it normal for such obedience? What the hell kinda master does that—erases any thought of free choice? What in the hell is Videus so afraid of?

"Not yet, but I'm very close," Videus mutters. He raises a hand to his head and his fingertips graze the skin on his forehead.

Videus straightens his shoulders, and replaces his head-dress. With his back turned, he looks almost weak.

I have to admit—this is not entirely the way I envisioned this meeting to go. At least, not after the last one. That—yeah, that was more like what I expected, I suppose. But this? It's almost as if he's tired of everything and he's willing to let his guard down, just a little bit with Caelum.

~Caelum—listen to me, we could end this. Right now. His back is turned to us. He wouldn't be expecting you to jump him.

Why wouldn't we take this opportunity? It's practically handed to us on a platter.

~What is it you expect me to do? This is not in my nature. I oversee things, hear things. I am not the brute force.

~Well, I am. If you're not able, move over and let me handle this.

I can feel the trepidation creeping into my body, arising because of Caelum. As much of a crony as he has been—he's right. He's not a fighter. He'd much prefer hanging back from the fray and being a casual observer. I can't blame him, but I can't sit here and do nothing.

~Alright, if you must. But he will not be as easily overcome as you may think.

Then, just like that, my consciousness is pushed out front and Caelum's has taken the rear. My hand slips to my back, as I reach for the electric blade I stashed earlier. I grip the hilt lightly, sure not to trigger the blade just yet.

I take a deep breath, preparing to lunge, but Videus turns around just as I'm about to flip the switch on the blade. I freeze in place, trying not to let my emotions and motivations show. There's no way I can attack him head on and win. I'm not that stupid.

Videus slowly walks toward me again, his movements once again slow, and deliberate. As if the headdress gives him more clarity than simply being himself alone. He takes a deep breath, watching me for a moment. The dark, bloody space where his face should be is unnerving. I suppose it's meant to be. Still, too bad he didn't turn around completely when he had his mask off. I would have loved to have seen the face of the real man.

"Hello Traeton. I figured you would make your appearance sooner or later. You do have a way of continually popping up, unwanted. No patience in you whatsoever," he finally says. "It's predictable."

I pull the weapon out, gripping it tightly as the ten inch blade of electricity flares to life.

Videus instantly laughs.

"Do you even know how to use one of those, boy?" he taunts.

"How about we find out," I say, widening my stance.

Videus takes a step forward and opens his arms wide, inviting any attempt.

I lunge forward, hoping to catch him off guard with an immediate response. Videus holds still, not moving—not even flinching. As I jab the knife into his rib cage, the electricity scatters, shooting off into random particles in the air. What's left is a rather awkward attempt at an uppercut.

A deep, boisterous chuckle eminates from Videus' core as he tosses me aside without even breaking his stance.

My body slams against the wall, effectively knocking the wind out of me.

"Do you honestly believe there's anything that could stop me? After all this time, all the attempts? And of all things, an electric blade? Sloppy, Traeton. Simply disappointing," he says.

Struggling to regain my breathe, I grimace at him. Safe to say this plan between Caelum and I wasn't one of my smartest. On the upside, at least we know Runa's still alive. And now, if I make it outta here in one piece, at least I know where she's being kept.

Crawling up onto all fours, it takes effort to stand. In a movement so fast, I'd say he wasn't even human anymore, Videus is at my side. He grabs my throat, his fingers digging into the side of my neck as he squeezes and pulls me to my feet. He slides my body up the wall, my feet dangling inches from the floor—all with one hand.

Personally, I'm amazed at the show of strength. If he could do this—why bother with taking over Fenton's body?

Without being able to see Videus' expression, it's hard to tell if he even cares. Could he crush my windpipe with one hand? Seems like he could.

"Why? Why are you doing this?" I spit, my words garbled and labored.

"I can't allow you—or the Daughter of Five to destroy everything I've worked so hard to accomplish," he says simply.

"What's that?" I fire back, struggling to breathe. "Your pretty face?"

"Everything I've done—everything here that you see—it's all to get him back. I have tried for centuries to repair the damage I'd—" he pauses for a brief moment, "The only way now is to push through," he says, squeezing my neck tighter. "Keep moving forward."

"Get who back?" I say each word slowly, trying to pull in as much air as possible.

"Do you not understand the nature of the delicate balance we cling to?" he says, ignoring my question. "The prophecy—if I don't stop the prophecy now, all will be lost. Everything. There will be no way to keep trying. Look around you. Do you know how many times I've been to the past to help this ant farm progress to the level it is now? They owe everything to me," Videus says. "And you want to take it away from me?"

His switch in motivations is confusing. Is it about some guy he wants to bring back? Or his pet project of the Helix. Anger floods Videus' words with more emotion than I've heard him display since we met face to face.

"What are you talking about? You aren't making any sense," I say through gritted teeth.

Either Videus has truly lost his marbles, or his entire grip on reality. Maybe both.

Suddenly, the lights go out and emergency lighting engages. The ominous red lights take this Crematorium to a whole new level of hellish appearances.

"What's happened now?" Videus snarls, tipping his head

to the side and his grip loosening enough to allow me to rest on the floor.

In the background of my mind I make out most of Videus' mental alert to the Salamanders and the rest of his cronies—thanks to Caelum still being connected.

~Find source. Make sure Daughter of Five locked away. Alert me...problems. Do not disturb me...ridiculous, mundane things. Much to do...expect not to be disturbed.

Salamanders flood the hallway outside, running in the direction of the rest of the vassalage cells and where Runa is being held. The sea of black creatures is in deep contrast with the washed out grey walls as the lights flicker back on.

Turning back to me, Videus says, "It's fortunate for you, keeping you alive is worth more to me at the moment. As soon as you become more of a problem than you're worth, I have no qualm in ending you. Even if—"

"I won't help you. Whatever you have planned, I'll do everything I can to get in your way," I say, his lighter grip easing my words.

"Well, that's unfortunate of you. Good thing I already have a man—well, a bird, actually—on the inside. I'll simply have to get rid of your consciousness completely and give your body up to someone I trust," Videus says slowly. "Would you like that instead?"

Inside, Caelum's fear is almost as palpable as my own. If Videus tries to extract my consciousness—he'll have full access to everything housed in our memories. That includes the location of the Archives as the Acropolis. For reasons still beyond me, it has a heavy relevance to the brewing war and I feel a need to protect it.

"Your man isn't in here anymore," I say, trying to throw him off. "I've destroyed him."

"You lie," Videus says, his eyes narrowing, "Caelum is more powerful than you'll ever be, boy. His awareness spans millenia, handed down through those who came before. No boy would put a stop to him. Certainly not you."

However, something falters in Videus' words. It's a split second flicker in inflection, but it's enough for me to play on.

"How else do you think I was able to regain control of my body? Do you think your crony would allow me to try and stab you?" I say, trying to sound reasonable.

"Alright. How were you able to destroy him then? Spare no details," he says, mockingly.

"Once I realized what was going on, it was like flexing a muscle," I say. Not entirely a lie. In some ways, I'd been working on expelling Caelum from the moment I became aware of what was happening. I just hadn't gotten complete control over everything. Sure, I'd been able to throw a wrench into things, I suppose.

"And this muscle—it did what exactly?" he says, his hand loosening a little more.

"I was able to regain control of my mind—take it back from him slowly until I could overwhelm him. From there, I was able to lock him away."

I cringe. That's not the way I should have described it.

"So, he's not destroyed? Just locked away?" Videus says, considering.

"Same difference. You'll never see him again," I say, shrugging.

"Perhaps," Videus says, wheels obviously turning in his mind. "Perhaps I've underestimated your mind, Traeton. If the SeizeScanner's frequency wasn't enough to open up your mind completely, perhaps we simply need to up the dosage."

My eyes widen.

The SeizeScanner? That's how this was done to me? How he was able to take control of my mind and insert Caelum.

I had no idea how this all started, or when. But now it all makes sense. The last time we were inside, Runa and I—

when I pushed her out the door— I got tagged by the Scanner. All I could think about was protecting her. I thought I was done for until I woke up at the Lateral. But it was all just a ruse, I was meant to go back home.

"So that's how you controlled my mind? The SeizeScanner?" I lament. "Was it meant to take over immediately? Or were you pissed your guy wasn't able to spy right away?"

"Oh—why not. You won't remember any of this once I'm done with you. The Scanner only allows me access to your coding so I could slip Caelum in. It wasn't immediate. So to answer your question, I was happy with the results. Up until now, that is," he says, leaning in close. "Oh, you fought me— fought Caelum. But I knew in the end the headaches would be overwhelming enough for you. I was, of course, right."

My eyes widen.

The headaches. Of course—it's all part of it. They started right after the Seize Scanner and only worsened over time. No wonder the NeuroWands did nothing to help. They weren't normal headaches. Why didn't I think of that? It'd never occurred to me they were connected, either. Even after realizing Caelum was in here.

I'm an idiot of epic proportions.

Dropping his hand from my throat, Videus takes a step back.

"None of this would have to be necessary if people would simply comply. Instead, they and are such resistant creatures, believing they know better than their fellow man. It's not true, you know. Some are not worthy of higher level thinking. There are some who are far too stupid to make intelligent decisions. They can't see the bigger picture and they don't know what's best for them."

"It's called free will, you should try it sometime," I spit.

Who does this guy think he is, really? The more he speaks, the more nuts he sounds. Sure, there are some pretty dumb people out there, but there are worse things to be—a homicidal maniac for one.

Placing a hand on one of the large stones of the wall, it lights up, scanning his palm. The wall dissolves, revealing a large arsenal of SeizeScanners, sonic resonators, and a myriad of other weapons for the choosing.

Videus grabs the largest SeizeScanner within reach.

"It's time to get this moving along. Don't you agree?" he says.

10

RUNA

*D*O I FOCUS ON THE ELEMENT OF SURPRISE? Or do I try to break out of here and be long gone before anyone comes back for another round?

I trace my hands over the point where the seams of the door should be, but nothing stands out. It looks like one solid pane of glass. If I try to break it, would it set off alarms?

~Don't do it. The last person who did was consumed by the rain.

A woman's voice enters my mind.

I don't know if it's reassuring to have so many people here to help, or downright creepy that they can answer my thoughts in this manner. The lack of privacy is unsettling at the very least. I need to learn to control the flow.

~Alright, so what do you suggest. Based on the information you've already attained—is there a way out? How does Videus make it work? Has anyone been able to ascertain that?

~There is a connection in his mind and the mind of the Labots. It's as if they can pass through simply by thinking it.

~So it's attached to the eLink in some form or another. Am I right?

~Perhaps. Unless it's on its own frequency. It's certainly possible, considering the length at which he's gone to keep us all here.

~You're right. I wouldn't put it past him to create a security all its own for this place.

Think Runa—you have to be able to get out of this mess. There has to be a way to trigger the opening. Maybe a fail-safe? In case something went wrong with the mental programming?

I look around the glass room. The only thing left is the glass chair. Otherwise, the room is utterly vacant. However, we already know Videus likes a good mirage—he's nothing if not consistent with that. Perhaps there's a button or panel hidden behind a holographic screen of some sort?

Walking around the cube, I run my hands over everything. The seams of the floor. The corner of the room. I drop to my hands and knees and test out every tile on the floor.

There has to be something here, I can feel it. Even someone as insane as Videus would have his clever moments. He wouldn't want to be stuck in a room like this without a way out if his programming stopped working, or the power cut out.

I run my hands over the back of the chair, the arms, the seat. Everything I can think of. Nothing.

I'm just about to give up when my right hand falls through a tiny space on the floor by the back wall. The veil of the holographic image doesn't lift, but inside I feel the lever. It's a simple pulley—rather than anything electronic. Probably because he knows I'd be able to manipulate it.

Well, this works just as well, too.

~Here goes nothing guys. I sure hope this is what I hope it is and not the 'incinerate' button.

I pull hard, shifting the lever from the up position to the down. The cube quakes, clearly not used to this mechanism being used. The door shudders, then shifts aside in a more mechanical, arduous way. Not the smooth gliding aside like when Videus does it.

Without a second thought, I'm out the door and running along the other glass cage units.

I chuckle a little bit as I run.

I guess I chose being long gone.

But I can't leave without setting everyone else free. It's my job—it's part of why I came here.

~The switchboard is near the back of the complex. You might be able to cause a mass shortage that will open the doors.

One girl says.

~How do you know?

~Because I'm next to it. The Ibis man didn't think I was paying attention, but I was. I let him think the torture had broken me.

I cringe. Torture. How could someone do this? How could anyone become *this*?

~Can you guide me? Can you sense where I am? I have a general sense on you—but it's vague.

I'm not sure how this connection between us all works, but if we could amplify it, it would be helpful.

~What do you mean? I—I can't sense where you are. Just that you're close. Maybe if I focus on showing you where I am?

~How do you mean?

~I don't know, I've never tried anything like this before. Let's find out.

Suddenly, without any additional information, a pillar of blue light shines from her location.

~I got you. On my way.

I race down the pathways, toward the beam of light. When I arrive, I rest my eyes on her glass cage. Its frosted glass is filled full of blue light, as well as shooting the beam toward the ceiling.

~Okay, I'm here. Now what?

The light extinguishes. I look around, trying to find the panel she referred to.

~*It's on the back wall, toward the left hand side.*

I run to the wall, my eyes flitting from one end to the other. There's nothing obvious on the left hand side.

~*I don't see it. Videus probably has it hidden. What does it look like?*

~*It's a panel with a bunch of command sensors on it.*

~*Okay, thanks. Give me a second.*

I walk the back wall on the left, running my hand over the wall to try to find the panel. Suddenly, little orbs of light—the ones that have helped me in the past—filter out of the wall and circle around one spot in particular.

It looks like more of the same sterile, grey wall.

How am I going to control the panel if I can't even see the commands? If I just start hitting them randomly, I'm sure the opposite of what we want will happen—*lockdown.*

The orbs begin to circle tighter, now that I'm focused on the right place. Sliding my hand inside the holographic image, I let their light guide my fingertips. Trusting them to lead me to the right place seems like the only option I have left. Especially if we're going to get out of here alive.

The orbs stop fluttering about and concentrate over one location. Without any time to lose, I tap the sensor, hoping it's the one we need.

Everything in the wide open space of cells shuts down, including all of the lights. Plunged into darkness, the people around me start to panic.

~*What's happened?*

~*Oh no, we'll never get out of here now.*

~*The man will be back—he'll kill us all.*

Their sentiments echo in fear and border on despair.

The orbs of light flit to another location on the board, then hover in waiting. I tap the next sensor.

Backup lighting kicks in from the floor—an eerie flame-like deep orange.

Then, the orbs quickly go to one more location. Without hesitation, I tap the next sensor. Unfortunately, this time alarms blare and the lights switch from orange to bright and flashing. The way they spin is disorienting, but I catch one good thing in this—assuming we can find a way out. The doors of all the cages dissolve, allowing people the ability to escape.

Some stumble out of their cells, carefully exiting with eyes open wide.

~*Baxten? Baxten where are you? Are you able to get out?*

~*Yes, I'm out. Where are you?*

~*In relation to you, I don't know.*

I look around the space, realizing if we're going to all get out of here alive, we need to work together.

~*Everyone—please, we need to be smart about this. I need everyone to come to the back wall of the vassalage.*

~*The back wall of the what?*

Someone says.

The woman who guided me to the wall steps out of her cell, instantly finding me. She has dark circles around her eyes, but a smile still breaks across her face.

"Oh thank goodness, I didn't dream you," she says.

I smile in return, "You didn't. But we aren't out of the woods yet. We need to get everyone out of here. Can you do another beam of light? Can you help us corral everyone together?"

"I can try," she says. Without another word, she closes her eyes and her entire body is consumed by the blue light. It comes out the tips of her hair, her fingertips, everywhere. It's brilliant and utterly amazing.

~*Does everyone see the blue beam of light? Can you come to it?*

There's a sentiment of mass agreement, and I sense everyone moving in.

"Have you always been able to do this?" I ask her.

She shakes her head, "Not like this. It has always been small things. Flickering lights, throwing holograms. Things like that. This didn't start until a month or two ago."

About the same time I stepped into the role of Daughter of Five, I imagine.

"What's the plan now? The man will be back very soon," a tall, blonde man says, reaching us first. He has the same sunken, haunting eyes.

"Once everyone gets to us, we'll find a way out together. I'm not leaving anyone behind," I tell him.

"Who—who are you?" he asks.

The girl creating the beam of light looks my direction, as well. Her eyes bright white sockets inside the beam of blue.

"My name's Runa. What's yours?"

"Rendan," he says.

"What about you?" I ask of the girl.

"Antricia," she says.

More people filter in, some rushing to join us. Others a bit more apprehensive as they gather. Baxten rushes toward me, his dark hair standing on end and his face as dark as the others. But the smile launching across his lips as he gains sight of me is enough to brighten the room.

I've never seen him happy to see me. Emotions were never his strong suit, being a faithful citizen. He followed the rules of the Helix to the letter.

"Runa," he says, reaching out and embracing me for the first time I can remember.

I sink into his arms, relieved to see him in one piece.

"Baxten," I say, pulling him close, "Are you okay? Did he hurt you?"

"Never mind that— Everything's better now that you're

here. What's the plan? How are we getting out of here?" he asks.

"This is as far as I've gotten. I'm open to suggestions," I say, looking around at the mass of people collecting.

"Well, whatever it is, we need to do it fast," he says, his eyes wide.

"As far as I'm aware, there's only one way out—the way we all came in," I say. "My guess is we need to go back that way."

"I don't remember anything about coming in here," Baxten says.

"Neither do I," another man says next to him.

"Me either," two other people say at the same time.

"Alright, then it's up to me. Look, we're going to move as a group. If Videus comes back for us, we'll all need to be ready to attack. He's strong when he has us all alone, but we're stronger together," I say. "If you have any kind of power, or special ability—be ready to use it."

There's a flurry of responses, but we don't have time to debate them all.

I place a hand on Antricia's shoulder and say, "Thank you for your help. Let's all get moving."

She nods, dimming her blue beam of light. It pulls back from outside of her, as if soaking up through her fingertips. Then, backing up through her veins until it finally fades in the darkness of her pupils.

Grabbing hold of Baxten's arm, I position us out front of the pack of people. Getting them to the point where they can find their way outside is critical. Videus won't want to deal with all of us, and Tethys. No matter how strong he believes he is.

After all, he's only a man and whether he realizes it or not, his team of Salamanders and Airgliders have been compromised—by me.

We move quickly and deliberately, stopping to help others out of their cells who are unable to move—or unable to walk. Suddenly, plumes of fire rain from the sky in random intervals. They burn through the cages and with the doors open, the flames spill into the walkways.

Chaos threatens to break our ranks and our resolve. Screams erupt.

"We need to move quicker," I yell.

Baxten pulls me in close, "I'll keep the crowd moving your way. Just keep going."

He pulls me into a tight embrace and runs off into the group.

"Keep moving—you gotta keep moving," he yells over the screams.

We race along the vast set of cell corridors until we come to the entrance to the main hallway. The access point is significantly smaller, and it's like trying to thread a needle with a large piece of yarn.

"Come on, keep going," I yell over the shrieks of people scared out of their minds. "Keep going this way, follow the corridor all the way to the stairs. Once you're up there, run—run like mad. Get outside and head for the tree line."

I don't know if I can make contact with any of them using only my voice, so I take a breath and broadcast it again. This time, on the frequency hopefully they'll all hear me on.

~Everyone—I know this is frightening. But you have to stay calm. Follow the group to the stairs. Once you're in the main corridor of the Helix, find a way outside. I know that might sound scary, but trust me. You need to make it to the trees. I'll join you there in a few minutes. I need to make sure everyone's out. If the man comes back, use everything you have to fend him and the others off. I know I will.

The barrage of responses come flooding in, but it's mostly

an overwhelming signal of relief. They have a goal or a plan of action. It's more than they had hours ago.

I stand by the doorway, ushering people through, and pointing them down the hallway. Hands start reaching through the bars of the massive doors in this corridor. The people inside weren't let out the way the others were.

Racing forward, I pull at the handles, trying to find a way to open the doors. They're locked, firmly closed tight.

"Let me help," says a small man, no bigger than me.

Stepping aside, I have no idea how he'd be able to do much more than what I did—which is nothing.

For him, however, the door simply opens wide, then promptly falls off its hinges. He turns and smiles, a lopsided kind of grin. Then, he works methodically, opening the rest of the doors in the same manner.

My eyes open wide, realizing all of these people—every single one of them connected by the bloodlines truly is special somehow. It's not just me.

Why am I the Daughter of Five when everyone here is so innately powerful?

Is this what Videus knew? Is this what he was trying to shield the Helix—or all of humanity from realizing? We each have our own powerful ways to do things? We're each special in our own ways?

"Runa—" Baxten calls, taking up the rear of the people streaming past me. "I think that's everyone. At least, everyone who made it."

He frowns, clearly shaken by the things he's seen.

"Okay, lead everyone to the tree line. I'll be there as soon as I can," I say, searching through the rooms nearby.

"What are you doing? You have to go, too. If that—creature comes back—he'll…"

"I need to find my friends," I say, continuing to search the empty cells nearby. "I can't leave them behind."

"Who?" he says, grabbing hold of my arm.

"Let go of me, Baxten. I can't leave them here."

"You have a lot of people depending on you to get them to safety. Are you sure your friends aren't already in the group?" he says.

In all honesty, I hadn't thought of that. Trae could have been in any number of the cells and on his way outside with everyone else. But Kani—

"You're right," I nod. "One of them could be out there."

"See? I know stuff sometimes. Come on, let's get out of here and to safety. If I never see this place ever again, it will be too soon," he mutters.

As we run, I spread my awareness through the building trying to locate Trae or Kani. But I don't even get a blip on any radar I have. Without some guidance, I'd be here for ages just trying to find the right spots.

I'll have to get everyone else to the Lateral—if Kani and Trae aren't with, and I already suspect Kani won't be, then I'll make another plan to save them.

We race up the steps, just behind the last few people in the rear of the group. As we spill into the hallway, everyone is clambering out the side of the building. A huge, gaping hole five meters wide has been ripped sheer through the structure.

"That's one way of getting around the checkpoints," I say, tipping my head in surprise and acknowledgement.

Whoever has the ability to blast a hole that size has some serious power behind them. It almost reminds me of Ammon and his ability to move stone and rock.

God, I hope he got out safely.

To no surprise, the hallways begin to flood with Salamanders. The sound is deafening as they race toward us, paying no attention to gravity, as they race along the walls, ceiling, and floors. Their electrical arcs zap back and forth between the advancement of darkness.

"Run— Jump out of the Helix, now!" I yell at Baxten.

The remainder of people still inside the building jump out the hole, as Baxten and I do the same. The cold air hits us like a wave of clarity and I take in the scene of people racing toward the tree line, just as I'd instructed. Unfortunately, further off, a conglomeration of birds begins to glide our way. *The AirGliders.*

I grab Baxten's hand and we both take off running for the trees. Some of the Salamanders throw themselves from the building, while others simply continue out the walls, running along the side of the glass until they reach the snowy ground.

When we make it to the trees, panic is breaking out in this group of misfits. Everyone has been through so much already, I can hardly blame them.

"Everyone, we need to make a stand. We're too far from safety. We have to work together," I yell, trying to speak over the cries.

"What do we do? There are too many of them." Baxten says, his eyes wide.

"If you have an ability, use it. I don't care how—just make it work to protect you," I say.

Turning to Baxten I search his eyes. The only thing he ever wanted was to lead a normal, boring life. As far as I can tell, he has no powers, nothing strange within him. He was merely sucked into all this craziness because of me.

"Baxten, keep your eyes open and prepare yourself. Do whatever you can. I can't promise how this is going to go down," I say.

His eyes widen, but he nods. He knows there's not much else he can do.

I pat his shoulder, and step around him. Facing the onslaught of Salamanders as they stream out of the Helix toward us, I sense the girl from earlier—Antricia—begins to set off beacons of light, blinding the birds from up above. Others take her lead and begin working whatever skills or powers they possess.

One man runs around, touching the trees and they begin to come to life—sweeping the sky and knocking the birds to the ground.

Another woman works the snow, shifting it out from underneath the Salamanders—pushing them back toward the Helix like a rug being pulled from their feet.

Suddenly, Tethys is at my side and I know it's time for me to call upon my own gifts.

"Wish me luck, Tethys," I say, closing my eyes. "We're going to need it."

*V*IDEUS TAKES HIS TIME, methodically tightening the restraints himself. Clearly, no longer willing to leave the rest to minions who may not do his bidding properly.

"What is it you plan on doing?" I say, watching him closely.

Videus looks up, his bloody holographic pool of a face staring blankly my direction.

"I'm going to ensure Caelum has all the space he needs," he says, without much concern in his voice at all.

"If I could be rid of him once, don't you think I'll be strong enough to do it again?" I ask.

"Oh, no. Not once I'm done with you," he says, brushing off his legs as he walks away.

My eyes widen.

"And what does that entail exactly? I mean, if I'm gonna end up gone anyway, what harm is it to share?" I say, narrowing my eyes.

"Why do you think the faceless ones are called Labots,

Traeton?" he asks, drawing his fingertips together in front of his body.

"What difference does that make?" I say, my eyebrows pulled in.

Is this just to buy time, or is he really so far gone he can't even pull coherent conversations together?

"Answer the question," he urges.

"I don't know, because they're your robot slaves?" I say, making a face. I vaguely remember reading something about it before in the mainframe—but I'd been having those damn headaches and for the life of me, I can't remember what it specifically said. Not that it makes a helluva lot of difference anyway.

Videus tilts his head to the side, "Come on Traeton, you can do better than that."

"I don't know, you're sick—"

"Tsk, tsk," he says, tick-tocking a finger. "No, they're called Labots because they're no longer themselves. Their brains—their identities—have been completely handed over to me. Their consciousness, their essence—whatever you want to call it—has been *lobotomized*. Gone. Surely it occurred to you when their faces were wiped."

"I—I thought the faceless thing was simply a hologram so you could see from their eyes. Or so those of us who see them are scared shitless," I say.

"Well, there's that, too. But it's not the driving force. You know, I'm not a complete monster. I didn't do it to everyone. Just the ones I knew would be," he pauses for effect, "helpful."

"Helpful with what?"

"With intelligence, stupid. Clearly it's not your strong suit," Videus says.

I roll my eyes.

"So no loss when I get rid of you completely and grant Caelum a new body."

"Did it ever occur to you that maybe your crony is happy with the body he already has?" I say.

Videus pulls up short, turning slowly to face me.

"Has he said something to you?"

"Yeah, he says you're a helluva ass," I say.

A sigh drifts from his lips and his shoulders sag. Evidently, I wasn't convincing enough. Caelum, on the other, wasn't happy with my words. I feel him struggling inside my mind, reminding me that toying with Videus is the last thing we should be doing. We need to be engaging in an escape plan.

Though I'm not sure what the hell kind of plan we could come up with, strapped to a chair.

"What the hell would have turned you into this...thing? I bet once you were the smartest guy on the block. Now, you're nothing but an ass. How the mighty have fallen," I say, ignoring Caelum's suggestion.

Without hesitation, Videus raises a hand. His fingers ball into a fist and he lands it squarely in my jaw. Instantly, I see stars.

As if kicked inside my head, an intense throbbing swells at my temples. I close my eyes, trying to shut it out.

~You must step aside, Traeton. It is for the betterment of all. I must take this over from here.

Caelum is adamant, but he has an intense amount of nervous energy around his decision.

~What about the Archives? Will you be able to hide that from him?

~Not if you allow him to lobotomize you. Trust me, your consciousness is the only thing keeping both of us from total annihilation.

~I don't get it. Why would you be in trouble over this?

~When we get out of this mess, I will explain more. But for now, know that with the Acropolis destroyed, there is nothing left

for Videus to overturn. No more ways to attempt revenge—or revival. Whichever. We must stop him.

I feel like I've been wrapped up into a war I have no place in being. I don't understand the rules, or the history involved. Yet here I am, smack dab in the middle with the fate of certain aspects resting on my shoulders.

This must be how Runa feels.

~Alright. Do what you need to do. But I'm trusting you here. If you screw me over—

~I will not betray you. You have my word.

~Yeah, okay. Not so sure how far your word extends. But I don't see much of a choice. So, how do we do this then?

As quickly as he had pushed my consciousness out front, I'm back in the rear—witnessing events through the eyes of Caelum. It's such a strange sensation. Almost like looking out of windows, while you're inside. You can see the outside, but you're not yet a part of it.

My head slumps forward, more for effect than anything else, I sense. Then, Caelum lifts his eyes to rest on Videus.

"Master, I have returned. It took some rewiring, but I believe I have caged Traeton. He should no longer be a problem," my voice says in Caelum's strange, monotonous tone.

Videus stands still, his blank face staring our direction. I assume under that mask, he's scrunching up his nose or something.

"Is that so?" he says.

"It is," Caelum says.

Videus watches my every mannerism with piercing discernment.

After a moment, he finally says, "Prove it."

"There is much to discuss. I believe the Daughter of Five has a plan in place," Caelum says.

I can tell he's buying time, but bringing Runa into this mess isn't the way to go. At least not to me.

"And what of this plan?"

"She has been looking for the root of everything. I believe if you are not careful, it will lead directly back to your origins."

Videus shakes his head, "That will never happen."

"I understand, master, but I would be leery. If the truth were uncovered—"

"Hmmm..." Videus strokes the place where his chin should be, "it's been so long since I was that man. So long since I thought about how the timelines played out when he was—it hasn't occurred to me they'd dig so far back."

"Perhaps the timelines have taken their toll. You have jumped in and out so many times, your brain must still be trying to make sense of all that you have seen and experienced."

Timelines? Jumping in and out?

Caelum is pulling information in that I'd have no clue about to give validity to who he is, but what in the hell does any of it mean?

Videus' shoulders relax slightly.

"You're quite right, Caelum. Things don't always make complete sense the way they used to. Time is no longer a linear event, but a very fluid, ever moving animal. It's hard to gain a good handle on it at times. The people who at one point mattered are nothing but a blip on the screen of a sea of people who've come and gone. It's hard to cast much care for them when I know their ethereal nature."

"What would you like me to do now? I do not feel it wise to let Traeton go back into the field without me present," Caelum says, peering down at our bound wrists.

"Your mission is over, dear friend. Now that I've captured the Daughter of Five, all that's left is learning the secrets on how she's been able to alter time. I suspect she's clueless about her connection to the Pillars," Videus says.

"What makes you believe this is so?" Caelum asks. "Would the Caudex not have given those details first?"

Videus snorts, satisfied he's truly talking to his second in command. He reaches down, undoing the restraints he so diligently tied moments before.

"It has always been the downfall of the Pillars to withhold information until the last possible moment. It poses such problems. Yet, they never learn. It's fortunate for me that I have pieced together the pattern. Besides, she still knows nothing of the Acropolis. If she did, she wouldn't have wasted her time coming here. It would have been the first place she went."

Caelum massages my wrists, and stands up.

"You are very right. The Acropolis rising would initiate the Beacon. It would be the end of everything you have worked so hard for. She was consumed with needing to save her friend. Kani, I believe her name was," Caelum says. "There was no talk about the Acropolis of any kind."

"Ah, yes. Kani," Videus nods. "She's made an excellent Labot. Her medical training and propensity for knives has made her quite useful. As a bonus, Kani was all too willing to be one of ours. Guilt was killing her—*as it should have*. That's why I've left a piece of her inside. So she can feel the torment of becoming a Labot, but remembering everything she's done. I even gifted her with memories once sealed shut."

"What memories are you referring to?" Caelum asks.

"Do you remember the first time you were able to fully possess this meat suit?" Videus says, waving a hand toward my body.

"Of course. I only managed to get partway to the Helix before I lost the connection with his mind."

"Very right," Videus nods. "It was also the day I paid my first visit to Kani—as the young me from her own timeline. I'd had the intention of taking her out, but Trae was still there. He—well, we fought. Then you must have gained control of him, and looking back, your mission must have taken over. Blue hair here, turned and walked out. I was surprised, because at that point, I thought you were still Traeton. The younger me doesn't have all of this—" Videus gestures to his own brainspace.

"I am sorry master," Caelum says. "I do not remember seeing you."

"It doesn't matter," he waves a hand dismissively. "What matters is Kani jumped me. She had her knife on me—and manage to get off my mask. It wasn't as secure as it is now. I had to strike back. She was astonished of course, but something—short circuited in her mind. I took advantage of her shock and horror. I nearly had her, when something in the stacks of the Archives began to... I don't know how else to describe it, and it sounds moronic—but it began to fight back. Objects began throwing themselves at me. To this day, I still have no idea how. We should probably investigate. At first, I thought it was some sort of booby trap. Or perhaps Kani has a latent power I wasn't aware of. Regardless, having only been in the Archives once or twice before, I fled. Over the years, I haven't really gone back. I have everything I need here—"

He splays his arms open to suggest all of the Helix.

"You gave her back the memory of the real you? Would not that have jeopardized your plan?" Caelum says, trying to draw him out further.

"The plan didn't exist. Not then. I was simply driven by blind rage and my own grief. I needed someone to pay and she seemed like the perfect one to do it. Then again, it wasn't exactly her fault— it was mine. At least the first—" Videus says, waving his hand dismissively. "Granted, none of it mattered in the end. Here we are now. I've never been able to accept...*his loss*. I won't."

A sudden surge of energy and the thunderous sound of flesh hitting the walls and floors permeates from the hallway. Salamanders flood the room, exhibiting signs of alarm. Electricity zaps between their bodies, surging from their feet and connecting one another. Their sides have illuminated with blue bolts of lightning.

"What—" Videus cries. "How could you let this happen? Get out of here— Stop them."

The Salamanders take their leave immediately, squeezing through the small door. They race over one another, squashing each other as they clamber out.

Videus turns to us, "Caelum—it appears I will need your assistance after all. The Daughter of Five has escaped."

Surprise and relief floods my body. I can't tell if it's coming from me, or Caelum.

"How can this be?" Caelum asks.

"That doesn't matter now, what matters is there isn't time to waste. You need to go to her. Find her. I need someone I trust to be there with her. I know she'll be looking for you— well, Traeton. She's taken some of the other subjects. I can't let this happen. It could bring about the—"

"The beginning of the prophecy. Yes, I understand the gravity of the situation, master. What would you like me to do with the Daughter of Five?"

Videus paces, thinking. Finally he turns back to us, "Nothing. I want you to slide in line. Be her confidant again. Find out as much as you can, so I can come up with a plan. I'll take them all out, if I have to."

"As you wish," Caelum says, making for the door.

"And Caelum," Videus calls.

"Yes?"

"If she uncovers the Acropolis, end her," he says. "You have my permission."

Caelum nods solemnly.

Without another word, Caelum leads us out of the vassalage tunnels. He doesn't look back to see where Videus has gone, nor does he even question to do so in his mind.

~Caelum, buddy. Are you still with me?

There's no answer, only stillness and purpose of mission. Shit. Shit.

~Caelum. We gotta warn Runa. We gotta help the others.

The lapse of conversation is unsettling, and despite myself, I begin to panic.

How do I get him to snap out of this?

My body moves forward on autopilot, not much of anything else going on inside. I don't know what flipped this switch, but it needs to stop.

I try to calm my nerves enough to reach out again.

~This isn't you, Caelum. Remember? The Acropolis? The prophecy? We have a chance at ending this hell for everyone— you included. Let me take over if you're not able to control your damn self.

It takes a moment, but I feel a shift occur. It's a tiny stirring at first, but it's more than I was getting a moment ago.

Caelum slows his steps, leans up against the cold wall, and takes a deep breath.

~Yes, I am sorry.

He finally says.

~What in the hell was that?

~Videus has abilities to override much. I am not sure of how it all works. Had it not been for the intrusion, I am quite sure he would have questioned us further and I would not have been able to stop the answers from coming.

~Shit. Damn good thing we got away when we did then, huh?

~You are quite right.

~So, Runa's managed to escape. What's the plan? We need to find her now.

~You would know better than I where to find her.

~If she's got others she's protecting, there's only one place she can go. The Lateral.

~You will have to lead us. The underground and I do not work so well together.

~Fine by me. Just get us out of here first.

Caelum nods and continues onward through the twisting turns of the Vassalage. It spills into the actual Crematorium, and it occurs to me—this could be our one shot.

~Caelum, we need to do something about this place. Destroy it or something.

~I am physically locked from doing harm to the Helix. Even in bird form. I would not be able to assist in that manner.

~Alright, then move the hell over. We can't let this opportunity pass.

~My master will hunt for the perpetrator and will show no mercy.

~Then let's make sure we're far from here when this thing blows.

Without any further fight, Caelum steps aside, allowing me to take control again. Sliding back and forth seems to get easier each time. In a strange way, I'll almost miss him when we find a way to get him outta my head. *Almost.*

The Crematorium is a labyrinth of rooms, hallways, and strange machines. I'm not entirely certain what any of them do. If Fenton were still here, he'd figure out how to take things down by following it to the smallest wire or some damned thing.

A pang of guilt twists sharply in my chest. Holy hell. How did everything get so messed up? Fenton should be here with us to set all of this right.

~Caelum, do you have any suggestions? You said you can't physically do harm—but do you at least mentally *know how? I could use some advice here. I don't know what any of this shit does.*

~It has never been my intention to destroy the Helix, nor any

part of it. But I would believe if the fires of the Crematorium were turned up, and the venting valves shut—

~Pressure would build up. That's good. It'll buy us some time to get the hell outta here before shit hits the fan.

~What does that mean? I am not familiar with this term?

~It means things get messy. Nevermind. I read it once and thought it was funny.

I shake my head. As much as Caelum isn't as bad as I originally thought, he's also been extremely sheltered. Granted, it's an old expression, but still. Read a book.

RUNA

$\mathcal{C}$ALLING UPON THE ENERGIES of the bloodlines for support, I feel a newfound sense of purpose and energy as I spread my awareness out across the snow. I tap into every living thing around me. The trees, the Salamanders, the people, the birds. Everything becomes an extension of who I am—and they're a part of me. Even without having the completed mark on my wrist from the trials, I've gained so much more strength. Perhaps it's because I'm surrounded by so many people connected to me. Perhaps it's simply time.

With my awareness heightened like this, I sense who each person is, their powers, and their identity. What's more, I sense every soul still inside the Helix—and buried deep inside the Lateral. I can even feel the people throughout the planet I had no idea until this very moment existed. There are thousands of others like us out there, with a slightly different genome.

Instantly, I know Trae is still inside, but he's not currently himself. I knew something wasn't quite right with him, but I couldn't figure out what. There's someone else there with him—occupying his headspace. It's an odd sensation because they're both deeply familiar.

Kani's body is still inside, in some sort of hibernation, awaiting commands from her new master. I realize now, she's lost to us. Whatever Videus did to convert her to a Labot has rendered her consciousness inert. I feel nothing inside her, just a blank, haunting nothingness. It breaks my heart, but there's nothing I can do to help her wake up. Nothing from this point in time, anyway.

The first of the Salamanders are almost upon us, and I start by tapping into their mind. Like an electrician tinkering with the wiring to make something work, I sense their misfiring and work to set things right. I'm not sure how I know how to do it, I simply do.

Disconnecting the control Videus has over them, the Salamanders suddenly halt. I leave Tethys to catch them up, swaying them to a new purpose, should they choose to help us. Continuing on in waves with the rest of the Salamanders, I work as quickly as I can to illuminate them all.

When I feel satisfied I've managed to help each of them, I turn to the AirGliders nearby. Understanding their history, I almost feel sorry for them. They were the first to try to help Videus—help humanity. They were the first to make connection and they were used like weapons.

A squadron of the little gray juncos dive at my head, as they conclude I'm the source of the confusion with their brethren.

Ducking down as they narrowly miss me, Tethys breaks ranks with the Salamanders to come to my aid. The Salamanders, in turn, begin turning on their feathered friends. Before I know it, the Salamanders and AirGliders have completely turned on themselves. Chaos breaks out as both sides defend their convictions.

The next wave of AirGliders—the large vulture looking

birds arrive on the scene, instantly adding backup to the tiny engagement of the juncos.

Full on war erupts between the two groups—and I realize I have to get everyone else out of the way. Electricity and fire burst from the Salamanders and the clap back from the AirGliders throws the energy around like a lasso on the loose.

In all the commotion, I didn't even notice as Delaney and her team arrives to add human back-up. Relief floods my system, as this means Ammon was able to get out of the Helix safely and complete his mission. However, it quickly abates when I see him amongst Delaney's team.

"Ammon—" I call out, running to his side. "You shouldn't be here. You should have stayed— Things are dangerous here."

"Are you kidding? You need all the help you can get," he says, widening his arms to the scene in front of us.

Without hesitation, his hands swing in front of him as he maneuvers his hands in correlation with his desire. The ground beneath us begins to move, then shifts aside, creating a wall of stone separating the humans from the fray of two of the Four Pillars.

Delaney runs up to me, her eyes wide.

"Are we too late?" she asks. "Where do you need us?"

I shake my head, "No, your timing is impeccable, actually."

I turn to Ammon.

"Listen, I need you and Delaney to lead everyone away. Bring them to the Haven or the Lateral as quickly as you can. Can you do that for me?" I ask.

I know this is something he's completely capable of, and with Delaney's team helping—everyone should be able to get out of here mostly unscathed.

Ammon's eyes flit from the destruction on the field behind me, back to me.

"But—" he starts, shaking his head.

Delaney nods, "Look kid, we don't need to get in the middle of a civil war. If getting the innocent bystanders out is the best option we have, we take it. C'mon."

She pats him on the shoulder, then quickly surveys the scene.

"I'm going to fill Ash in so we can get moving out. Stay safe," she says, then leaves to talk to Ash. Together, the two of them run off, yelling for others to follow.

"Please, Ammon. Not everyone knows how to get there. Now's our chance while the Salamanders and AirGliders are fighting. You're one of the only ones I trust right now. You need to help protect everyone so they can get to safety."

"Is there anything I can do?" Baxten asks, suddenly at my side.

"Both of you—corral the people together. Follow Delaney and Ash's lead—those two over there. Make everyone listen and get them to safety," I say, grabbing onto Baxten's forearm. "Follow Ammon here, he'll lead the way."

Baxten turns to the small frame of ten-year old. I see the skepticism on his face, but for once, he trusts my call.

"Okay, kid. You heard the woman. Let's go," he says, patting Ammon on the shoulder without a second thought.

Relief floods through me as the two of them start to jog away together.

Ammon slides me a sideways glance, his face scrunching in irritation, but he does as he's asked.

"Everyone—this way. Follow us, we need to get out of here," he calls out.

The two of them run off, corralling as many people as possible, along with Delaney and her team.

~*Everyone, you need to get out of here. Let me handle the rest.*

It's important you each get to safety. Follow Ammon and Baxten,
or Delaney and her team. They'll lead the way to a safe place.

I broadcast the message, knowing it will be far more
effective than everyone trying to yell over the crowd. I also
push out images of who Baxten, Ammon, Delaney, and Ash's
are. They don't need any further confusion on who's whom.

Instantly, the group as a collective turns their heads,
searching for those I've described. As the masses pinpoint
Ammon and Baxten, or Delaney, they begin to move like one
giant unit. My brothers, along with Delaney and her team
manage to make their way to the front, leading them away
from the fray.

Tethys stays by my side, ready to unleash her protection.
But I dismiss her attempts to engage her shield. I know I
need to be out in front—vulnerable, if need be. I have to
connect to the rest of the AirGliders and disconnect their
link with Videus. I can't do that as easily when Tethys' shield
surrounds me. It muddles things up and makes it slightly
more difficult to sense them all.

~Just stay by my side and keep a watch.

I pat her on the back, and smile. Tethys grunts in
acknowledgement. She doesn't like it, but she doesn't question it, either. I close my eyes, trying to silence out all of the
beings who are not the controlled AirGliders. I want to
engage only with their frequency—no one else.

After a moment, the others begin to fall silent—not gone,
but simply muted. Interestingly enough, I can still sense
Traeton—which makes me pause. What's happened to him?
Has an AirGlider gotten to him? Has Videus taken control
of him?

I try again to disengage Trae from whoever, or whatever
is inside his mind. But I'm instantly shut out. It's almost as if
he wants the intruder there.

Shaking off the surprise, I refocus my intentions on the AirGliders. I filter my consciousness from the one inside Trae, to the others nearby. I work on each, disengaging them from the commands of Videus. As they're freed from his direction, the birds stop fighting in mid-flight—taking to the tree branches, confused and dazed. They begin to chatter amongst themselves, trying to make sense of what's happened.

Pausing, I don't know whether to follow everyone to the Lateral, or to head back to the Helix for Trae.

What would Trae do?

He'd tell me to take care of the others. To get them to safety first.

But if roles were reversed, he'd go inside after me, of course.

Tethys warns me this is not the wisest of decisions. She keeps close to my side, unwilling to leave me to the chance of anything Videus may have planned now.

If he captures me again—I doubt he'll let me live. And yet…it's a chance I have to take. I can't leave Trae behind.

"Tethys, we need to get Trae out. What more can I say? Are you going to help me?" I say to her.

She grunts, shaking off the extra energy and adrenaline from the fight, and gearing up for another one. I pat the side of her head, and pull myself up onto her back.

Everything inside her is screaming to get as far away as possible. But she pushes through it, engaging her shield and propelling us toward the Helix. I keep my senses locked on Trae, tracking where he is so I can get a better idea of how to get him out.

He begins to move, though—making his own way from the Vassalage, toward the stairwell leading out. As we get closer, I realize he's making his own escape.

Relief floods my body. After everything, he's still Trae. If he makes his way out of the Helix, he won't have to escape alone, but luckily, we'll be here to get him out.

Tethys reads my mind, following the signals I give her on Trae's whereabouts. As we reach the Helix, Trae bursts out of the hole we created. He jumps out, hitting the snow in a roll, then getting up and running.

My first instinct is to race to him, but for some reason, I hesitate.

Where is Videus? Surely he knows the others are missing by now. Perhaps the disengagement of the Salamanders and AirGliders has set him back? Maybe he's trying to find a way to get them back online?

The disconnection for them is permanent, I felt it. But if I'm not careful, they could be manually returned to the flock. If Videus captures any of them, he could start all over again. I need to find a way to unite them to our cause.

Shaking away the thoughts, I say, "C'mon Tethys, let's get Trae—"

She takes off, pulling the snow's energy and shooting us toward Trae at high speed. He's running as fast as he can, as if he's being chased. It makes it more difficult to pull him into Tethys' shield with me.

Behind us, an explosion rocks the Helix. I look over my shoulder to see fire blast out the hole and a portion of the Helix fall in on itself. The explosion sets off a chain of reactions throughout the building, collapsing sections as they go. The devastation is worse than just the building itself. I feel every life as it's extinguished in the destruction. I gasp as I realize Kani is one of them.

Trae falters, stopping to witness the destruction. His body and face are so mangled, and he holds his side as he catches his breath. His wrists have marks from restraints and there are more cuts and bruises across his handsome face.

Tethys takes the opportunity to pull him into her shield. I

slide off her back, walking up to him slowly. He twists around, blinking wildly when he realizes I'm by his side.

"How? Where? Where in the hell did you come from?" he asks.

Tethys urges me to do something to subdue him.

I ignore them both.

"Did you do that?" I say, pointing back to the smoldering Helix.

Trae's good eye opens wide, but he nods.

"We—I had to do something. Couldn't just let him keep torturing people—" Trae says, shaking his head. "But I didn't mean for the whole thing— There were innocent people in there. I just wanted the Vassalage to blow."

"I know, Trae. We need to get out of here. I need you to trust me," I say, leaving his side to climb on Tethys' back.

"But we need to help the innocent—"

"We have to let them go, Trae. Those who can, are already finding their way to safety," I say.

It's true—I can feel the energy of the place. It's as though a common cause has united them and awoken them from their slumber.

Trae's eyes widen further and he looks as though he's about to lose it. Tethys urges me to use my gift—the one she gave to me. To pass it on to him. She relays information of how her bloodline—the Waterbears—they're a part of me as well. Confused, I pause.

What does she mean? Her bloodlines?

Another explosion bursts from the side of the Helix and I realize we don't have time for any of this. We have to get out of here.

Without further hesitation, I slide off her back and touch Trae's forehead. I only wish I could take away the physical pain he's enduring. Remove the bruises, and broken ribs. But this is the next best thing for our situation. I feel the veil lift from his eyes and he steps back, slamming against the bubble of Tethys' shield. I'm not sure what's changed—why I can do so easily for him what Tethys had to do so brutally. Perhaps it's the trials? Or the mixture of all the bloodlines. Whatever it is, I'm grateful.

"What—what is this?" he asks, taking in his surroundings inside Tethys' shield.

Then, something shifts inside of him. His shoulders unclench and he relaxes slightly.

"She's my guardian, Trae. I don't expect you to understand, but—"

"She's the last Waterbear," Trae finishes, his eyes flooding with wonderment.

"How did you—?" I say, quirking my eyebrow.

"Runa, I have something I have to tell you—but we need to get out of here first. Videus won't be far behind. Can —*Tethys*—get us to safety?" he asks.

"How? How do you know her name?" I say.

"I just sorta knew," he says, shrugging. "Didn't you say it?"

"I—don't know. Maybe I did. Well, c'mon. We need to get out of here. And yes, she'll get us to safety," I say, pulling myself up on her back, then lean over, offering a hand to help him.

His tongue slides across his lower lips, drawing my attention. So much has happened these past few months.

I miss him. I miss being just us, stumbling through what I thought was life. It was messy and there was so much I didn't know—but those lips. They felt like home to me. In a strange way, they showed me what it was like to be me—just me.

Shuddering away the flood of emotions, I flick my fingertips to urge him up. Trae grabs my forearm, and places one hand on Tethys. He pulls himself up, sucking in a sharp breath. Without a second thought, he slides his arms around my waist, taking a moment to let his body rest. Then, he takes a closer look at Tethys, and shakes his head.

"This is so—she's so—wow, amazing actually," he says.

"She is," I agree. I don't know what I'd do without her.

Tethys takes off, propelling us quickly toward the Lateral's entrance. By now, I hope everyone else has at least managed to get to the safety of the cavern system.

"Runa—I'm so sorry I couldn't protect you in there," Trae says after we've cleared the vicinity of the Helix.

Looking over my shoulder, I tug my eyebrows in.

"You have nothing to be sorry about," I say.

He shakes his head, but falls silent.

I know there's more he wants to say. More he needs to discuss, but I don't want to pry him open. I want him to finally talk to me. To finally open up and tell me what's been happening on his own.

Tethys begins to internally debate the best route to get us to the Lateral. Oddly enough, she finally decides on the Haven's entrance, rather than the small outlet by the Archives.

"The entrance is blocked, Tethys. Remember?" I say out loud.

"What's that?" Trae says.

"Sorry, I was talking to Tethys. She wants us to go through the Haven's entrance, but I'm not sure how. Has anyone dug it out after it collapsed?" I say, trying to look over my shoulder.

"Not as far as I'm aware. It's been pretty much useless."

Tethys just chuckles internally at the fact I don't understand her abilities better. Then I remember the last time we were trying to get to the Lateral. She'd come up from underneath, breaking through stone, ice, and much more to get us there.

"Actually, come to think of it—why not bring us that way again?" I say.

Tethys shakes off the suggestion. She sends the impressions of Videus, and the need for discretion— for some reason we need it, even in the Lateral.

RUNA

ITHIN A COUPLE MINUTES of silence, we arrive at the entrance to the Haven. Instead of pummeling through the way she had when we broke through the channel, Tethys pauses. Taking in the scene around, her body is tense and alert as she spreads her own consciousness through the snow, making sure the coast is clear.

Then, the snow rumbles from the base of her shield, making a direct path all the way to the packed snow filling the entrance. As if exposed to a flash of heat, the snow in the entrance boils itself away. The water that remains pools on the floor of the entrance. It curls itself up like a wave, crashing down on the remaining boulders blocking the entrance. Then, Tethys calls the water to herself, rebuilding her shield and taking in the extra elemental nourishment.

A couple of smaller rocks and rubble remain, but nothing so large that we couldn't manage to squeeze our way through.

I slide off Tethys' back and Trae immediately follows after.

"Are you ready?" he says.

Standing at the entrance, the irony isn't lost on me. In a way, this is where my connection to everything began. Because of Trae's selflessness, I was introduced to this side of the world and became part of the prophecy.

Sighing, I nod at Trae, and take his hand. I push my own consciousness out to the immediate vicinity, sensing any energy signatures or consciousnesses nearby. Deep in the ground, the Lateral lights up in my mind like a bright focal point. But the Haven is now a barren, isolated place.

"Yeah, let's go," I say.

Tethys releases the shield, sending a warning to be careful and be swift. She reminds me the actions I take now affect not only me and Trae, but the entire planet. Too much has been set into motion. The longer I stay in the Lateral, the more I put at risk. There's more to the story somehow and I need to find out what I'm meant to do next.

Trae remains stoic as we make our way to the entrance. We climb over the rocks and boulders, slowly working our way to the main tunnel of the Haven. A few yards from the entrance, Trae pulls up short. His lips purse and his eyelashes flutter quickly.

"You okay?" I ask. "Being here for me it's—So, what about you? Are you going to be alright?"

He sighs slowly and nods.

"Yeah, I just—I guess I didn't expect to feel like this. We're just a few meters from Fenton's mainframe room. Being back here—it's like nothing happened. But everything's changed. It sucks."

"I know what you mean. I wish there was something I could do. All this," I say, waving my hands at my body, "the Daughter of Five stuff—and I can't do anything that truly matters to us. I can't bring Fenton back."

"That's not your burden to bear, Runa. It is what it is.

People live, people die. You can't save them all," he says, his eyes gazing at the floor.

"Come on," I say, grabbing his hand, "Let's get through this together."

We walk slowly, taking our time. When we finally open the door to the Haven, I suck in a breath. Everything—everywhere—it looks like the whole space was tipped upside down and shaken. Fenton's mainframes are smashed. Books, candles, pots and pans—papers, it's scattered everywhere.

"Videus' doing?" Trae says. "Looks like the Archive's—and that was his doing, turns out."

"I—I don't know?" I say, looking around. "It doesn't look targeted. It looks more like a fit of anger. Is anything missing?"

Trae shrugs, "Hell if I know. Doesn't matter now anyway. This isn't home anymore."

We move through the rooms, checking each to assess the damage, not for how to fix it—but for our own curiosity. Kani's room is the worst. Her swaying fabrics and paintings are ripped to shreds and crumpled in heaps across the room. Frames are broken into shards and lying in scattered sections.

"Whoever the hell did this has a serious grudge against Kani," Trae says, swiping his hand out in front of him.

My brain is pinging back and forth, trying to play out more scenarios than I could possibly consciously work out. It feels like it's going backward and forward in time, trying to sort out different versions of the past and present. The energy is almost overwhelming, and I feel myself start to sway.

It's been a long time since I felt like passing out from the energy bombardment.

"Runa, you okay?" Trae says, grabbing hold of my wrist.

I suddenly get flashes of the Caudex. No words, no

advice. Just flashes. The wave passes, and my head starts to clear.

"Yeah, I— I think I need to get back to the Archives."

"What? Now? I thought you wanted to—What about all the people in the Lateral now? I thought you needed to check on them?" he asks.

"I know, but I have to get back. My guides—they're telling me—I need to get something," I say, sitting down on Kani's bed.

Trae's face lightens, his eyes open wide, "You mean the enormous book?"

I stare at Trae for a moment, unsure what to say. I'd hidden the Caudex from him specifically—but now I don't know—it's almost like he's back to being his old normal self.

I nod.

He nods in return, his tongue skating across his lower lip.

"It was glowing. When you left, I woke up confused. Then, Ammon found me and the book, it started glowing so bright. I hid it for you, in case anyone came back to the Archives to finish the crazy destruction. Kinda glad now, since Videus was the one who was there." Trae says.

"How do you know it was Videus?" I ask.

"When I was in the Helix—when he thought I was— he let it slip that he was the one who messed with Kani, and my mind."

My gaze softens, as I think about the consequences. This mess at the Haven could very well be his doing...

"Why would he want to hurt Kani—or mess with your mind?" I say.

Trae shrugs, "I suppose to get intel on you. Runa, I have something I need to tell you about—"

"Where did you hide the Caudex?" I blurt out.

Trae sighs, his gaze flitting around the room.

"You know, maybe you're right— let's ditch this place. I'll show you where it is," he says, grabbing my hand.

I'm inexplicably nervous. Why would the book shine when I wasn't around? Why didn't Trae tell me about this before now? Is it simply because it didn't get brought up? Or is there more to it than that?

Should I be suspicious after everything that's happened? He was inside the Helix, after all. What if he's an agent for Videus now? Could that be why I sense the AirGlider energy?

So many thoughts ramble around in my head and it occurs to me, I need to ask something I've been wondering about for a while. It will confirm or deny my suspicions.

"Trae, I need to know what's been going on with you. How did you know about Tethys being the last Waterbear? And what's with all the strange behaviors since I got back?" I ask, staring him directly in the eye.

Trae's tongue slides across his lip—a signature move of his and I realize it's a bit of a tell. Part of who he fundamentally is.

He shifts awkwardly, then takes a seat next to me.

"There's not really an easy way to say this, so I'm just gonna spit it out," he says. "I've—I'm not the only one inside my mind. There's someone else in here."

He taps the side of his head.

I inhale sharply. It's one thing to contemplate and even conjecture about this being the case, but it's a whole different animal when it's confirmed from the man himself.

"I kind of assumed. Well, no, more than that actually, I sense something else. I didn't at first, but I do now," I say.

"What do you mean?" he says, his dark eyes surveying mine.

"I sensed something in you—not long ago. I wasn't trying to pry, I was just trying to connect mentally with the

AirGliders," I say, casting my eyes to my hands folded in my lap.

"I see," he says, licking his lip again. "So you know it's not human."

"Do you know a name?" I ask, suddenly curious.

Trae pauses for a moment, holding my gaze, then shakes his head.

"No, no idea," he says, shaking his head. "They're just kinda there. I've managed to take back control, though. I can sense them—but that's about it."

"I suppose it would be difficult, knowing who they are when they've taken over?" I offer.

"Yeah," he nods, "I know I'm not in control at times, but things are hazy. Kinda like being in a dream, I suppose. Then, when I am myself, I can't remember what I've done when I'm not me. I think I have it under control now, though. At least, I hope."

He runs a hand along the back of his neck as he scrunched his face.

"We need to find a way to get whoever it is out of there. We can't allow Videus access to our plans, regardless of how much control you think you have. I wonder if Landry could help?" I say, thinking out loud.

"He's been pretty damn preoccupied. Dealing with Fenton's death and the EMP situation. If we can figure this out without him, that'd be better," Trae says.

"That's true," I say, remembering the warning from future Trae.

Was this what he was referring to?

Regardless, Landry's been through so much, he needs a little respite.

I take a deep breath.

As much as I want Trae by my side, is it really wise? Am I putting everything in jeopardy, just being near him right now? What if this AirGlider can access everything we say and do, even if Trae's in control?

"Trae, maybe I should go alone. Can you tell me where you hid the Caudex?"

Trae shakes his head, "I don't think that's a smart idea. What if Videus shows up and you're alone?"

"What if whoever's inside controlling you makes a reappearance and it's you who attacks me?" I counter. "Could you live with that? What if I have to stop you? How could I live with myself the way Kani's had—"

"I really don't think that's likely to happen," Trae says, shifting slightly. His eyes drop to the floor.

"How could you be so sure?" I say. "Who knows how Videus controls them? Or how much he sees even through your own eyes? What if he's able to record everything?"

Trae stands up, and begins to pace. His eyebrows flicker upward as he considers.

"Look, if you really don't want me to continue on with you, all you need to do is say so. I don't want to jeopardize your mission, or put you in danger."

I stand up, taking his hands in mine.

"I know you don't. Which is why I think it's best to go our separate ways for now."

As soon as I speak the words, I get a flash of Trae being on the ground, surrounded by blood.

Rubbing a hand across my face, I realize there's no good answer here. No good way to handle things. If Trae's on his own, he's vulnerable. If he's with me, I'm vulnerable. At least with me, I can control my actions and reactions. But if he got hurt—especially because I sent him away—I don't know I'd be able to live with myself.

"Alright," I say, "I've changed my mind. Maybe it's better we stick together."

"But what about everything you just said?"

"Well, if Videus is doing those things, he already has enough information to make a move. Don't you think? We just need to make sure we're faster than he is," I say, trying to be optimistic.

"Alright, but I'm grabbing Jayne," Trae says walking to the room he shared with Fenton. He tugs a box from beneath the bed, and lifts out the sonic resonator. Cradling it in his hands, he takes a deep breath.

Then he hands it to me.

"Take this. I want you to be in charge of her. If anything happens, even if it's me, I want you to pull the trigger," he says.

I shake my head, "Trae, I have my own way to fight. I don't need this. It's better left here or with you."

I try to hold it out to him, but he pushes it back at me.

"At least hang onto it for me," he says, "just to be safe."

His eyes glisten with concern.

"Alright," I agree. "Let's get back to Tethys."

We take our time, slowly walking the tunnels that lead us outside, lost in our own thoughts. Will it be the last time I see the Haven? It feels like everything I've gone through has been preparing me for the next few big moments. The time of reckoning is almost here.

As we pass the kitchen, I linger in the doorway, remembering my first encounter with food. The trip to the Oasis that interrupted the barrage of insults from Kani. Fenton's teasing and references that didn't make sense at the time. But they're starting to now.

I miss both of them. I may not have liked Kani at first—and I'm certain the feeling was mutual—but I know now she was just protecting herself and the men in her life. She always was a true badass.

I smile, but it fades as quickly as it arises. I wish I could have saved Kani—brought her back with us. Taken her away from everything. How did this all get so messed up?

Trae stands by my side, silent and strong. I feel the energy rolling off of him—like a mixture of agitation, anticipation, and excitement. The AirGlider inside him is dormant, quietly sitting in the background. I can't put my finger on it, but there's something so familiar about his or her energy.

We continue down the main passage, past the common room, the mainframe, and to the main door. Trae locks everything up and we continue to the exit in silence. Both of us lost in our own thoughts.

As we leave the tunnel together, walking out into the snow, Tethys is instantly by our side. One moment, my feet crunch across the snow, the next, we're inside her bubble.

We both climb up on her back, and she senses we're on the mission for the Caudex. Her mood lightens, as though this is something she's been waiting for.

My mood on the other hand—it's quite different. Closer to Trae's, I suppose. I want this over. I want to put things right and—move on.

Is that even a possibility? Moving on?

With Trae's arms around my waist, I think about what it would have been like for the two of us. If we were allowed to simply follow the normal course of time, of humanity, where would we be?

"Where did you hide the Caudex, Trae?" I ask.

"It's with the Tree—your tree," he says. "I figured it was the safest place for it. Videus couldn't see it before."

My eyes widen, and I gasp. Had Videus taken me up on my offer to get the book—it would have been right where I said it was. And I had no idea.

"You okay?" Trae says.

"Yeah, I just—it's nothing," I mutter, shaking my head.

That was a close one.

We sit in silence for a moment or two, while Tethys course corrects to the Tree of Burden.

"What are you thinking about?" Trae asks.

I sigh.

"I've been wondering what things would have been like for us—you and I...if we were allowed to be ordinary humans. No prophecies or crazy sociopaths controlling things. Where do you think we would have been?"

I look over my shoulder, and Trae's cheeks flush slightly.

"What is it?" I ask, my eyebrows tugging in.

"Nothing," he says shaking his head, "I guess I could see us together. You know, like Kani and Fenton," he pauses for a moment. "Maybe one day, having kids. Have you ever thought about kids? I can say honestly I haven't...until I met you."

My eyes widen.

"Until you met me?" I say, surprised.

Trae shrugs, "I could just see it, I guess. Like it became a pathway I could travel down, if we wanted to. You know?"

"Hmmm," I say, considering.

What would it be like having children with Trae? I only have a few memories with both of my parents and in all honesty, my mother wasn't the best. Though I do understand her motivations a bit more, now that I've met Ammon. It was a survival instinct for her. Knowing now she was also a Labot in disguise... I'm not sure what her distance would mean for me. Would it impact the way I handle things? What kind of mother would I be?

My mind follows the logistics of things, but it occurs to me I've never seen the necessary equipment at the Lateral to support the reproduction of humans.

"Trae, how are the children born outside the Helix? Does the Lateral have an incubation lab?" I ask, looking over my shoulder.

Trae sucks in a quick breath and a hand flies across the back of his neck. Once again, his face flushes.

"Ahhhh," clearing his throat, he finally says, "When two people—well, when they—See, Runa, humans…"

He struggles to search for the right words, and I wonder why. Is it something bad?

"What is it?" I ask, casting my gaze out at the snow in front of us. The trees zoom past with amazing speed, and I know we'll be at the Tree of Burden soon.

"Runa, do you feel anything with me? When I kiss you— does something stir inside you?" he asks, his eyes searching mine when I look over my shoulder at him.

I smile, "I do. But what does that have to do—?"

"Humans, in order to have babies in, I don't know what you'd call this—*nature*, I guess. It's not just about babies, either. But that's the purpose, I guess. Ugh, this is all coming out wrong. Our bodies are meant to connect, yours and mine. Men and women. Hell, sometimes men and men, women and women, too—but that's not the point. Uhm, to make babies, our bodies sorta intertwine. Genetic code is passed from," he clears his throat, "are—are we there yet?"

"Nearly," I say, hanging on his words, "Genetic code is passed how? For what purpose? How does this connection take place? Is there some sort of port?"

He scratches the top of his head, and snickers slightly.

"Kinda, I suppose," he says.

It's nice to see him more himself, but I can't place why it's such a difficult conversation for him. Children are a logistical component of continuing the population. Family units seems to be more complicated out here than in the Helix, but that's to be expected, I suppose.

Trae takes a deep breath, then something shifts in his demeanor. His shoulders release a bit and he takes another cleansing breath. Deeper than the first.

"In order for an infant to be born, genetic code is passed from the male to the female by way of sexual intercourse. It is a mating ritual occurring across all species of mammals. The combination of the male genetic code with the female code melds together to create a new human child," he says in an oddly monotone voice.

"Okay? How does sexual intercourse work? Why do I get the impression it's uncomfortable?"

"It is not uncomfortable—quite the contrary. However, it is difficult to explain, yes," Trae says, biting down on his lip.

We arrive at the Tree of Burden, and Tethys comes to a halt. Her energy is beginning to border on excitement again. I look around, wondering if there's something she senses out here that I can't see.

She drops her shield and Trae drops off her back, making his way through the snow. He edges toward the Tree of Burden, his eyes on the sky.

I slide off as well, walking over to Trae to finish our conversation. Raising an eyebrow, I wait for more.

Shaking his head, almost as if he's struggling with himself, he holds a finger up.

"Give me a moment," he says, walking away.

I stand beside the Tree of Burden more confused than ever. I thought it would be a simple question, but instead, I'm met with even more questions.

After a few long moments, Trae walks back. His awkward demeanor has returned as he points up at the Tree. He runs a hand along his neck, his cheeks flaming.

"You know, I really think we should just get the Caudex," he says, his lip darting out and running along his lower lip. "We can revisit this later."

I take a deep breath, shaking off the curiosity, and confusion. He's right.

"Where is it, then?" I ask.

"It's sorta...up there," he says, pointing up to the top of the Tree.

My eyes flit from him, following the trunk of the crystalline Tree, up to the very top branches. Cradled in its upper most embrace is the Caudex.

"How—?" I say, my mouth dropping open.

Trae shrugs, "The Tree sorta took the book from me. That's where it ended up."

"Let's hope we can get it back down," I mutter.

RUNA

*L*IGHT REFRACTS FROM THE TREE, sending cascades of iridescence in all directions. The low sun makes everything seem magical, as I take in the Caudex hidden in the Tree's upper branches. It's amazing none of the AirGliders spotted the book—surely they've been on the lookout for the Tree of Burden since my talk with Videus.

"Maybe if you get close enough, the Tree will give the Caudex back?" Trae suggests.

"Maybe," I say, walking closer.

From here, I can see it's pages glittering brightly, but it's masked well within the light from the Tree.

"Was this your idea?" I ask, turning to Trae.

He makes a face, "Not exactly."

His right hand runs along the back of his neck, as he squints his eyes.

I watch him, waiting for more.

After a moment, he finally says, "The AirGlider—the one in my head, he's not so bad. He's actually helped a couple of times."

My eyes widen, and I turn to square up with him. "You're not seriously saying you've been talking with him, are you? You know they can't be trusted until their connection to Videus has been severed."

"Yeah, yeah, I know that. But I think his already has."

"Why do you think that?" I ask, watching his every micro expression as they flit through his face in rapid succession.

"Look, Runa, you're gonna have to trust me a little bit."

"You, I do trust. But I don't trust the AirGliders who have free reign and are tied directly to Videus. Here—let me help, maybe I can," I begin.

Trae steps back, his hands up as he shields himself from me.

I stop moving toward him, throwing my hands up in defeat.

"Look, if you're happier with the AirGlider in there—"

"It's not that, I just don't think it's a wise idea to remove him just yet. There's a lot we don't know and he's been very helpful so far."

"This is ludicrous. After the conversation we just had— and now you want to defend one of Videus' programs being in your head? Do you not understand how crazy that sounds? We should be working to get it out, not hang on to him for further exploitation. He has his own body, Trae. He's *disembodied*," I say, emphasizing the last word.

"Technically, what we should really be doing is getting that damn book down from the top of the tree," Trae says, jamming his finger up into the air.

"Fine," I say through gritted teeth.

Turning on my heel, I reach for the Tree's trunk. It's cold and smooth to the touch. As soon as my hand comes into contact, the aquamarine crystal at my neck glows brightly. The branches of the Tree twist in a dance all their own, as they work to gently carry the Caudex back down to me.

I reach up, taking the glowing book from its embrace, and step back in awe. This Tree has been through so much, but it's still a wonder all its own.

Taking a cleansing breath, I tug the aquamarine crystal from behind my top. It glows and hums at a frequency only I can hear, I think, as it prepares to unlock the Caudex.

"You said this was glowing before you left the Archives," I say, glancing up at Trae's wide eyes.

He nods.

The lock disengages, and I slip open the heavy cover. The pages fly open to the one with new insights.

It takes a moment for the light to subside so I can read the information. Trae hovers to the side, close but granting enough space for privacy.

"Can you see anything? What does it tell you?"

"Just a second," I say, holding up a finger.

The dark writing reveals itself, one word at a time— as if it's being written by an invisible hand.

Daughter of Five, the moment to end Videus' reign grows near. The next move will be the igniting of the Beacon. This will set a chain reaction to allow the Acropolis to rise once again. The Pillar factions need only a cause to unite them. The Acropolis will stand as a clear message to all that the prophecy is true and the process has begun.

I take a deep breath. This isn't the first time I've heard about the Acropolis, but everything is always so vague. How do I ignite this Beacon? And where is it even located?

As if answering my questions, the book keeps going.

The Beacon's location is hidden under humanity's feet, ready to engage whenever the prophecy is initiated. Upon proximity to the

Beacon, the Daughter of Five's blood and the mark of completion will act as the key.

"What's it saying?" Trae asks, curiosity getting the better of him.

Instinctively, I rub my wrist where the partial mark is hidden. Will the Beacon still ignite if I only have a partial mark?

Shaking my head, I look up at Trae.

"It's saying I need to ignite a Beacon. It sets off some sort of chain reaction to rise something called the Acropolis," I say.

Trae's eyes widen.

"The Acropolis?" Trae repeats.

I nod, "My only problem—well, there are a few actually. For starters, I have no clue where the Beacon is, let alone the Acropolis."

Trae shifts slightly, his eyebrows scrunched together in thought.

"And, well, it says the mark I was meant to receive through my trials would ignite the Beacon. But the final trial was never revealed. I don't know what happened."

"Can I see it?" Trae asks, moving closer.

I hold out my wrist, pulling back my jacket cuff. The glowing, blue ink glitters like sunlight in water.

"It's a flower?" he says.

"The Everblossom," I say, sliding the cuff back into place.

"Wasn't that the flower that was said to have been everywhere when humanity first arrived? Even in the snow?" he asks.

I nod.

"Thus the name, I suppose."

"So, if this mark was meant to be the key to ignite the

Acropolis, how do you finish up the final trial? Is it something you can just hop back into quick and—"

"No Trae. It doesn't work like that. I was told if I left before I was finished, I would not be able to get back."

"Then why did you leave?" he says, taking a seat in the snow next to me.

"I had to get back to you. Something big was going to happen and I couldn't let you believe I wasn't going to return," I say, thinking back to the future crater where the Lateral used to be.

"Okay, so what do we do now?" Trae asks, "Are we back to square one?"

I push myself up to a stand and take a short walk to engage my mind. Trae follows, keeping pace with me.

After a few minutes of silence, I say, "I don't understand. If the mark was the key, why wouldn't they tell me before I left? Why didn't the Caudex deem it more important then? Everything is hinging on it now. Without it, I'm basically inert."

Trae shrugs, "Maybe it didn't occur to them?"

I lower my eyebrows and make a face.

"After everything I've been through, that's not likely," I say. "I don't know why it matters, I don't even know the location of the Beacon or the Acropolis. Maybe they put their faith in the wrong person?"

Trae clears his throat.

"If it helps, I know the location of the Acropolis," he says.

My eyes widen as I turn to look at him.

"You do?"

Scratching the back of his head, he nods sheepishly.

"Okay, where?" I say, raising my eyebrows.

"It's the Archives," he says.

I blink rapidly, taking in this new information. At first, I want to laugh. To tell him the AirGlider in his head has done a number on him. But the more I think about it, the more I realize he could be right.

The place was much larger than I gave it credit for. And Ammon and I stumbled on that massive room. It didn't look like the rest of the Archives, filled with relics of humanity. It was elegant, beautiful, and full of power.

I turn to Trae, and say, "How do you know this? Did the AirGlider tell you?"

Trae shakes his head, "Not so much told. I sorta sensed it when he realized."

Sucking in a sharp breath, I say, "Does this mean Videus knows? We should go. We need to get a step ahead of him"

I turn on my heels to head back to Tethys.

Trae chases after me, grabbing hold of my wrist.

"No, Runa. Stop. Videus doesn't know. The AirGlider, he —when he realized, that was when things changed with him. He knew he couldn't bring the news back to Videus."

"Didn't Videus have control over him?" I say.

"This—revelation, it's what broke the connection," Trae says. "That's what I believe."

I bite my lower lip, thinking.

"Okay, good. That's good," I say, beginning to pace. "A relief, I guess. But we still need to find the Beacon."

"Well, I'd imagine it can't be too far. Can you? I mean, everything's been kinda going on here on this side of the planet."

"Plus the Caudex says it's under humanity's feet. Could it be in the Vassalage somewhere?" I say, thinking out loud.

"I doubt it. That was all Videus' creation. Did you sense anything like that when you were down there?" Trae asks.

I shake my head, "No. But it was difficult to discern much. Many of the people—they have powers of their own."

Trae's eyebrows flick up, "Really?"

"That's why Videus wanted them. Their bloodlines are

connected to mine. It gives each of them their own special gifts."

"Wow, handy," Trae says, shrugging. "You know, if it came down to a fight with Videus."

"Let's hope it doesn't come to that. They've been through hell. What Videus did to them—it's unconscionable," I say.

"What about the Lateral?" Trae says, his tongue skating across his lower lip.

"What about it?" I ask.

"Could the Beacon be there somewhere?" he says.

I shake my head, "No, I really don't think—" I begin.

But the memories of being underwater with Tethys as she brought me to the Lateral flood back. There were gears and other machine-like qualities under the floor of the Lateral. What if it actually is the location for the Beacon?

"We need to go," I say, grabbing his hand.

"Go? Go where?" Trae says, surprised.

"To the Lateral. You might be right, but I need to be sure."

"What happens if you can't get it to ignite? You know because of the mark thing?" Trae says.

"Then, I guess I only have one choice left," I say, frowning.

"And what's that?" Trae says.

"I have to do whatever I can to get rid of Videus before he destroys everything."

I tuck the Caudex under my left arm, and make my way to Tethys. She stands up, stretching slowly, and shaking the snow from her fur.

"Whoa, do you ever get used to seeing her?" Trae says startled.

"From the moment I made the connection with her," I say, smiling, and petting the fur on the side of her head. "It's like I've known her my whole life."

He shakes his head, eyeing her.

"That doesn't bode well for me."

Tethys bends down, allowing me to climb on first, then Trae follows. Without hesitation, the bubble of her shield surrounds us and we take off for the Lateral. She already knows the mission before I have to tell her. The snow is an extension of her—it allows her to feel, sense, hear things.

Making our way through frozen trees and snow dunes, Tethys maneuvers us to take the underground waterway again. I need a closer look at everything to know if Trae could be right.

The cliff's edge is nearing. The sky is a beautiful shade of purples, oranges, and golds thanks to the locked sun and its halo casting its illumination in the sparse clouds.

"Hold on tight," I say to Trae, knowing what's about to come.

Trae grabs hold of my waist.

With that, Tethys throws us all over the edge of the cliff. We shoot downward at such a velocity, yet it's odd—just like last time, in the moment, it's as if time stands still. My hair rises as gravity gives way, and my stomach turns. Trae howls, gripping me tightly.

We crash through the ice and snow, then slowly submerge into the watery depths below.

"What in the—?" Trae says, opening his eyes and releasing his grip a little.

"There's a channel of water underneath the Lateral. I'm not sure if anyone else realizes it's there. The last time Tethys brought me this way, I remember seeing things. Statues, and a strange structure under the floor," I say. "I remember thinking it was odd."

"Okay, I coulda used a little warning before we cliff jumped, though," he says, taking a deep breath.

"Sorry, it didn't occur to me until we were coming up on it," I say, gripping Tethys tightly and peering into the blackness of the water.

Tethys moves surely through the depths, allowing the water to guide her to where she needs to be. Both Trae and I remain silent, waiting for a glimpse of the Lateral.

Light streams into the water at large intervals, casting shadows and illuminating some of the underwater sculptures. I can't tell if the light comes from outside, or the Lateral itself, but I'm happy for the visual disruption. The intensity of darkness becomes disorienting after a while.

As we get closer, I claw at my wrist, holding it tightly to my body as the skin starts to burn, like it's searing away. Soon, the sensation becomes unbearable. I grope at the fabric of my jacket, pulling it back and exposing the partial mark.

As though it had a mind of its own, the light of the mark floods outward from my wrist, painting the walls with the same shimmering blue light. The light embeds itself into markings etched into the stone and statues. It starts off bright, casting away the darkness. But after a few moments, the light begins to dim.

"Guess it knows I haven't completed the trials," I say, frowning.

"But at least we know we're in the right place. That's gotta mean something, right?" Trae says.

"Yeah, I guess. But if I can't ignite the Beacon, I don't know how much good it is," I say.

"Well," Trae begins, but sighs. "That's why we have a Plan B. If we can't get this thing to work, then we take Videus out."

"Maybe there will be more in the Caudex soon," I say.

Tethys begins hunting for the best way into the Lateral. The last time she burrowed through the middle of the street, but this time, she's more restless. Not only because the stake of our planet lies within these moments—these actions, but also because there are more people milling about in the streets now. She doesn't want to hurt anyone.

After what feels like forever, she finds her entry point.

"Hold on, things are going to get a little bumpy," I say, pulling Trae's arms closer.

Tethys swerves, guided by something I can't see.

Suddenly, the mark glows again, casting the blue light across a series of stone steps along the left. They spiral along the wall of the cavern system, heading upward toward the Lateral.

"Are those stairs? How would they even—? Who would have built those?" Trae asks.

"One way to find out," I say, as Tethys gets us close.

Once we reach the stairs, it becomes clear Tethys won't be able to follow. The stairwell is far too narrow—built for a person to walk up alone. But for as far as I can see, it's under water.

"Can you swim?" I ask Trae.

"I think I can manage. How about you?" he says.

"How hard can it be?" I say, shrugging.

Trae takes a deep breath, but coughs.

"If we're going to try this, we need to get moving. Tethys' shield will eventually run out of oxygen. Are you ready?" I ask, keeping my eyes trained in the glowing stairs.

"Let's do it," he says.

"Follow the light of the stairs. If anything goes wrong, swim back to Tethys. She should be able to help," I say.

Trae nods.

I take my own deep breath, trying to fill my lungs with as much air as possible before we give this a try. I grab hold of Trae's hand and clutch the Caudex with the other.

"Okay, ready? 1...2...3."

On the count of three, both Trae and I inhale deeply and Tethys releases her shield. Water rushes in at us from all directions, throwing us about like rag dolls.

I struggle to hang on to Trae. The vortex pulls us apart,

our fingers slipping away from one another. I try to open my eyes to see where we're meant to go, knowing he'll be doing the same. The blue light is beginning to dim, but I vaguely make out the steps.

Pushing myself as hard as I can with my legs, I make my way slowly to the stairs. As I reach them, I scramble with my free hand, trying to find something to grab onto to pull myself up and out. The stones are slippery, covered in some sort of growth. I try the walls, finding a hand hold wide enough to slip my fingers inside and push me upward with my free arm.

I continue along the wall, searching for my next hand hold, and kicking myself upward through the water. The blue light finally goes out completely, and I'm plunged onto darkness as I scramble to get myself out.

Panic starts to claw at my chest as the last dregs of oxygen dwindle and carbon monoxide is bursting to get out. I fight the urge to inhale, but I'm losing the battle.

Just when I think I can't take it anymore, I push myself through the surface. My inhalation is loud and sloppy, and I scramble, desperately trying to find something to hold onto. The steps above the water are no longer slippery, but dry and solid.

I throw the Caudex up onto one of the stairs. With wobbly arms and legs, I pull myself completely out of the water. Spinning around the way I came, I stare into the darkness, waiting for any sign of Trae.

"Come on, come on," I say, shivering.

I'm met with complete silence.

"No, no, no," I say, shaking my head. "Come on, Trae."

This can't be it. After everything we've been through, all that we still need to accomplish. This can't be how things end.

"Trae—" I scream. ·

TRAETON

*L*OSING RUNA'S HAND sucks both of us into the dark abyss without any sense of direction. Not only is the motion and water completely disorienting, but so is the lack of oxygen and lack of time.

~This is not an ideal situation.

~Thanks, Caelum. I didn't realize.

Is sarcasm lost on him? Seems like the kinda guy who wouldn't get it.

I take a moment to allow the water around me to settle, trying not to let panic set in. If there's one thing I'm good at, it's being under this kind of pressure. It's the only time clarity comes. When the pull of the water subsides, I search for the illuminated stairwell. The bluish light is fading, but at least I have a direction to move towards.

It's much further than it was, so I'll have to make up ground quickly. As I start kicking my legs, trying to propel myself toward the stairwell, I get a gentle nudge from behind. Tethys tries to aid me in getting there quicker.

I reach the stairwell, only to inhale accidentally. Water floods my lungs, burning inside my body. I need to cough desperately, but I know if I do, I'm in for a much worse fate. Clenching my torso tight, I try to grab hold of the stairs, but they're completely covered in algae, making it impossible.

My lungs feel like they're going to burst into flames, and I've reached the point where Tethys will no longer fit. I know I'm on my own here, but I don't know if I'll have the energy left to make this happen.

I reach out, trying to find something—anything—to grab hold of. There has to be something in here. A railing perhaps—-

~If I knew we were going on a suicide mission, I think I may have risked going back to my own body.

~Not helping Caelum.

~I was not trying to help. I was merely pointing out a fact.

~Wonderful. How about you just keep your mind shut and let me worry about getting us out of here.

I've barely made it to the stairwell, and all of the blue light vanishes. Plunged into darkness, the one thing I can be grateful for is at least I'm not lost in the open water without direction.

My body searches for another way to cough, bursting at my already painful side. The broken rib from Videus' attempt at gaining information makes it difficult to not only hold my breath, but reach out for anything.

I use my legs, trying to kick the water and push myself up that way.

Dizziness starts to set in as the oxygen in my body begins to fail. I need to breathe—

Scrambling for the stones, I try to find a railing, or something—anything to give myself an edge upward. Who knows how far I have before I find the surface of this thing. Hell, there's no guarantee there's even a surface. What if we go up these stairs, only to find a locked door at the top?

What in the hell were we thinking? Why would we do

this without at least testing out the scene first? Caelum's right. This was a suicide mission.

Without warning, the water begins to rush past me in a flurry of bubbles. Almost as if a drain has been pulled, all the water in the stairway recedes. Air floods into the space, and I take a deep breath, coughing and sputtering out the water in my lungs.

"Trae—Trae are you okay?" Runa yells from somewhere in the darkness, relief in her voice.

I bob up and down in the water, unable to clear my lungs enough to catch a good enough breath to respond.

Suddenly, the stairway is illuminated with the immensely bright light I've only seen coming from the Caudex. Looking up the stairwell, I'm a good five meters away from Runa— much too far to have swam in my current state.

Gratitude floods my body, as I rest in the water, allowing it to hold me for a moment.

"Trae, are you alright?" Runa repeats, an air of panic edging back into her voice.

"I'm okay," I say, my voice harsh and scratchy.

Rushing down the stairs, Runa nearly slips and falls as her feet hit the algae covered rock.

"Everything's so slippery—will you be able to make it up the rest of the way?" she asks.

"I'll have to," I say, trying to work out the best scenario on how to do so. I don't really have any other choice.

Runa takes a deep breath, kneeling down and touching the stones at her feet. The algae beneath her fingertips turns a flame orange, then spreads out, burning it all away.

"How'd you do that?" I ask, my eyes wide with awe.

Runa walks tentatively down the stairs as they're cleared away.

"I don't know…it's sort of evolving," she says reaching out.

I offer my right hand and she pulls as hard as she can. Every muscle in my body screams, and mustering the energy to pull myself out of the water is nearly impossible.

~You are very lucky to have been in the Daughter's proximity. You nearly got us both killed.

~Oh shut up. I don't overly need your verbal assault right now.

Caelum sulks in the background of my mind, but very clearly happy we both made it out of that situation. I'll admit, it came far too close for either of our liking.

With Runa's help, I scramble up the steps on my hands and knees, then stop for a breath. She wraps her arms around me, and I sink into her embrace.

"I—was so worried. I thought I lost you," she says.

Sucking in another deep breath, I turn to her and say, "There were a couple times I thought that too."

She shakes her head.

"That was so stupid. I should have just had Tethys—I don't know what I was thinking. I mean, really?"

"Runa, forget it. You can't second guess your decisions. You made a call and we went for it. Now we're here," I say looking up the stairs. "Where *is* here anyway?"

"I'm not sure. By the time I got to the top, it was so dark. When the Caudex lit up, I was focused on you," she says glancing up the stairs, unwilling to let me go just yet.

"Well, should we check it out?" I say, feeling like I could get most of my body to cooperate.

She nods, releasing me enough to fumble to a stand. Then she grabs hold of one of my arms gently helping me. My body feels like it's been sent through a meat grinder, but I manage to stumble up the remaining steps. We walk slowly, making sure everything is dry before taking the next step.

When we reach the top, Runa leans down to grab to the Caudex—but just as she reaches the book, she freezes. Her eyes are trained in the darkness beyond her.

"What is it?" I say, leaning into her.

She lets my arm go to point the Caudex's light into the darkness.

"What in the?" I step forward, waving a hand in front of the motion light sensor.

Lights flickers to life, turning on a series of lamps in a large room. To the right is a large table with one chair. To the left, a small kitchen space. And in the back, a bed and small door to what I can only assume is an allay from here. There are smattering of books shelves and small tables around the room, each with a lamp.

"What is this place?" I say.

Runa's eyebrows flicker upward mimicking the same surprise I feel, and she shakes her head.

"I honestly have no idea," she whispers.

She walks into the room, her right hand brushing against the surface of the table. There's not a spec of dust as she places the glowing Caudex in the center. Without a word, she moves on to the back of the room. I prop a hand on the table, resting for a moment.

Her eyes take in the bed, and she points.

"Would you like to rest?" she says.

I look down at my soaking wet clothes.

"I'd love to. But probably not the wisest until I dry off," I say.

She continues on to the small doorway on the far end of the room. A light flickers on, and sure enough, it's an allay.

"No stairs outta here?" I call to her.

Walking back into the room, she shakes her head, and drops onto the foot of the bed. Then she buries her face in her hands.

"What is it?" I ask.

Walking over to her, I place a hand under her chin and tilt it upward.

"It's a dead end, Trae. Why are we in a stupid dead end? We're going to have to go out the way we came."

Tears swell in her eyes and she bites her lip to hold them back.

Shivering, I look around. There has to be a reason we were led here by the light from her mark. At least, I have to believe that.

"Are you sure there's nothing in the allay? A ladder?"

She shakes her head.

"Just the allay, a shower, and a closet of towels and clothing."

"It's like someone was meant to stay here. *Live here.* But who? And why? Have you checked your book? Does it say anything?" I ask, pointing at the glowing monolith on the table.

Taking a deep breath, she wipes at her eyes.

"I haven't. But it's not glowing because it has new information," she says.

"Then why is it—? Oh. You did it. Got it turned on like a flashlight," I say, realization dawning.

"It was all I had. I needed to see," she says, shrugging.

"Your powers are definitely getting stronger. Too bad you weren't given the ability to heal," I say, wishing I could get rid of this annoying swollen face and sharp pain in my ribcage.

Runa's forehead wrinkles.

"Tethys has the ability to heal, but it was associated with her saliva. I should have had her—"

I hold up a hand, "Pass."

She chuckles.

"I could try licking you if you want?" she says, jokingly.

The images that conjures are unexpected, considering our circumstances. I shudder away the feelings it arouses.

~How can you possibly be thinking about procreation at a time like this?

Caelum's sudden words in my head make me jump. I'd almost forgotten he was there.

~I—I wasn't. God, get outta my head, would you?

~You most certainly were. I saw—

~Yeah okay. Enough. My procreation thoughts are private. For phugsake.

Runa's eyes watch me closely, concern sparking in their depths.

"Are you okay," she finally asks.

Clearing my throat, I nod.

"Mind if I check the shower? If it works, I could really use the warm up," I say, rubbing my arms.

"Of course. You do that and I'll," Runa blinks rapidly, then points to the table, "I'll consult the Caudex."

"Great," I say, nodding.

I take a moment, realizing it's a bit selfish to leave her—to take all the hot water for myself. Maybe it has a limited supply.

I turn back to her, "You know, you've gotta be frozen, too. You could always—join me."

Her eyes widen, and she bites her lip.

"I...I better consult the Caudex first. Like you said," she whispers, her cheeks suddenly a beautiful shade of pink.

I nod, trying to hide the jab of disappointment, as odd as it is. Turning around, I take a deep breath, hobbling along to the allayroom. As I walk in, the lights flicker back on. The space isn't overly big, but still large enough. I turn the shower on, dialing up the temperature to where I like it. Then I walk over to the small closet. It holds the towels and plenty of clothing in drawers along the back wall. Men's and women's clothing are all mixed together, as if it makes perfect sense to have them in this small room beneath the Lateral.

Who was this place meant for? And why is the only access

point through the water? How the hell did they get every-thing in here? The bed, and tables? Hell, the electricity and water.

"I've found the heat," Runa calls from the other room. "It should regulate the temperature while we're here."

"That's a relief. Thanks," I call back.

Grabbing a towel and some fresh clothing I hope will fit, I head to the shower. Glancing at the open allay doorway, I take a deep breath.

Guess putting in an actual door didn't occur to the people who built this place, huh?

I peer out the opening and find Runa sitting at the table, her face illuminated by the lamp nearby.

"Suck it up, Trae. It's no different than the Oasis. Right?" I say to myself.

~Are you afraid of getting undressed?

~Shut up. I'm not afraid.

Nevermind what I told Runa, I can't wait to be the only one in my head again.

Peeling off my wet jacket and shirt, I set them aside hoping the auto dry will kick into gear. Bending down, I take off my boots and place them beside the wall. Then I undo my trousers and let them drop to the floor. Standing in the allay-room naked, I feel more than just exposed. I feel oddly—*alive.*

It's like every cell in my body is humming, and I can't stop it.

"Okay, Trae. Get a grip," I whisper to myself.

My eyes slam shut. That's exactly the kind of thing Fenton would have said. Only it would have been meant as a double entendre. He would have loved to watch me squirm over it, too.

Is it sad I kinda miss that?

I open the shower door and step inside. The instant steam assaults my senses, then the hot—damn near scalding—

water. After everything I've been through lately, I don't think anything has felt so good.

I stand in the water, letting it pound my back and cascade over my body for a few moments without moving a single muscle.

A knock on the glass outside makes me jump. Then the glass door slides aside and Runa steps in.

Do I cover up? Do I care?

"Runa? What are you —" I say, realizing she's as naked as I am.

Runa's eyes don't leave my body, and mine don't leave hers.

Turn about is fair play, I suppose. No time for dignity.

She steps forward, concern creating lines across her face. Her eyebrows tug inward, but her lips play upwards. Placing her left hand over my swollen eye and her right hand across my broken ribs, she closes her eyes.

The water cascading around me begins to glow a brilliant, pure white. It pools under her hands as if she's commanding it the way her Waterbear can. Inside my body, my broken ribs snap back into place with very minimal pain—just enough to know they're repairing. My swollen eye instantly feels better.

The water continues to pool under her hands, glowing to the point where I can even see the bones in her hands through her skin. When she's satisfied, she releases her hands and meets my gaze.

"How did you know that would work?" I begin.

She smiles softly.

"When you were in here alone, it got me thinking about all of the trials I've been through. Then it got me thinking about my connection to each of the four Pillars. I didn't know it would work, but I hoped," she says.

"So you're saying the trials are what gifted you these

powers?" I say, trying hard not to focus on the way her skin felt and how exposed we both are.

"Maybe? Something like that…maybe they just made them stronger," she says, placing her hands on my chest. Water flows from my body to hers, as it cascades down her arms and escape at her elbows to the floor of the shower.

A shiver runs through my body and I'm extremely aware of the space where her fingertips touch my skin. And how little separates my naked body from hers—

I bend down, kissing Runa's lips gently. An undercurrent of passion threatens to sweep me up. I could very easily give in to its energy, if I'm not careful.

I take a deep breath, and shiver.

Runa stands on her toes, pressing her lips to mine. Her scent of vanilla wafts gently around us, but it's more potent now—mixed with something else. Electricity? Power? Maybe both.

Her kiss is soft at first, but something ignites between us —just like it had before—and it's as though the months apart —everything keeping us from being together—they all melt away. The worries of Caelum, Videus—it all vanishes from my mind as I'm consumed in the moment with her.

We may never have a future. Hell, if things go as planned, and the Beacon thing is ignited—it could end everything we know. Even if it puts Videus in his place.

My hands wrap around her face, pulling her in to me, allowing the fire to consume us both. No fear of rejection, no fear of hurting her down the line—this moment is literally all we have. We nearly died in the water. We could die at any moment. And I have to let her know how I truly feel.

Her body presses against mine, and she kisses me with such force, such ferocity. God, I've missed her. Not even just this—but *her*. Everything about this—its all so unfair.

My heartbeat picks up, pounding through my veins—

working its own sense of magic on me. Making me wish things—want things I have no place in wanting. Not now. But I can't help it. I need her and I hope like hell she needs me too.

I may not have been able to explain things in words—but I could show her.

I place my hands on her neck, then gently run them along her bare shoulders. She shivers, but her eyes twinkle, and her lips curve upward.

Taking in her naked body adds fuel to the fire already burning intensely inside me. Her hands add their own dimension, soft and oddly sure of themselves. I've envisioned how this could go down before—how could I not? But I'd always anticipated more awkwardness. From her, from me. I'm not sure why. Maybe because I assume that's how I would have been fresh from the Helix. I also assumed it would be a more appropriate time...

Runa takes a step closer, her body inches from mine as she steps into the stream of hot water along with me. I search her eyes, wanting permission to keep going.

Without any words, after a moment of silence, a slow, sexy smirk slides across her lips. God, if she only knew what she does to me.

"I want you to teach me, Trae. Teach me what it's truly like to be human. To embrace all this. I need you to," she says breathlessly.

I hold still, taking in all of her—the soft skin of her torso, the curves of her body. I'm not even ashamed to take it all in. I don't feel embarrassed for myself or for her. It's like everything has led us to this point.

I've never wanted anything more than I want her, and it's been that way from the beginning. There's a connection with her and it's not just about sex. It's everything about her. Her warmth and comfort. Her strength and resilience. Her beautiful smile and body. I want every single piece of her. And I want to hand every piece of me over to her.

I run my fingertips down the silhouette of her exposed torso until they rest on her hips. Then, I draw them forward until her hips touch mine. She watches me closely, her multi-colored eyes wide with anticipation. Her breath is slow and deep, and her face flushed with excitement.

"Are you sure about this?" I ask, pausing for a moment to catch my breath. "The intruder, you know he's still here with me somewhere and—"

She answers my warning by placing her hands on my buttocks and squeezing.

"I know," she says. "But I also know it's you with me right now. I can sense he's taken a back seat…That's what matters."

My heart races, threatening to thump right out of my chest. It's done its job, though, preparing me for what comes next. My body is humming with my own sense of anticipation.

With neither of us wanting to be apart any longer, I reach for her, pulling her body even closer to mine. I press her against me, and bend down to place my mouth to hers. The sensation of her skin on mine sends electricity through me. My skin's vibrating, my blood pumping.

Runa's fingers intertwine through my hair, tugging and pulling it in movement with her mouth as she kisses me. Her tongue teases mine in a way I've never experienced before. She makes it all flow so easily, so uninhibited.

Flashes of kissing her before, in a lush, green place permeate my mind. White, five-petaled flowers hug her body as we entangle together on the ground. Like this is something we've done before—hundreds of times, millions of times. Her touch is the same.

A groan escapes my lips, and I give myself permission to explore. To let her know she gives me strength to love. She's my light—my own personal beacon home. She was from the first moment I met her. I couldn't explain it then, and I can't explain it now.

Runa arches her back as I drag my fingertips up the soft skin along her sides. The hot water steams around us, adding a multi-sensory dimension I can't even explain. Her head tilts back, and she closes her eyes. I caress her back, pulling her close to kiss her neck.

"You've always been the one, Runa," I whisper in her ear, my voice gruff. "I wish I had the sense to tell you that sooner."

Runa opens her eyes, and softly grins. She places a fingertip to my lips.

"You don't need to apologize for anything. Or justify anything. Be here with me—now. Just us. No past, no future to worry about. Only right now," she says.

CUDDLED up next to Runa's naked body, I can't imagine a more blissful place. Deep down, I know this is how we should have been. How our lives were supposed to be entwined. Perhaps how they once were in a different life.

I'm also acutely aware of what's hidden in the silence. If I'm not careful—if we don't watch ourselves—this could be more than our first time. It could be our goodbye.

RUNA

*T*RAE'S HAND STROKES MY BACK, warm and steady. I never knew this place—this feeling—was something to be experienced between two people. There was an entire piece of humanity I'd been missing. How could I go so many years and not know?

The memory of Trae's body sends electric currents up my spine. It's like we're magnets and even despite everything that's going on, I can't control this urge to be together. To let these problems of the future, the past—let it all go, even for a while. This *desire* to be with him, to give *myself* to him is almost illogical and reckless—but it's also there and I can't deny it.

"What are you thinking about?" Trae whispers.

I lift my head from his bare chest, gazing into his beautiful brown eyes. His blue hair stands on end, a byproduct of our entanglement. His eyebrows tug in as he searches my face.

"I was just thinking about how much you've opened my eyes to all that I've been missing. I thought—I thought I knew what it meant to be human, but—" I shake my head.

"Everyone's in the dark at the Helix. I can't say I understand the motivation from Videus, but I can relate to how you feel," he says, his gaze soft and open.

I bite my lip, thinking.

"How long did you know?" I ask.

Trae quirks his head slightly, "Know?"

"How you felt about me. That it could lead to this, if we just—"

Trae chuckles, shaking his head before laying it back on the pillow.

"Runa, as much as I hated to admit it to myself, I knew there was something about you from the moment we met. I couldn't explain it. Hell, still can't. Sometimes, you just know. It's like an energy or an air binding you together before your logical brain can catch up. "

"When we met, I was covered in blood and unconscious," I say, raising an eyebrow.

"Hey, I didn't say it made sense," he laughs. "You've always felt like home."

I can't help but smile, but his words suddenly remind me of the exchange I had while on my trials.

"I feel like home?" I reiterate.

Trae's eyebrows tug in, but his dimples flash, "Well, yeah."

"It was you—" I gasp.

"Me? What was me?"

"You were, *Something*, weren't you? The one who visited me in my mind while I was on my trials." I say.

His eyes widen, "That—that was real? I thought it was just made up; something in my head while I was stuck there."

"It wasn't—you found a way to reach me." I say.

My heart warms at the thought of Trae realizing the connection between us before I even knew connections like this existed—and he even found a way to reach me when his mind wasn't even his own.

Trae slams his eyelids shut, and shakes his head.

"Are you okay?" I say, lifting myself up.

"Yeah, I'm—it's okay Runa. I just," he licks his lip, "I still have this—*intruder* in here. Mostly he's locked away, but sometimes he—I don't want him to taint anything. Not now."

Ever since Trae came out of the Helix, he's been the man I remember. There's been none of the previous signs of strangeness. It's been so easy to forget he's still struggling with the AirGlider inside him.

"Are you—are you alright? Is he fighting you?" I ask.

"No, nothing like that. He's just acting like my conscience and I don't need one of those right now," he says, rolling his eyes.

I tug my eyebrows in, concerned.

"Don't make that face. It's nothing bad. He just—he thinks we've spent enough time away," Trae says.

"Do you hear him all the time? Did you—*during*?" I ask, unable to help myself.

Trae sits up completely. The soft blanket falls to his waist in the motion as he twists to look me in the eye.

"No. He—*we* were alone," he says.

"How do you know?" I ask.

"Because I do. It was," he raises a hand and scratches the back of his neck, "it was a request of mine. I needed him to get the hell outta the way and stay there."

Trae's brows pull in as his lips tug downward. His eyes plead with me and I know he means what he says. Taking a deep breath, I nod.

"He's not wrong, though. As much as I'd like to stay here with you in this beautiful bubble, we need to figure out our next move," Trae says.

Taking a deep breath, I let all my air out slowly. I hate to go—we haven't had nearly enough time together. And if what comes next is as big as I fear—

"Okay, how about we get dressed and we figure out our next course of action. There has to be another way out of here," I say trying to hide the disappointment welling up inside me.

Trae leans forward, kissing my cheek. Without a word, he slips out of the bed and disappears into the allayroom.

Laying back in the bed, I take another long inhalation and blow it out.

The more I try to push Trae's naked body from my mind, the more it becomes front and center. The memory melds with the moments in the trial where I felt him behind me. Giving in to this urge is what allowed me to pass the first trial. Hunger. Desire. It fueled everything from the start.

So why does it feel so unyielding now?

"I'm sorry, Runa. I didn't even say thank you for healing me," Trae says as he enters the room. He buttons the top of his new shirt, sauntering to the table with an air of confidence about him. He's always been strong and confident before—but it's slightly different now. I don't know that I have a word for it.

"You don't have to thank me. I wish I'd been able to do it sooner," I say.

"So, did you see anything new in the Caudex?" he says, taking a seat.

I clutch the blanket for a second, unwilling to let the moment fully pass. Nodding to myself, I push up to a stand in one quick motion. The blanket falls from my body and I walk to the doorway where my clothing lays in a heap on the floor. Trae inhales quickly, and I smile to myself before grabbing them and turning around.

"No, nothing new, but I was looking over what it was saying about the trials. Trying to piece together what the trials meant. Or what they were leading up to before I deviated from them," I say, walking to the allayroom with the still damp pile in my arms.

"And?"

"And I think everything was tying in elements from the five factions," I say, finding some dry clothes in the allayroom closet. I pull on my undergarments and walk back into the other room?

"Factions?" Trae asks, his eyes caressing my body the way his hands had not long ago.

Tugging on my new trousers, I say, "The Four Pillars, and humans. I think its about embracing pieces of each. That's why they're giving me power. I'm also beginning to think Videus knew more about the prophecy than he originally let on."

Trae's eyebrows flick upward.

"Really? Why's that?" he says.

I slide into my new top, a soft, pleasant button up shirt with a neckline that accentuates my collarbone. The purple fabric feels like a second skin—so smooth. Placing my crystal necklace on is the finishing touch.

Trae watches my every move, those handsome dimples emerging.

I grin at him, and take the seat beside him.

"When I was in the future, at least I think it was the future —Ammon and I stumbled on a garden of sorts. There were snow sculptures in the courtyard. Only, it wasn't really snow. They were made from blood. People Videus had killed who fit the profile in the bloodlines leading back to me," I say. "The Caudex has mentioned in a veiled way—something about buried shards. I think that's what it means. Something gifted through the bloodlines."

Trae scratches the top of his blue head.

"Interesting theory."

I tip my head to the side, "You don't believe me."

"It's not that. It's just— doesn't it seem a little implausible? I mean, how does one send 'shards' through bloodlines?"

"How do I have powers? Why do others Videus has captured have powers?" I say, thinking back to the group that escaped the Helix.

Trae shrugs, "I honestly got nothing. Point taken."

I crook an eyebrow in appreciation for my reasoning, though I can't fully explain it. It's something I simply feel—a knowing since the snow sculptures.

"Thanks," I grin. "Now, if I can just figure out what I'm meant to do with all of this power—It's obviously been gifted down to do something important. But the trials are what determines the Beacon. Without the mark, the Beacon doesn't ignite. So, the powers…They have to be something else. A fail safe?" I say, brainstorming aloud.

"What if it's just a side-effect?" Trae says pragmatically.

"So you don't think it was meant for anything?" I sit up straighter.

He shrugs.

"It's not so much that I don't think it's meant for something more. Just that humans, we don't have any kind of power on our own. But these, what did you call 'em again? Pillars? Those guys did. If their essence, or shard, or whatever is in your blood, maybe it's just a simple reaction to it."

I bite my lip.

"That makes a certain amount of sense, I guess," I say.

"You sound disappointed?"

"No. Well, yes. Maybe a little. It's just—I have this gift, so to speak, and I have an incredible urge to make sure it's used. But for the right reasons. You know?"

"Sure," he says, nodding.

"Really?"

"Don't sound so skeptical. I get it. You're looking for meaning in all this. It makes sense."

"I hadn't thought of it that way before," I say, grinning.

"Leave it to me, I make mud—uh, clearer mud," he says, scrunching his face.

I can't help but laugh. It's been so long, and feels so good. Even in the midst of all this chaos. In the middle of—who knows what comes next. It's nice to have someone near who can still make me laugh.

"Okay, so what else?" he says. "You were saying Videus might be aware of the prophecy. Is it because he was hunting the bloodlines?" Trae asks.

"Yes. I don't think he has all of the pieces, though. Otherwise, he would have done something to stop the Beacon. And wouldn't he know where the Acropolis is?" I say.

"From what I'm gathering—he knows about both, but like us a little bit ago, he's just unsure of where they are. Maybe he was hoping you'd—"

Trae's face goes white, and his smile drops.

"What? What is it?" I ask, standing up.

Traeton goes completely unresponsive—his face like stone.

I grab hold of his shoulders and shake.

"Trae? Traeton Revasco—"

After a moment, he blinks wildly.

"We—we need to go, Runa. There's—"

Suddenly, the rocky cavern wall shivers, and a hologram hiding a stairwell on the right disappears.

"Traeton? Runa? What are you doing down here?" Landry asks, shock written across his face as he takes a step into the room. His forehead wrinkles as he recovers, and his hands are filled with supplies.

Trae's mouth drops open, but no sound comes out.

"Landry, we could ask you the same thing. You surprised us," I say.

I feel the urgency rolling off Trae. He received a message, or something from the AirGlider—but now's not the time to discuss it. We need to go.

Landry shoots a glance from Trae, to me, and back to Trae again.

"Well, I built this. So—"

Trae's eyes widen.

"This is *your* place?" he finally says.

"What's gotten into the both of you? C'mon, guys. What's going on? You shouldn't be here. It's not ready yet."

"Ready? Ready for what?" Trae asks.

"Habitation, obviously," he says, making a face. "How'd you get in here? Did Alina let you in?"

Trae blinks back his surprise, and begins to nod. "Yeah, Alina said it was a surprise and to check it out."

I turn to Trae, my cheek twitchy as I narrow my eyes, trying to follow his reasoning. I feel as though there's information lost in translation happening. It's been a long time since I felt like this.

"It's definitely a nice, uh, place. What made you think to create it?" I ask, trying to keep the mood light.

"I needed to get away from everything. I don't know—after Fen—," his eyes drop to the ground, and his shoulders stiffen, "after losing him, nothing felt right anymore. Everywhere I looked, I saw him. I needed a place I could go that was devoid of his memory. Something new. You know? I needed to tinker."

I nod, "Makes total sense."

I look around the space. The attention to detail, the amount of work that would have been necessary to make a venture like this happen—it wouldn't be possible in the mere months since Fenton's death. This has been in the works for much longer.

Taking a calming breath, I grab Trae's hand.

"Well, I guess we should really be going. We have some people we need to see," I say.

Trae nods, "Yes, people."

"C'mon guys. I just got here. The least you can do is stay. Have a drink or something. Let me know what you really think of this place. It's my first attempt at creating something on this scale. Did—er—did you use the bed?"

Trae's eyes widen and he turns to me, his mouth open to say something.

"We did. It sorta happened—um, I'll just—" I get up, retrieving the blanket from the floor and making an attempt to lay it back the way it was before we arrived.

"Yeah—I think we're better off just washing those, Runa. But thanks," Landry says, placing the items in his hands on the counter.

"Sure," I say, pulling everything off and laying them in a crumbled ball.

Trae places a hand over his face, his red cheeks peeking through his fingers.

I can't help but want to laugh. Honestly—I can't even find it in me to try to hide anything. The absurdity of the situation is too profound.

Trae grabs hold of the Caudex, shoving it toward me and stepping between Landry and I.

"We'd really love to stay Landry, but we need to go," he says, taking a strong, solid stance.

Landry watches our every move with skeptical eyes.

"Be my guest," he finally says, swiping his hand out toward the way he came. "I suppose I should get back to working on that EMP. It's really been a tough one to crack the right frequency. The builder of the Helix really thought of everything."

"Yeah, you'll have to fill us in on that one soon," Trae says, oddly agitated. "Sorry, really wish we could stay longer."

He takes my hand and starts walking toward the newly revealed exit. Tucking the Caudex under my left arm, I grip his hand tightly.

"Yeah, no worries. I guess," Landry mutters, shaking his head.

We walk the small stone stairwell as it curves slightly to the right and we end up at a small, wooden door. It's simple, and nondescript. I reach for the handle and push it open.

The room is dark, but as we enter, dim lights flicker to life.

"This is Alina's place," Trae says. "We've been right underneath her house."

"What's going on Trae? Why did you want to leave so quickly? It seemed Landry wanted us to stay and talk. Isn't that a good thing considering how he's been?"

"No, now's not the time to chat with Landry. You'll just have to trust me," he says.

Trae takes the lead, having been inside Alina's before. The house isn't big, but it's still nice to maneuver through it without needing to orient ourselves. We walk through a small kitchen, which unlike Landry's house, is a room all to itself. Then, on to a hallway which leads to the main entry.

Trae's breath is shallow as he guides us through each room.

"I feel like there's something you're not telling me. Please, what's going on?"

"I just—got a bad feeling about hanging out down there."

"A bad feeling? How?" I ask, tugging his arm and making him stop. "It was the AirGlider, wasn't it? Did he say something to freak you out?"

"Runa—I know you're skeptical. Hell, I'd be too. But Caelum really does want to help," Trae says.

"*Caelum*? Are you kidding me?" I say, dropping his hand.

Laughter bubbles up, a strange, almost maniacal laugh.

"He just wants us to get somewhere safe," he says, his gaze shifting to his feet. "Something's not right and he—"

"Safe? You think anywhere is safe? I knew—I knew you were compromised, but I figured it was just some miscellaneous AirGlider. Videus is coming for us. From every angle. Every timeline. Every direction and we don't even know how we can stop him. All I'm supposed to be—this Daughter of Five— it's all useless if his number one in command is inside your head. Why didn't you think to tell me this sooner? Why the hell did you keep this from me?"

"I knew you wouldn't understand," Trae says, his voice low. "And I didn't want to worry you. Honestly, Runa, I have this under control."

"Like hell you do," I say, glaring at him.

All this time, he knew who was inside his head—he knew it was Caelum and chose to keep it from me. How could he do this?

"Do you think I like this? Having some damn bird inside my mind, invading my thoughts whenever he wants? It's obscene, that's what it is. Especially because of us—and everything we've just—but I'm making the most of it. And look, he warned me, warned *us*, right before—" Trae takes a step back, taking a deep breath and lowering his shoulders that had risen.

"Right before?" I say through tight lips.

Trae blinks, his dark eyelashes rapidly fluttering across his cheeks.

"Look, we can talk about it elsewhere. We really need to go. It's not safe here," he says.

"Because Caelum says so? Of course not. We're in the Lateral—with *friends*."

"Runa, please," Trae pleads. "We need to leave. Something is coming, if we don't. Lets go, then I'll tell you everything."

I search his eyes. Desperation clings to their inner reaches, and despite my anger, I hear myself say, "Fine, let's go.

Trae exhales and reaches for the door handle.

"Guys, what are you doing in here?"

17

RUNA

BOTH OF US JUMP, startled at the voice from the darkness of the room. Trae flings the door open, and light floods into the entryway.

Alina enters the light; her eyebrows tucked in.

"Guys?" she repeats.

Trae grips the door handle tightly, but doesn't move.

"We were looking for you and Landry," I say, stepping toward her.

"Well, Landry's not here. I think he's over at his place. He's still trying to come up with the EMP you guys need," she says, her shoulders relaxing a bit.

"Oh, great. That's—great," I say, turning to look at Trae.

His eyes widen and he tips his head toward the door.

"We'll just go check in with him to see how that's going," I say with a smile.

I start backing toward the door. Alina's eye twitches slightly, and she shakes her head.

"Okay, well, if you need anything else—knock next time," she says.

I nod, "Yes, you bet."

Trae's out the door before I even turn back around. I race out of the house and down the steps into the cobbled streets of the Lateral. My eyes widen as I take in the sheer number of people milling about. They're all walking around, their eyes wide as they take in their new surroundings. Most of them are slightly emaciated, and look as though they haven't seen sunlight of any kind for years.

Perhaps they haven't.

"We need to find someplace quiet. Somewhere we won't be spotted by someone else we know. Keep your head down, I have just the place," Trae says, plucking a hat off a kid on the street and covering his bright blue hair.

I initiate the hood from my NanoTech jacket and drag it up over my head. Keeping our heads down, we meander through the crowded streets. Intense energy rolls off each person we pass connected through the bloodlines. I sense their connection to me, and I have no doubt they sense mine to them. No hood or hat could hide that.

Some of them lift their heads as we pass, searching for something they can sense, but not physically see. I want to reach out to them, tell them we're here to put things right. But I know now is not the time or place. I need to regroup and figure out how to initiate the Beacon without Videus being alerted through Caelum.

Yet, as we continue on, like being drawn to a magnet, we start being followed. It starts with one confused straggler, and continues to expand.

I grab Trae's hand, "Trae, stop. We need to stop."

He turns around, confused. His eyes widen as he takes in the large crowd gathering behind us.

"What! How'd they follow us?"

I shake my head and say, "Instinctively. I could feel it, too."

"Feel what?" he says, his eyes wide.

"Each of them. The ones who share the bloodlines."

He licks his lower lip, nodding to himself.

"Trae, we need to face this head on. Time's running out. There's no place left to hide and we both know it. Without the mark, we have to take a stand. Maybe they're part of it," I say, sweeping my hand out to the sea of people.

"Runa, you do what you gotta do. At this point, I'm just here to back your play."

"You'll tell me what you needed to say later?" I ask.

"Yeah, sure."

I take a deep breath. It feels like I've been made for this moment. That everything I've been through was leading me to this point.

Turning to face the crowd, I look into each of their faces. Despite everything they've been through; the isolation, the torture, they all gaze back into my eyes with hope written across their faces.

Stepping up onto the ledge of the fountain in the middle of the Lateral, I take a moment to watch the gathering crowd.

"You've spent the last few days, weeks, months, or maybe even years wondering what you'd done to deserve the treatment you'd received. You've probably wondered if there was something different about you—or maybe wrong with you. Maybe you already knew," I begin. "Now is the time where we lay everything on the table. The hands we were dealt have been difficult. But they're nothing more than circumstances. They don't define us, even if they're a part of who we've become. What defines us is the direct actions we take in our lives. The way we move through those circumstances we've been given."

I take a deep breath, searching for the words. There's so much to say, but without threatening to overwhelm them, I need to relay what's most important.

"Things are about to become dangerous. The man—

Videus—that's his name, he's going to be coming for me—coming for all of us. I wish I could tell you being here was the end of your suffering, but I don't know what's in store yet. I just know whatever he has planned, I'm going to stand and fight him. This is *my* life. They're *your* lives. I'm not going to give Videus any more pawns to play with. You each have power inside you. I know you've felt it. Maybe you even know what that power means for you. You need to tap into it now. It's what you were captured for. It's what Videus is most frightened of. He kept everyone separate because he didn't know which of you would lead him to me. Little did he know, together we're stronger than one person."

I look out into the sea of confusion and understanding. Those who are with me begin explaining to those around them.

"If we rise together, standing against his tyranny and violence, we can take back our lives. I have a plan. I can't promise it will be easy. I can't promise I can keep you all safe. But I do promise that if you're with me, I will do everything in my power to break this cycle and give you your lives back," I say. "We need to come at Videus head on. We can't sit back, waiting for him to come to us. That's what he'll expect. Instead, we leave at dawn to retaliate. Think about it for a moment. Talk about it with those you love before you decide."

Everyone erupts in chatter, drawing attention our crowd by the rest of the Lateral residents. Some begin to leave their homes, making their way to us.

"What's going on here?" Delaney says, walking up beside Trae.

"Lane, we're all in danger—I'm sure you're well aware. We need to take a stand and put an end to all of this. Everything we hold dear is at stake," I say.

Without a second thought, Lane tips her head and says,

"We always knew it would come to this. The records are old, but still clear. Whatever you need, the Council is at your disposal."

"Council?" Trae says, taking Delaney by the arm and pulling her aside.

I step down from the fountain, and follow.

Lane points to me and says, "She's the Daughter of Five, is she not?"

My eyes widen.

"How do you know that name?" I ask, suddenly cautious.

Delaney inhales slowly, then straightens her jacket. Her dark, curly hair is piled on top of her head, the way it was when I first met her. She looks calm and put together. Not like someone who should know anything about the Daughter of Five.

"I've been a part of a group inside the Lateral called the Council. There are four of us and we've been seated by those who came before us. We're meant to watch for signs of the prophecy," she says.

My head is spinning, and I step away.

A secret group of humans who knew about the prophecy? How could this even be possible?

"Who are the other three?" I ask, turning around to face her.

Trae glances from me to Delaney and back again.

"You won't know them," she begins.

"Try me," I say.

"They're from different cities on Pendomus. So unless you've been to the outskirts of Kanlantia or the highlands of Franish, I highly doubt it will matter. What matters is we need to sound the alarm. I knew—I knew from the moment you told me you were attacked by the Morph," she says.

"What about the Morph? You told us the Morph was

fabricated—Oh, right," Trae says, his eyes widening in recognition. "You already knew about the Waterbear."

Delaney nods.

Thoughts swirl around in my head like a wild current.

The Morph was designed deliberately based on Tethys. Delaney has known all along about the Waterbear and other Pillars. She's known about the propaganda of the Daughter of Five. It was all right here, under our noses the whole time.

Shaking away the surprise, I say, "Look Lane, if you're aware of the prophecy, then you know we need to find a way to get the Beacon initiated so the Acropolis will rise. We need to release Videus' control on the Four Pillars so they can choose for themselves who they support."

"If you're the Daughter of Five, you know you're the only one who can get the Beacon initiated. Do you have the mark?" she asks.

I hold out my arm, allowing her to lift my sleeve. The glowing Everblossom with its missing petal shimmer under the surface of my skin.

"It's not complete?" Delaney says, lifting her eyes to mine.

"It's not," I say.

"Then it's no good to us," she says shoving my arm back to me.

She begins to pace.

"How can you only have a partial mark?" she says, crossing her arms.

"I didn't finish the trials. I needed to come back," I say. "I got word my friends were in danger."

"Of course you did," she says, rolling her eyes. "They're always in trouble. That doesn't negate the importance of what you were meant to be undergoing."

"Look, are you going to back me up, or are you going to second guess my judgment?" I say, anger welling inside of me. "We don't have time for petty squabbles and second guessing. What we need now is direct action. By now, Videus could know where we are, and how to get to us. With or without the Beacon, we need to find a way to join everyone in a common cause."

Delaney's face is unreadable, even as she cocks an eyebrow and glances toward Trae.

"What exactly do you have in mind?" she finally says.

"I was thinking—the Beacon is meant to be partially a symbol. It's a way to alert the Pillars the prophecy is true and is in action. To me, that means it's time to stand up and do what's right. It gives them all a reason to break ranks with Videus, if they can, and fight for their independence again," I say.

"You realize that's easier said than done. Many of the Pillars have been enslaved and had years of mental and physical conditioning to keep them in line. If it were as easy as you say, to just—break ranks—many would have done it before now. What about all those who can't do it on their own? The Beacon was meant to be more than just an alert system—it's meant to amplify your power. That's how the Acropolis will rise again."

I take a seat on the edge of the fountain.

"Well, that's news to me," I say, biting my lip. "I didn't know."

Why does everything have to be so mysterious? Trickling in at the most inopportune times? Why can't they just spell it all out and say, *Runa—get your butt in gear and make this, this, and this happen?*

Why can't I just be omnipotent or something? Ugh.

"Alright. Here's what I think we need—"

High above the city, the lights flicker, immediately followed by a rumble knocking debris loose from the cavern ceiling.

"What was that?" I say, looking up.

"Nothing good," Delaney says. "Trae, stay here with everyone. I'm going to fill in Ash and the team. We need to be ready. By the looks of things, dawn just came early."

Delaney rushes off, maneuvering through the crowd of people until I lose sight of her.

Another loud crack above us rumbles the very fabric of the Lateral. One of the large lights hanging high above the city crashes to the ground, leveling the roof of a smaller house on its descent.

Someone nearby screams.

"It's started," I say, eyeing the group of people beginning to lose their calm.

"Everyone—everyone listen to me. We can't panic," I yell over the sounds of crying, screaming, and shouts.

The volume settles only a little, so I close my eyes, trying to connect with each and everyone in the Lateral. Bloodline tied or not, we all have a stake in what comes next.

I push the boundaries of what I can do, searching each molecule of this place for sentient life. When I'm satisfied I've found everyone I can, I open my eyes.

Above each them is a bright white and blue light—letting me know they're online with me. In a strange way, they remind me of the orbs of light I first saw when my vision was adjusting to this new power inside me.

~Everyone, we aren't prepared. None of us are, but that's the thing about life. Things shift and change all the time without our permission. Things are never clear. Never one-hundred percent concrete. What matters is what we do when things shift. Videus is coming. He's already here. It's time to take our stand and protect those we love. Are you with me?

With that, the ceiling of the Lateral itself tears apart like someone opening a metal can. Large boulders launch as debris, landing all around us. Snow from outside careens inward, splattering around in odd places, bringing the outside into the Lateral.

Flashes from the future of the gaping hole where the Lateral used to be instantly come to mind. Everything is beginning again—and even though I'm here, I'm not able to stop it.

Large holes rip through the cobbled streets, revealing the large, open water below. Screams erupt as a young boy loses his balance and falls into the water.

I rush forward, unable to help myself. If something isn't done he'll die and I can't have that on my conscience. I reach out to Tethys, knowing she's nearby, still circling somewhere in the watery depths below.

As I reach the massive hole's edge, another huge chunk of the cavern ceiling comes crashing down, leveling a nearby home to its foundation. A huge chunk of ice and snow skitter across the floor, landing near my feet. More screaming.

There's so much screaming.

The pitch digs at my core, and my body begins to shake from the rush of adrenaline.

I need to get the boy—get the boy, and then focus on the rest.

Staring into the depths, I push my consciousness into the water. As much as I've connected to the inner realm of Tethys' watery magic, I don't have the kind of strength she does to push him out. This will have to be done from beneath.

Tethys acknowledges she'll protect him and get him to safety. I sense her as she hunts beneath the Lateral, searching for the boy. After a moment, the water below turns a bright blue and begins to boil. Just as she had done before with me, she bursts upward.

I scramble back as she widens the hole and delivers the boy. As her shield disengages, his limp body flops to the floor. An older woman, his mother most likely, rushes out, searching in the air for what just lifted him from the water. Tears stream from her face as she pulls him close.

A man beside her rips the boy from her arms and begins a maneuver to remove the water from the boy's lungs. After what feels like forever, the boy sputters and coughs. So much water comes spewing from his mouth, it's unreal.

I blink away the moment, realizing this same scene and many more are playing out all around me. People everywhere are suffering, and I've let it all happen.

There are no ranks, no orders. Just complete chaos and everyone fending for themselves.

I waited too long—spent too much time reveling in my own humanity with Trae. I should never have let myself forget, even for a moment, how dangerously close to annihilation we all are. For all I know, he was biding time to warn Videus about where we were.

"Runa—we need to get everyone out of the Lateral or this is about to be a massive grave," Delaney says, rushing back to me.

I look around, regaining my senses.

"Where's Trae? Have you seen him?" I ask.

Delaney shakes his head, "No, not since the attack."

My heart drops.

Did he use me? Has Caelum taken over again? Did he ever really leave?

"I need to find him and Ammon. He'll be able to help protect everyone as they're getting out. Is the path to the Haven open? Can people go that way?"

"I assume the entrance is still blocked, but—"

"It's been reopened. Have everyone head that way for now. It's our safest bet. Unless you have a hidden set of ships that can go under water," I say.

Delaney shakes her head.

"Alright, look for Ammon, and I'll search for Trae."

"Are you sure? Runa, there's so much going on here. We need to be helping the others, not hunting for your brother. I'm sure he's a nice kid and all, but there are more pressing —" she begins.

"Trust me, he's your best hope— he can move stone and rock with his mind. He wants to help," I say, trying to center myself in the midst of all the chaos. I need to reach out to him mentally because there's no way either one of us will find him in all this chaos.

"Runa, we're wasting time. Look at everything going on —" Delaney says.

I shoot her a sideways glance and she stops whatever she was going to say.

"Runa, you do what you need to do. I'll do what I need to. If I find Trae, I'll send him your direction. I'm sure he's off helping someone who's been hurt."

Delaney takes off, not waiting for a response from me.

So much for my Daughter of Five status. I can't even command a leader of a secret group who had intel about me and the prophecy. This truly is a one-for-all kind of mentality.

Deep, rolling clouds billow overhead. They look like purple pillows as they circle into enormous balls. Here and there, pieces of the clouds break off, detaching and careening through the sky toward us.

Those who notice the oddity, stand back in shock.

"Oh my god. What is this?" I say, my mouth gaping open wide.

RUNA

*I*N THE DISTANCE someone screams, "White elephants."

I turn to find the source of the scream, but meet a sea of faces with eyes wide in horror. Returning my gaze to the sky, one of the white blobs from the clouds careens directly at me, as if it had a specific target and just found it. Before I can move out of its path, it latches onto my arm, howling and screeching like a feral animal. For a moment, I'm awestruck. I've heard of elephants before—from the Earth downloads— but this is no elephant. Instead, it looks more like a human infant made of mist; only it has weight and mass.

The white elephant's empty eyes peer into mine with a triumphant grin spreading across its eerie face. Then it tips its head back, and howls. Quickly, its face slams forward as its teeth sink into my flesh. Blood gushes from the wound, painting the ground and coloring the face of the white elephant. To my horror, the white elephant begins to change color completely as it pulls the blood from my body and ingests it. Before it can morph completely, a group of random people from the Lateral come to my aid. They grope at the small cloud infant, wrenching him from my arm and disrupting his feast.

I stumble backward, dazed and horrified, as I grope my arm in an attempt to stop the bleeding. My skin itches, my veins burn, and my vision tilts. Someone nearby offers a shirt to tie against it, but I shake my head and reach down to a snow chunk on the floor beside me. It begins to rumble, then melt, pooling at my feet the way I've seen Tethys do so many times before. The snow creeps up my arm, entering my open wounds and flushing out a white, viscous fluid before coagulating my blood and sealing the wound. In seconds, my arm looks as though the bite had been ages old, as only a vicious scar remains.

Some of the white elephant children flee back to the clouds; some soaked in blood, others as white as before. I glance around at the band of miscreants by my side. The air hangs heavy with a mixture of horror and happiness at their retreat.

Another scream erupts, dissipating the relief like the vapor they're made of. The world around me feels as though it halts as those closest to me point again to the sky. Directly in front of us, a large cyclone appears darkening the sky as it widens in an eerily horizontal fashion—rather than facing toward the ground the way I've seen of the tornados of Earth.

From inside, masses of white elephants erupt like a swarm of bees, raining down on us without discrimination.

Far off in the distance, cannons of some sort shoot off, aimed at the sky, without much thought. One of them, while taking out a few of their targets as they descend, also takes out a large wall of stone and ice beyond. Water erupts from the hole, pouring into the city.

"Who's firing the cannons?" I yell.

Someone nearby shrugs, and yells back, "Probably someone on Delaney's team."

Some of the white elephants flee upward, backing away from the onslaught of water flooding in on us. Others, don't seem bothered, latching on to their victims, turning red, and holding tight. We need to get everyone to higher ground. The water rushes in fast, flooding everything as though it was a captive animal that had been waiting to be unleashed.

The flood gives no opportunity for any to escape, it's far too quick as it consumes us all. I crouch down, bracing for the tide of water, only to find myself engulfed in a shield as I rise to the surface. I open my eyes, finding myself floating around the upper walls of houses. Tethys, able to finally move freely in the water, has taken some of us in. But many others aren't so lucky.

"Tethys—the others, we need to save the others," I say, edging on the air of a panic.

This is all wrong. This shouldn't be happening.

My mind swirls around all the details. How can any of this be happening? Nothing prepared me for these creatures —no record, no warning. I'd never even heard of them before. Clearly others have known about them, though. What's the point of the Daughter of Five, any of it, if my friends and the Lateral are still wiped out in the end?

No, it will not end this way.

"Take me back, Tethys," I say. "I have to go back. People I care about are still down there—Trae, my brothers. So many innocent lives. I might be the only one who can do something about this."

Tethys grunts, clearly torn between her mission to protect me, and knowing what I'm here to do. All around us, people flail about, trying to stay above the rising water.

"There's no time—I have to try," I say, patting the side of her neck. "This can't be the end. It just can't."

Tethys maintains our position and relinquishes control. I close my eyes, letting go of the panic and mayhem around me. I reach out, finding each and every soul who struggles in the water. Much the way it did with them before, as if they come online with me, I see a bright white or blue light hovering over each of their heads. I feel their pain, their panic.

Instead of trying to communicate, I focus on gifting them the power to save themselves. To use the water around them to create their own personal shield, to use the power of the water to heal themselves and protect them.

All around me, small bubbles pop to the surface, surrounding the others and protecting them one by one. Many continue to flail in the water, trying to find a way to save themselves—those without innate power in their blood. Quickly, I send out the urgent response to save those who don't have our bloodline ties.

Somewhere in the distance, I sense Trae, trying desperately to stay afloat.

I give the same command to Tethys, who takes in three people nearby before darting to Trae's location. The family we picked up scream wildly, clutching on to one another.

"What is this thing?" The man asks, his voice nearly a screech. "Who are you?"

I don't have time to answer, needing instead to focus on Trae's location and giving Tethys the most accurate coordinates.

The white elephants dive in and out of the water, undisturbed by its effects as they search for their victims. The small shields of water are strong, summoned by the water itself. They keep out most attempts the white elephants make, but the shields won't hold forever. I know all too well how the limited amount of oxygen the shields can pull won't hold. There's too much CO2 to filter out. Eventually, the oxygen will need to be replenished.

Tethys veers around screaming people, knowing we can't take on more than five of us inside her shield. All around us, people are flailing, screaming. Some are being helped—some are not. My heart aches watching it all, knowing there's not much else I can do.

We finally reach Trae, and his body is beginning visibly to tire from exhaustion. Without any fanfare, Tethys absorbs him into the shield and dives deep, taking off like a rocket.

Trae sputters and coughs.

"Took you long enough," he says, reaching for my hand.

He grabs my forearm and climbs up behind me, wrapping his arms around my waist.

"We need to get everyone out of the Lateral. I don't know how he'll do it, but Videus is about to level it," I say, realizing I'm powerless to stop the inevitable.

"How could you possibly know that?" the other man asks.

"Someone once showed me," I say.

"Say what?" he says, his eyes wide and almost blank.

He's in shock.

"Nevermind. What's important is I know what's coming and we need to get to safety."

"And where do you propose safety is? Have you looked around you? I've never seen these creepy baby things in all my life. And with the Lateral underwater—what's safe anymore?" the other man cries.

"Hey, if anyone can do it—it's this woman right here," Trae says.

My mind is going a million miles an hour as I try to formulate a plan quickly. With the water rising, it will eventually flood everything. There will be no where left to go but up through the ceiling. But I doubt the water will ever get that high.

While half of me is trying to come up with a plan, the other half of me is wondering how Videus managed to create those abominations. Has he expanded his powers? Has he brought in reinforcements since I liberated some of the Salamanders and AirGliders?

What kind of power does it take to rip apart the Lateral's cavern ceiling like it was nothing?

A deafening, high-pitched squeal pierces my brain and my hands instinctively fly to my ears, trying to shield them from the sound. Everyone in the immediate vicinity is doing the same.

~It didn't need to end this way. Still doesn't. For those of you who cherish the breath in your body, I only ask for one thing and I'll let you all go. I don't care that you escaped. I don't care that you demolished my vassalage. I only ask for a simple deed to be done and I'll stop this onslaught. Bring me Runa, the Daughter of Five's head. A simple task and you're free to live out the rest of your days in peace. You have my word.

Videus' words broadcast, clearly tapping into the eLink network for some, and finding a way to get through to those of us without it. Everyone begins to look around them.

"This is not good—Runa, with a bounty on your head, you need to run. Get as far away from all of this as you can," Trae says, clutching me closer.

I shake my head. Surely no one will take this madman's request seriously?

"You can't be saying I give up? Do you have that little faith in people?" I say, surprised.

"I know exactly how people are. They're gullible and fallible. Give them the choice between their own lives and the life of someone else, they'll choose their own. Wouldn't you?" he says.

My jaw slacks open. Tethys grunts a warning to others inside and the man holds up his hands.

Would I make that same choice? I'm not so sure.

"No, I wouldn't. I'd stand for what's right," I say, defiantly.

"Then you're the exception to the rule. Maybe that's why you're special," Trae says.

Tethys shoots another warning grunt to the others, but they just huddle closer.

The water level has risen to the tops of the houses, and continues to climb. Without accepting a command from me, Tethys descends into the water, rather than rise with it. We plunge into the depths as she searches for a means of escape.

Around me, people inside the safety of their bubbles stare wide-eyed as we pass. A look of both acknowledgment and conflict scatter across their faces. The man is right. They're fighting with their internal instincts.

I hang my head, disappointed. After everything, the connection I know they feel with me, some would be willing to turn me over to Videus—just like that.

Clutching Tethys' fur with my hands, I clench my jaw and allow her to take us away from all of this. I can only hope they'll be able to find their own way out. Maybe Videus will even allow them to survive as they hunt for me.

Within a few moments, Tethys finds one of the large gaping holes in the street, and propels us downward through it. She maneuvers us swiftly, aptly weaving in and out of the statues and large rock outcroppings deep beneath the Lateral.

"Where are you taking us?" the woman asks.

I shake my head and softly say, "I'm not sure where we're going. But we'll be safe."

Right now, I can't say I care where we go. Disappointment and disbelief wash over me.

How could this happen? How could *I* let this happen? I should have stayed and finished the trials. If I had, none of this would have happened. I would have been able to initiate the Beacon ages ago and set everything right. Instead, I'm running away when I should be standing up and fighting. I should be making things right—not worse.

In her own way, Tethys tells me I've done everything I could.

"You and I both know this is all my fault. I should have been ready. I should've had the mark. But I let myself get in the way. I thought I knew what was best. Stupid," I say to her.

Tethys ignores my irritation and travels quickly, propelling us through the underground currents as quickly as possible. My wrist aches, and I lift the sleeve of my jacket, revealing the partial mark as it glows beneath my skin. It burns and itches like crazy, almost as if it has a mind of its own. In a way, it's like it senses we're near the Beacon and it has a purpose to serve.

We follow the tunnel we came in, eventually popping out onto the surface. Her shield disengages to release the family —Tethys trusts them as much as she trusts Videus at this point. But at least she was willing to get them to safety.

The family stumbles out into the snow, surprised. Tethys doesn't stop long enough for me to say goodbye, or give an offering of where to go to find safety. She's done her part, now on to the next.

We plunge back into the depths of the water and disappear.

After a couple of minutes, Tethys slows down, searching for something I can't see. Light filters from the ice above, illuminating some of the large statues buried in the water. For the first time, I realize not all of the statues are human-like. Some of them are in the shape of Waterbears.

"Are you taking us to your—?" I begin.

"Take us where?" Trae asks, echoing my sentiment. "I can't see anything."

I shake my head, but as we continue on more evidence of

the Waterbears arise. Large, cascading homes in the shapes of bubbles cling to the side of the underwater rocks.

We pass an enormous statue of a Waterbear, holding its young on its back. Much the way we are with Tethys now.

She careens around the statue, finding a location near the surface to slow down and stop. As she gets closer, the Caudex lights up inside the pouch on the side of Tethys' shoulder. We rise out of the water, as she glides across a large icy walkway toward a cavern made of pure ice.

Tethys releases her shield and the cold air assaults my senses. Instantly, I begin to shiver as I grab the Caudex and slide off her back. Trae slides off behind me, following.

"What is it? Is there something new?" he asks.

I sit down on the cold ground, and pull the aquamarine crystal from my neck.

My eyes flitter first to a paragraph that's been here before. The prophecy itself.

Locked within space and buried in blood, the keys to creation anew bide time. They linger in wait for when the wheels of Pendomus are set in motion and the threads of existence unravel. Through intentions and fear, safeguards become the Captor's demise. The Daughter's deliberate agreement to deliver her life's Burden will liberate the Five and reconstruct time in its accordance. Through human blood and ultimate sacrifice, the Acropolis will rise and all balance shall be restored.

I read it twice, before I realize there's nothing in the prophecy about the Beacon. Absolutely nothing.

"Why does the prophecy mention the Acropolis, but not the Beacon?" I say. "The Caudex elsewhere gave instructions on the Beacon. So it needs to be ignited in order to raise the Acropolis but it's odd that it's not at least mentioned."

"Is that odd?" Trae asks.

"Maybe?"

Tethys grunts.

I shake my head, "Nothing at all…"

Human blood and ultimate sacrifice.

I'd almost forgotten about that part.

I run my fingertips across my lips, staring at the page.

My heart skips a beat. I know what needs to be done. In a weird way, I think I've always known.

My eyes pause over a different portion of the paragraph, "Deliver her life's Burden…"

It solidifies my belief that I'm coming to the end. I'm not meant to survive this.

Once the Beacon is ignited, how do I deliver my life's Burden? Where?

"What do you think it means?" Trae asks, a hint of worry hidden in his tone.

"I don't know," I say out loud. "But it doesn't sound good, does it?"

I take a deep breath, and meet his gaze. His eyes are wide and the corners of his lips tug downward.

"You can't possibly—" he begins.

"I don't know," I repeat.

Regardless, I need to figure out for sure what it means. He and everyone else back at the Lateral are in danger—real, immediate danger. And those who aren't, they're going to be hunting for me now thanks to Videus.

I set the Caudex down beside Tethys and stand up.

"I'll be right back. I need—I need some time," I say.

Trae looks as though he's about to protest, but thinks better of it.

"Okay, I'll be right here," he says instead.

"Thanks," I whisper.

Turning my back on him, I head deeper into the ice cavern to clear my head.

There has to be more. More to everything and it's staring me in the face, but I just can't see it. Does it really want me to sacrifice myself?

My mind plays over the prophecy again and again. I stop walking, mulling over two words that give me hope that perhaps everything happening might be avoidable. Or at least fixable.

Reconstruct time—

Is the whole point of this to set all of the timelines right? To unravel the time loop Videus has begun? Something inside my soul vibrates and I know I'm on the right path. I don't know how yet, but it's all wrapped up in this.

What will resetting time mean for everyone? Will they even remember me when it's all said and done? My eyes flit down the tunnel to Trae, then to Tethys. Then past her to the wall of ice beyond.

What would resetting the timeline mean for Trae and I? After all we've shared, and become…will he even remember I existed? What if my sacrifice means he'll never know of me? That we'll never come back to this place with each other?

If I make it to the other side, will I even remember him?

What about everyone else? My mother? Fenton? Kani? Could setting the timeline right mean saving them all?

My mind escapes back to a time when I dreamed my mother and I could have been close. Where life is simple and my friends are happy and safe.

Casting another gaze at Trae, I stop and take a deep breath. If it's even a possibility to gain all that back—it's worth the risk of not knowing.

I'll do whatever it takes to deliver my Burden in whatever form it might take. I'll lay it all on the line. Wherever I need to go, whatever it costs, I'm ready to pay the price.

19

RUNA

UDDENLY THE GROUND BEGINS to rumble.
My wrist sears with pain, and I drop to my
knees, clawing at my jacket. As I pull back my sleeve, light
streams from the mark, and I watch the final petal slowly
appear. As it does, each of the five petals fill in with a crystal
white light—so pure and unadulterated I have to shield my
eyes. Light travels up my arm, flooding my body, filling into
my irises. It streams out my fingertips and ends of my hair.

Before I know it, Tethys and Trae are by my side. Their
presence is a safety blanket as I tread into unknown territory. Trae wraps his arms around me as all of the information once trapped inside the Caudex floods my
consciousness, granting me access to everything written and
unwritten. The waves of energy are intense, and I grope the
sides of my head, trying to move with it—to allow it to do its
job. In a strange way, I've become the Tree of Burden's vessel.

The mark does more than simply allow the Beacon to
ignite, it's a gateway between what is, what was, and what
will be. Within my mind, I can clearly see distinct threads of
timelines and each of their subsequent tangents created by

Videus. We're so off track and it all stems back to a single location in time.

The location is still fuzzy—not able to fully open up to allow me to see the what and why with clarity. But there's no doubt this is the moment that broke Videus. The moment where he left his humanity behind and became something completely contorted.

As the light subsides, it settles itself in place, illuminating only the mark. The five-petaled Everblossom shimmers under my skin a gentle white, with subtle hints of blue.

I take a moment to let the intensity of the energy settle.

"Runa—are you—are you okay?" Trae asks, breathless.

I nod, taking a deep breath. My body trembles, the adrenaline and energy finally dissipating. There's so much to do—so much to *undo*.

Standing up, I take in our surroundings once more—this time, with different eyes. I understand why Tethys brought us here. I know what this place was before it was hidden and completely enveloped with ice. I also know what needs to be done now.

The ground around us continues to rumble, and Tethys leans in, steadying us both.

"We need to go—" I begin.

Suddenly, the ground beneath us shifts. I feel Tethys' excitement—she knew this would happen. She knew the choices I'd make—even despite the direness. It's why she brought me to the outskirts of the Acropolis. The energy, the molecular memory— everything would lead me to the conclusion she expected.

"We need to get back to the Lateral," I say, rising to my feet. "I need to ignite the Beacon."

"Are you sure? I mean—what the hell just happened? There's this light, and—" Trae says, pointing from me to the cavern. "Is there even a point now? Hasn't Videus won?"

I take his hand, but hold his gaze.

"Trae, you have to trust me. I have work to do, and I'll need your help," I say.

These next few moments are what I was made for. I understand what needs to be done in order to set things right. I need to ignite the Beacon. Once accomplished, the energies of the Five will be ready for their sacrifice in order to open the timelines to alteration.

Even in the midst of all this chaos, I can't help but smile to myself.

I finally realize why I've been called the Daughter of Five. You wouldn't think it would matter, but it does.

The Four Pillars buried shards of themselves—their genetics, their essence, their powers—in the one place they felt would be safe until the time had come. In the bloodline of my ancestors. Four separate people on the planet were gifted the unique qualities only the Pillars could bestow— and it's taken this long for all four to combine into one. I have the pieces of each of the Four Pillars—along with my own consented humanity—buried inside my blood.

The Four were biding their time until they could provide insurmountable pressure and change the time discrepancies Videus posed. My bloodline back to the first four people, who knows how far back, made everything possible. That's why Videus was after them all. He knew somewhere, some-how, Pendomus itself was gearing up to fight back.

Stepping forward to Tethys, I slide the Caudex back into the pouch on the side of her body. No longer necessary for the information it holds—instead, the Caudex has become a key. My life's Burden is simply this, the Caudex. Once I place it inside the Beacon, timelines will reset, and the Acropolis will rise. Things will go back to the way they were meant to.

Glancing up at Trae, I smile.

Trae's eyes narrow and he tips his head to the side, "What comes next?"

"I need your help, but you aren't going to like it," I say.

Trae rolls his eyes, and takes a breath, "I don't like it already."

"I need you to go back to Videus," I say, holding his gaze.

"What?" he snorts. "You can't be serious."

"I need you to go back to him and tell him I fled. Make him believe the attack on the Lateral was effective."

Trae huffs, twisting in a circle with his hands clasped behind his head.

"Dammit," he mutters.

"If you go as Caelum—he might believe you."

"Dammit," he repeats. "Okay, I'll do it."

"Thank you, Trae," I say, taking one of his hands in mine.

"This is goodbye, isn't it?" Trae says, his eyes searching mind.

"I don't know," I say.

That much is true. Once the timelines are reset, it's anyone's guess how things will end up.

Trae nods, considering. We stand in silence for a moment, not quite ready to go our separate ways.

"Before you go, I need to tell you—" Trae says.

I look up into his gaze again.

"Caelum, he's happy you know. He wants me to tell you— he never meant to be a part of Videus' schemes. He wishes you luck," he says.

Smiling, I say, "I know. I've always known."

Trae pauses again, looking as though there's more to say.

"Okay," he sighs, "I guess we should get going."

"I guess we should," I nod.

Taking a final look around the ice cavern—the Waterbear lair—I look forward to returning it to its original glory. Without another word, I climb on Tethys' back, and Trae does the same. She saunters off, choosing not to engage her shield, but to walk us to the water's edge. Just before she jumps, her shield engages, and we plunge into the water.

~Tethys, we need to get Trae to the surface. He's going to buy us some time.

Understanding, she veers to the right, finding an outlet not far from the Archives—or the Acropolis. After a few moments of silence in the water, we come to the end of the line. Cautiously easing out of the water, Tethys guides us as close as she dares to the tree line.

As we come to a halt, Trae slides off her back. Tethys keeps watch, her shield still engaged as he takes my hand. I slide off her back, facing him.

"How can you be so brave?" he asks, his dark eyes serious and solemn.

My eyes drift to the floor as I consider his words.

Is it brave to accept what is? I suppose maybe it is. It's an act of rebellion, in a sense to embrace reality rather than run from it. Even if this reality wasn't meant to be.

"Trae, we can't let Videus continue to destroy everything. We both know he needs to be stopped, and together, we're the only ones who can do it."

Trae's eyes widen. He swallows hard, but eventually nods.

"I know, you're—you're right," he says. "But I still wish there was another way. I don't—"

"I know, I do too," I say, shaking my head.

"I need you to know—" Trae begins, trying to find the right words. "I need you to know how much I wish things had been different. That we'd been able to have our time together, just you and I. Without any of this shit that's kept us from truly being together. I wish we were given the time to see how our relationship could play out. Maybe we'd even grow old together. Have a couple of kids," he grins, his dimples flashing briefly.

"Kids," I smile, my eyes threatening to tear up, "I wish we'd had our time together, too. Maybe, once this is all said and done, we'll still get our chance?"

"Runa, if we don't—if we don't see each other again—I want you to know that I lo—"

I step forward and stop his words with my fingertips. This can't be the way to hear this—on the brink of destruction.

"Don't say it," I whisper. "Show me instead."

I lift my face to his and he presses his lips to mine, putting his hands along my face and pulling me close. In this mess of existence, Trae's been the one thing to be happy about. Even in all the darkness. He may not realize it, but his strength gives me strength, too.

My lips tingle, my body pulses with energy. He's shown me what it can mean to be a woman, to be human. To be more than just a person alone on her own mission.

After a moment, I break our connection, leaning my forehead against his chin. He wraps his arms around me, pulling me in tighter.

"So this is it," he says, "We're really doing this."

A moment of silence passes, and I say, "We are."

Trae takes a deep breath and his shoulders relax.

"Well, let's get it done," he says.

Tethys releases her shield, and Trae gives me one more gentle kiss.

"See you soon," he says with a hint of smile. His dimples appear briefly, and he releases my hands.

Without further fanfare, Trae walks off, leaving me standing beside Tethys. When he's a few meters away, he turns back just in time to see Tethys engage her shield. He watches us for a moment, then he nods to himself as he walks towards the trees in search of Videus.

My heart thrums loudly in my chest. I could be sending

Trae off to his death. If things don't go the way I hope, the way they're meant to, I could be dooming us all to death.

I take a deep breath to calm my nerves, and climb back onto Tethys' back.

She doesn't linger, as she takes off through the snow and reenters the underground river.

Everything feels different. I *feel* different. Let's hope it's enough.

Faster than ever, Tethys propels through the water, making her way as quickly as she can. She knows she's on the clock now, having precious cargo to deliver. At least, that's the way she describes me. In a way, this is her mission as much as it's mine. We've been connected from the very beginning, she and I.

This time, as we travel, everything around us illuminates brightly and stays lit. The blue light we saw before ignites in all the scribing, the etchings, and special marks of the statues and walls. Gears I didn't even see before begin to spin, setting off a system of levers and pulleys. They seem oddly mechanical for the magic they begin to work. Tethys maneuvers us quickly, making our way back to the Lateral to finalize the process.

I need to be in proximity to the Beacon in order to deliver the Caudex and set everything in motion. Once it begins, there's no way to stop it. I already know the devastation the Beacon itself will force. It'll level everything around it once it gains the energy from the Pillars. Everyone still in the Lateral will die.

Before gaining the mark, I never would have taken this risk. It means ending people's lives—but when the timelines reset, none of it will matter. At least, not if everything goes according to plan. It's the one thing I couldn't bring myself to say to Traeton—if I'm successful, all of this goes away. Even us. Maybe we get to start over. Or maybe my work here is done and I'll never be born.

As Tethys gets closer to the Lateral, the large gears from beneath the city light up and spring to life. The massive mechanisms begin to rotate, building power. The water around us hums with anticipation.

"This is so beautiful" I whisper, taking in the mysteries underneath the city. I'm the only one who will ever see this and it's such an odd splendor to witness.

It's been a while since I was first here—and I noticed the gears, but thought nothing of them. They were simply a part of what I thought was a city now long gone. Or perhaps part of the Lateral's initial construction. But now, they're stunningly ancient.

Tethys continues to maneuver us up through the flooded floor of the Lateral. Thankfully, there aren't many people here anymore. Either they found a way to use their shields to get out. Or perhaps Videus—

I shake away the thought.

Tethys brings me to the center of the city. The absolute middle. As we hover over the location, my mark begins to burn, and the water beneath us and around us begins to boil.

As the gears below do their work, beams of light travel upward from beneath the city. They flood the five structural posts outside the city and they begin to glow a bright, sky blue. My job here is done for now.

The Beacon's process will continue to do the rest on its own and I need to be clear when it erupts.

Tethys leaves the confines of the Lateral's inner city, heading to the surface of the water. Since we left, the water has swollen up through the better part of the enormous open cavern, nearly reaching the exit toward the Safe Haven. More than likely, it's how the others escaped.

Tethys shoots through the water, making quickly for the

exit as the energy in the Lateral builds to a crescendo. Just as we reach the landing, the light from the five posts bursts from their ends, conjoining in midair in a single beam of light. As the light extends upward, a large dome of energy bursts through the water, encompassing the city.

The shockwave that follows, thrusts the water—and us with it— toward the exit. Tethys rides the wave as far as she can allow, but as the water settles, it pulls back, leaving us in the dry tunnel leading back toward the Haven.

Disengaging her shield, Tethys lets me know she'll find her own way out—but that I need to head to the topside and deliver the Caudex to the Beacon.

I pat her head, gathering the Caudex from its pouch.

"Thank you, Tethys. For everything. Stay safe, okay? I'll see you soon," I say, running my hand through the fur at the side of her neck.

She grunts in acknowledgement as she turns and disappears into the watery depths. I follow her descent as far as my eyes allow, and finally take in the scene beyond.

The Lateral's dome shimmers under the water, a shield of sorts—not all that unlike the Waterbear's shield. Perhaps that's what it's meant to mimic.

"I hope everyone was able to get out safely," I whisper to myself. "Sure looks beautiful from here, though."

Even with all the devastation, there's a miraculous beauty in all of it. We're coming to the final steps—the final few moments testing our truth. The Beacon is set to ignite fully, and the Acropolis will rise. We're almost done.

I turn around and run through the tunnels toward the Haven. I pass the Oasis first, then on toward my first home beyond the Helix. As I reach the Haven, I'm flooded with a strange mixture of nostalgia, excitement, and even sadness. The quiet stillness of this place is all wrong. Being here without Trae, without the others—it feels wrong.

If the timelines are reset—all of this will never have happened. Leaving the Helix. Being taken in by Traeton and his friends. They may not even exist. With the timelines as they are, it's hard to tell how the decisions humans have yet to make will play out. There are gray aspects in the timeline; areas needing to fill themselves in once I do what I'm meant to.

I slow down, walking through the Haven in silence. I know this will be the last time. Unable to allow any remorse to reach me, I continue on with my mission. The Caudex needs to be destroyed in the Beacon. It's the only way to set everything right.

Closing the heavy door to the Haven is like closing out a final chapter of one of Trae's books. Bitter sweet.

As the exit to the outside comes into view, I break into a full run.

When the cold, outdoor air hits my body, I'm surprised to find some of the others huddled in small groups. Relief floods my body, as I see Delaney, Ash, and those from the vassalage—Antricia and Rendan—amongst many others.

My eyes flit to the trees around me. I'll need to be careful without Tethys' protection. Videus' numbers are down, but I don't know how many he had in his control before. And after the Lateral—who knows what else Videus has up his sleeves. Those white elephants were a surprise.

Jogging up to Delaney, the others begin to chat and point at me.

"Lane, I'm so glad to see you," I say, embracing her as I approach.

She returns the hug, a sigh escaping her lips.

"Runa, we've lost so many—I hope you have good news," she says.

"It'll all be over soon. The Beacon has been initiated."

As if in response, the ground shudders again. As I turn

around, large chunks of snow and ice crack apart and slide off the side of the broken dome that used to house the Lateral.

The locked sun with its halo smiles down on me while snowflakes kick up and flitter through the air. Even though it's been the symbol of our locked planet, the sundog has always been a reminder to me—even in stillness, there's beauty.

I'll actually miss it.

"But—I thought you didn't have the mark?" she says surprised.

"I didn't," I say, lifting my sleeve, "but I do now. The process has been started."

"So the city—it's intact?" Delaney asks, her eyebrows tugged inward.

I nod, "For now it is. There seems to be a shield of energy protecting what's left."

Delaney's eyes widen and she shakes her head.

"You saw a shield of energy surround the city?"

I nod, "Yes, it pulled itself up from the five posts around the city."

"Runa, that's no shield. The Lateral is about to blow—we need to move everyone out. Now," she says, spinning on her heels. "Ash, get everyone back—"

The hillside behind us explodes—sending everyone hurtling through the air with the rest of the debris.

20

TRAETON

*C*WALKING AWAY FROM RUNA feels like I've ripped pieces of myself outta my body and left them behind. I know this is the right thing to do—but I can't stand the thought of her doing what she needs to do alone. Heading into the Lateral again to ignite the Beacon—raising the Acropolis. Whatever that means. What does that even mean? Does the building have lifts under it or something? Or is it all metaphorical? This's all something straight outta one of my fiction novels. Yet, here I'm living it. Crazy.

~I never believed I would be alive to witness the arising of the Daughter of Five and the return of the Acropolis.

Taking a deep breath, I ease into the conversation with Caelum. I'm never ready for his initial contact, even though I know he's still lingering with me.

Ever since my time with Runa—our time together—I've wanted desperately to be the only one in my head. To cherish the moments we had together without the casual onlooker of Caelum.

I take a deep breath and sigh it out.

"Well, bud—time not only to witness the Acropolis, but

225

put an end to Videus' tyranny. Do you think he'll buy us coming to find him?" I say.

Caelum takes a moment, considering all we've seen—all that's yet to come.

~I am not sure. He is not a stupid man, quite the contrary. In order to seem believable, we may have to do things we would otherwise not do.

"What in the hell does that mean?" I ask, climbing a drift of snow up toward the top of the small hill leading to the Archives.

~Simply that it may mean going along with Videus' plans momentarily. He is not always a nice man.

I snort, "No kidding."

Suddenly, the ground I'm climbing on begins to rumble. The snow in my grasp crumbles through my hands and I lose balance, sliding downward a meter or so. Shifting and cracking beneath my feet, I struggle to find a good hold onto anything as everything around me breaks apart.

~The Daughter of Five must be getting close to igniting the Beacon.

"No really? What gave it away?" I say, searching for a way out of this mess.

~It was the breaking apart of the ground. Did you not notice?

I shake my head, and just about see my brain with the eye roll that follows. These AirGliders seriously need to get themselves a clue. They're smart, but so stupid at the same time.

Leaping from one rock to the next, I barely miss careening down into an abyss as the building buried in the snow begins to unearth itself. I knew the Archives was big— but until now, I had no idea the true extent of it.

Large turrets and towers are the first to rise up out of the ground, aspects of the building I had never even seen while I was inside. The outer building is much more ornate, and artistic than I gave it credit for.

"How is all this possible?" I say out loud to myself.

It's hard not to stare in awe of it all.

~The building was hidden for its own protection. It has centuries old mechanisms to allow for it to—

"Thanks, genius. I wasn't actually needing a lesson on it. I'm just surprised," I say, scrambling to solid ground and running away from the commotion of the Archives—*the Acropolis* as it rises from the ground.

When all is said and done, this place is going to draw some crowds—that means Videus too. As I get to the tree line, and feel far enough away, I turn around and take it all in.

The enormous building looks like a medieval castle from the history books of Earth. Only more ornamental, and embellished. Large birds, Salamanders, Waterbears, and a creepy looking spider adorn the four outer towers and various aspects of the building.

"What in the hell are those?" I ask to Caelum, pointing at the spider. I involuntarily shudder at its size.

~They are TerraDwellers.

"Well, thanks. Glad you cleared that up," I say sarcastically. "What in the hell are TerraDwellers?"

~They are the last of the Four Pillars. No one has seen them for a very long time. I am not even sure they are still on the planet.

"Well, we better sure as hell hope they are. They need to make it here in time to help Runa with the Beacon," I say.

~Indeed.

"Alright—any sign of Videus? Can you sense him or anything?" I say, surveying the scene.

He has to be here somewhere. No way he'd let something this huge happen without noticing and developing a plan of attack. I know I wouldn't.

Caelum takes a moment. I swear I can hear his wheels turning as he tries to connect and figure out what Videus is up to.

~I am not sure where he is. It feels as though he is guarding himself from me, though I am not sure why.

"Dammit. I'll bet I know," I say. "He's worked out you've been compromised—probably saw footage from the Helix. He knows I'm the one who blew up the vassalage—which means this plan of Runa's has just gone down the allay."

I search the tree line. If Videus can hide himself from Caelum, could he still locate him? Or are they both operating blind? Somehow, I'm guessing Videus knows exactly where we are. I wouldn't get that lucky.

How did everything get so phugged up? How could one man lose himself the way Videus has? I just don't get it.

~My mast—Videus—has bound things too tightly. He can no longer see the lines of reality clearly. He has been in and out too many times and he has forgotten himself. He only knows he cannot save his brother, and in turn, he refuses to allow anyone else to be happy. Especially the Daughter of Five. She became his obsession to keep from feeling.

"Feeling what?" I snort.

~Anything.

"That's a shit plan."

~I didn't say it was otherwise.

"Okay, so if he knows his second in command has been compromised—what then? He'd fly solo to stop Runa?" I say, musing aloud.

~That would be my assumption as well.

"Then we're in the completely wrong place. We need to find Runa now," I say.

"Oh, that would be a grand idea, Traeton. Do that, won't you?" someone says behind me.

I spin around quickly, coming face-to-face with Videus.

Adorned again with his headdress and dark cloak, I realize who he has chosen to embody—the Egyptian god known as Thoth.

I don't know why the insight hit me—something in the irony of this all. Or maybe the absurdity.

How did he learn about Egypt? Did he have books, too? Kani and I only learned by the books in the Archives, and even then, it wasn't easy to understand at first. Their culture and way of life was so different from ours. It took Landry to explain it to us in a way we could understand. Granted, we were pretty young.

I swallow hard, unsure of my next move.

How do I bide enough time for Runa to do what she needs to do?

"Videus," I say, finally acknowledging his presence. "How are you?"

"Cut the pleasantries, boy. Where is the girl?" Videus says.

"Screw you. How about you cut the pleasantries. If you're going to do this, drop the act. Let go of this Videus persona—and lose the Thoth complex. You're not as clever as either of them."

"Big words for such a small, fragile being," he says in a low voice, "I could snap the arteries to your brain in half if I wanted. You'd bleed out inside your skull until your body completely shuts down. It's not pleasant, but I would still enjoy it so," he says.

For the first time in a long while, fear rushes through me. Could he honestly do something like that? Hell if I know. Wouldn't put it past him, though.

"If you were going to, you'd have done it already. It's not going to get you to Runa," I fire back.

Videus stands motionless, a dark tower of a man in the midst of the sea of snow.

"Where are the rest of your cronies, by the way? No birds

or Salamanders to come to your aid? Is that why you had to send the spectacle show with the clouds? Nice touch, by the way. They were creepy as hell," I say.

"The white elephants are more than a spectacle, but I don't expect a simpleton like you to understand. You have yet to see their beauty, but you will," Videus say, his voice now low and smooth.

"What does that mean?" I snort.

"Only that you've yet to discover what they're capable of, boy. Now, why don't you tell me where to find my little Everblossom."

The way he says 'my little Everblossom' makes my skin crawl. It's like a creepy old man, lurking in wait to do unspeakable things. I suppose he is.

"No clue where Runa is," I shrug nonchalantly. "She had her own mission and I wasn't about to get in her way."

"She didn't want you screwing things up for her, eh?" Videus says.

"What the hell is that supposed to mean?"

"She sent you on your way so you weren't a detriment to her. You're a liability, Traeton."

I swallow hard. That wasn't why she sent me off on my own, was it?

"You have no idea what you're talking about," I say.

~Do not play into him, he's baiting you.

Caelum's warning both pulls me back to the present and solidifies my tactic. He's right, I can't take what he says personally, but I can make Videus think I do.

"Oh, I think I do. Did you tell her about Caelum? Does she know how hard you've been working to keep him in there, despite knowing who he was?" Videus says.

My insides recoil, but I keep hold of myself.

"Yeah, actually, she does," I say, my eyebrows raising.

"Hmmm," he says, pacing slightly. "And she was fine with all that, was she?"

"Of course not—she was pissed."

"Ah," he goads.

"Not at me, you imbecile. She was pissed at you," I spit.

Okay, so in truth she was sorta pissed at me...but we'd worked passed all that, right?

Damn, come to think of it—I never got the chance to talk to her about it. I never got the chance to warn her about the impending doom I sensed from Caelum when we were in Landry's bunker.

~Do not begin second guessing yourself. It is what he wants.

"Oh, I'm quite sure she was upset with me, that's a given. But I wasn't the one who betrayed her. Am I right?" he says.

"Screw you. You have no idea what you're talking about," I say, anger arising, despite my best efforts to keep under control.

Videus chuckles.

"You know, I always thought if the Acropolis rose, it would mean the end. Yet, I find it oddly satisfying," he says, beginning to pace. "You see, everyone's close—*very close* to being able to destroy everything I've worked so hard at. Yet, right at the eleventh hour, I'll be able to sweep the rug from under your collective feet."

"And just how do you suppose you're going to do that?" I ask, calling his bluff.

If he had more, he would have done it by now. All of this is just a way to bide his own time until he's able to take out Runa. I know it, he knows it.

"Do you see a Beacon anywhere, Traeton?" Videus asks, a small chuckle escaping him again.

I look over my shoulder. The Acropolis darkens the entire horizon, but beyond that I don't see anything standing out. Though, to be fair, I have no idea if I'm even supposed to.

"You don't," Videus answers for me, "because it's not fully ignited. It's weak and dissipating without the proper strength. It won't ignite until the Five offer their support—in blood."

I turn back to face him, "What are you getting at?"

"Well, Traeton, your little lover will have blood on her hands in order to make this work. More than she already does, that is. The Pillars—and her own. But I can stop her—and you're going to help me, of course," Videus says.

"And why the hell would I do that?"

"Because you no longer have a choice," he says, simply.

With that, Videus raises his arms to the sky, and a cluster of those cloud-like abominations split apart and careen toward me at an ungodly speed.

There's nowhere to run—nowhere to hide out here in the space of dead trees. At least, no where close enough. The cluster of white elephants latch onto my arms, my legs, and torso. The pain is absolutely excruciating as their bizarre cloud teeth bury into my skin. My veins tense up, as something foreign oozing into my blood stream ignites a burning sensation throughout the rest of my body. Dropping to my knees, my back seizes up, but I still try to pry them off of me with the little strength I have.

It's no use.

Whatever this is—whatever he's doing, it causes the white elephants to turn red, the longer they're latched on.

"You may be wondering," Videus begins, "what makes these little guys so beautiful."

I glare at him.

"Not overly top of mind," I say through clenched teeth.

"Well, let me enlighten you anyway. See, blood is such a

pesky thing. Who needs it really? I have something far more productive to replace it with," he says.

"What in the hell are you talking about?" I say.

"Very soon, you won't have to worry about growing older, about dying. In a few moments, you'll be fully synthetic. Of course, you may experience side effects such as complete loss of mental control—but I'm sure you can handle it," Videus laughs. "I'm sorry, Caelum, unfortunately it means you'll be annihilated as well. Turns out, I can only trust myself to get things done right.

Videus slowly unhooks his ibis mask, and lets it fall to the ground. My energy and consciousness begin to slip. I watch, helpless, as the mask lands softly in the snow, a bizarre remnant of his hidden identity no longer needed.

MY BACK SLAMS AGAINST A TREE, knocking the wind out of me. I land in a heap in the snow. The Caudex flies from my hands, landing a good few meters away. All around me, people, rocks, snow have been thrust backward.

The energy expelled by the Beacon bursts through the hole already created in the ground by Videus, and huge plume of blue light thrust into the sky. White double spirals rotate around the blue light, reminding me of the way the Helix looks in the distance.

Gasping for air, I push myself to my hands and knees. My body aches and it's extremely difficult to gather air into my lungs. Cries of pain, surprise, and suffering erupt all around me.

"What's happened?" someone wails nearby.

"Not again," someone else cries. "It's the girl—the one with the white and purple hair. This is all her fault."

People nearby shout their agreements.

Scrambling to my feet, I survey the scene. Trees are toppled on their sides, some hanging onto the ground at odd angles. Blood spatters the ground of some of the people who weren't so lucky with the blast. Survivors attempt to get back up, some struggling to stand while others hover over the people they've lost.

"Lane?" I call out, my voice a raspy whisper. "Delaney?"

I spin around, looking for any sign of where she may have landed. A meter or so from my location, I catch a glimpse of her dark curls buried in the snow. Rushing forward, I drop to my knees beside her body.

"Lane, are you okay?" I ask, gently turning her over. Blood begins to darken the snow beneath her. Half of her face is missing—ripped from her in the blast.

My eyes close, and I release her body. Sitting on my heels I cover my face. I knew people could be hurt in this timeline, but I never considered I'd be here to watch those I care about perish.

Returning to a stand, I realize I have two choices. I can be consumed by the pain here in this place, or I can do something to change it.

I don't have the luxury of letting any of this matter. It can't deter me from what needs to be done. Walking past the suffering, the cries for help, and the angry shouts my direction, I make my way to the Caudex. My heart tugs, screaming at me to help them here and now—but my instincts tell me I need to finish what I've started. Otherwise, this is all these people have. I won't let that be true.

Lifting the heavy tome from the ground, I clutch it to my body. The wind whips my hair around, and I stand dazed in the field of trees and wounded people. I stare at the tower of energy venting high up into the sky. Even from here, the intense energy rolls off it in waves. The power of it, evident to anyone with eyes. They certainly don't need my enhanced vision.

The mark on my wrist burns, calling me forward; calling

me to the light with the rest of the Pillars. Do the others feel the same pull?

Amidst screams and cries for me to do something to help, I leave everyone behind, walking for what feels like ages. Eventually, I reach the decimation, climbing over the rubble of what used to be the cavern system. The entrance to the Haven has completely caved in—and a huge crater has opened up where the Lateral used to be.

It looks exactly as it had in the future—and I'm suddenly acutely aware if I don't make the right moves, this will still be the future.

I reach the precipice, the energy of the Beacon pulsates, drawing me in closer.

"Not so fast, Everblossom, dear," a voice calls over my shoulder.

I pause for a second debating on whether to turn and face him, or run onward anyway.

Slowly, I turn.

Of everything I'd envisioned Videus to be, nothing could have prepared me for this moment. I'd given in to his faceless game—playing the part that while he was human, he wasn't a man. Not really.

But he is. And far worse than that.

He's my friend.

"Landry," his name escapes my lips, but I can only stare.

His features contort. Aged through more years than I dare count, and far more angry.

Beside the man wearing Landry's face, Trae stands at attention. His blue hair flickers in the wind, but his eyes are vacant and devoid of their sparkle.

My heart tightens.

"Are you surprised, Everblossom? Shocked to see the man behind the mask, here to bring you down?" Landry says through his teeth.

"I—I—" I stumble for words. "Why? Why you?"

"Who did you expect? Someone hideous? Scars, perhaps?" he points at my face and the slash marks covering the left side of my face.

"But we—we were friends," I say, searching for the words.

All of my anger and hatred for this man feels displaced, and I struggle to meld the two worlds together.

"Friends?" he says, "That's a funny way of putting it."

His calculating blue eyes narrow, as he begins to pace in front of me. For a moment, I'd almost say there was a hint of surprise hidden in those eyes.

Doesn't he remember? Why doesn't he remember?

I shift, glancing at the ground, trying to work things out.

It all suddenly makes so much sense. The technology. The connection to me. He's always meddled with minds. Always taken an interest in things he could control and connect to.

His brother—

Recognition dawns.

The vision was of a young boy—one laughing and playing. It wasn't the age he lost him. It was the age Videus admired most. It was the unraveling threads of happy memories he's had of his brother. *Of Fenton.*

He blames me for his death.

It's one of those strange paradoxes—which came first? My connection to Fenton? Or Landry's decision to lose his humanity?

I try to wrap my mind around it all. Make sense out of why Landry would do this—why he'd go through such an elaborate plan when he could have simply taken me out when we first met. He could have destroyed me then, and no one would have been the wiser.

Why go through all of this?

"Hand over the book," Landry says, pointing to the Caudex in my hands.

"Bite me," I fire back, indignation forming in the pit of my stomach.

How dare he blame me—he was the one who gave Kani no choice.

"Ooooooh. Interesting selection of words. Where did you hear this archaic diatribe?" Landry says mockingly.

I hold still, standing my ground, acutely aware I'm one woman standing against Videus, and his second in command. I glance again at Trae's handsome face, knowing he's gone. I don't sense his humanity rolling off him—nor the AirGlider who was inside. Instead, he's something completely mechanical.

I take a deep breath, exhaling my heartache.

There's nothing left for me here. Nothing left to fight for in this version of reality.

"Alright, don't speak. I'll speak," Landry says, turning to Trae and placing a hand on his shoulder. He takes a long pause, allowing his hand to linger there, as a sly grin slides across his lips.

He tips his head to the side and says, "You care about this one, right? I can understand why. He was smart, strong, and generally loyal. It took a while to break him and get access to his mind. Ages, actually. Now, no matter what you do, he's mine. You can't do a thing."

Rather than listen to his diatribe, I focus on the worn lines beside his mouth. The wrinkles carrying weight near his eyes.

This isn't Landry. At least, not my Landry. The one I've known, talked to, stayed at his home with my friends. This is an older version—years older. Worn and warped.

My mind begins to whirl through all the questions surrounding Videus and Landry. Why are there so many inconsistencies? Why didn't he take me out when he first met me? If he can time travel, why hasn't he taken me out yet?

Traeton as an older man. He has the same vibe.

Is this why the Landry I know didn't attack me? Is it the course of an older man? Did this shift happen after we met? I push my mind to the furthest reachings in understanding of time travel and keep coming up with the same conclusion. Younger Landry should have known. He should have carried the memories with him and found me far sooner. With far less casualties.

None of this is making any sense

I tune back in.

"...But he doesn't matter to me. See, all it takes is another jump on time to wipe out his lineage before they even make it to Pendomus. He'll never exist. Not now, not ever."

I watch his mannerisms closely as he steps behind Trae, trying to taunt me out. It may have worked before the mark, it may have worked before the bloodlines. But I see through him now.

"If you wanted to take out Trae, you would have done it already. The simple fact you haven't been able to change the one thing that matters to you—saving your brother—it speaks for you. See, when you jump through time, I don't think you have access to the editing program. You know enough how to tinker, to set off the dominoes and see what happens, but you have no idea how to access the parts you really want," I say, bound with the energy surging around me from the Beacon, the Caudex, and the mark.

Landry's eyes minimize to slits as he glares at me.

"I may look like a single girl, standing in the snow, but I'm much more than that. I'm the one who's going to finally put an end to Videus. I have the keys to the editing software, so to speak," I say, taking a step forward. "So this is how things are going to play out. All it takes is one wrench thrown into this time line tangent and *you'll* never exist."

Landry laughs.

"Not likely. There's only one way that would ever happen and, honey, if I can't make it happen—you can't," he says.

I watch him shift slightly—almost imperceptibly. He doesn't believe what he's saying.

And he obviously hasn't wanted to jeopardize his earlier timeline in order to take all of humanity out. Had Landry never gone dark, there would be no Daughter of Five. Had Fenton not gotten involved, he wouldn't have died. So where did it really begin?

Suddenly, the energy around me shifts. I can't put my finger on it exactly, but I know the tides are turning.

"Then what are you so afraid of?" I ask, smirking.

"Me? Afraid? What would I have to be afraid of? I have the upper hand here," he says, snorting.

"Do you now?" I say, raising my eyebrows.

Behind Landry, the scene in the field has changed to a very different one from when I walked away. A sea of people have begun to rise out of the debris, making their way to us. They stand shoulder to shoulder—ready to fight.

Videus looks over his shoulder and returns his gaze to me, "You realize, they're here for you."

"Perhaps they are. But then again, maybe they're here for you. Where are your other minions?" I counter, turning my head toward the sky.

As if on command, the sky fills with birds as the flocks make their way toward us. Large and small—both the juncos and the vultures. Beyond, in the snowy filled trees, Salamanders crawl out of the woods. Their electrical storm no longer blue, but the color it was meant to be—the color of fire.

At first, Landry smiles—a hopeful grin.

I shake my head, reminding myself not to underestimate him. He may look like Landry—he may even *be* Landry—but fundamentally, something has broken in him. He's not the same man.

As the large spiders known as the TerraDwellers crawl out of the crater, reality sets in and Landry's smile drops. These are not his minions. They're free to do as they please. And they've been called here to help me.

Tethys joins in, making her way from the river's opening near the Acropolis. She's seen it, she relays—and it's more beautiful than she remembered.

"What is this?" Landry asks, narrowing his eyes and edging closer to Trae.

"You should know," I say, "Isn't this what you wanted all along? This moment when the world takes in all you've done and fights back? Because it's here."

"And just what exactly do you think all of you are capable of?" Landry says, a hint of fear bleeding into his words for the first time.

"Everything you aren't," I say. "We're going to stop you. Not here—not now, in this place. But from the very beginning. Are you ready to be wiped from the face of existence?"

His eyes widen, but he holds himself taller than before.

"You've always been an impetuous one, Everblossom. Are you so sure you have everything you need to get this little —*spellwork*—done?" he says, flicking a hand toward me.

Trae immediately lunges forward, racing at me with lightening speed. Before I can stop him, his full weight is thrown on me and I land face first in the snow. Trae's body stumbles, and he rolls in the snow beside me. The Caudex skitters from my hands, landing a meter away. As Trae pushes up to a stand, I grab his ankle, dropping him back to the ground.

Suddenly, Trae's foot lands squarely in my face and all I can see are stars. I hear him scrambling in the snow—and I know I've lost the Caudex.

Videus' laugh is deep and foreboding.

"It all comes down to this? A fragile, insignificant book.

And this—this is why civilizations have fallen before us. This is why the good guys never win. Because you never learn from past mistakes. This technology—" he taps the side of his head, "*my technology*—is the way of the future. It was the way to preserve everything and keep it sacred. But no one would believe me. Now look around. This prophecy, the Daughter of Five business—it all hinged on the final flaw of this book making its way to the big tunnel of light over there."

I open my eyes in time to see him jab a finger at the Beacon's light behind me.

"Pretty soon, this Beacon will wane. It can't output this kind of energy forever. And when it does, nothing will be left of your beloved city, and the people you care about. You'll be all alone in this world, just as I am."

"I'm not alone, look around you, Landry. I didn't ask for this, and yet here they are. You, on the other hand—you're not alone, either. You're adamantly opposed. You're the *reason* everyone is here, coming together," I say, climbing to my feet.

"Touching, isn't it?" Landry says, shrugging nonchalantly.

My eyes flit to Trae, who has returned to Landry's side, standing completely still—a machine in sleep mode.

The wind whips my hair across my face and I know no reasoning will ever work on Landry. He's too far gone. He doesn't just hurt, grieve, and get over it. Fenton's death consumes him. And it has planetary consequences. All the time loops, all the tangents—he's smart enough to be dangerous, but he's emotionally and empathetically stunted. Unstable.

Action is what has to happen now.

Quietly, I center myself and send out the signal to those around us who'll participate. It's a simple countdown, but I know they'll understand.

I need to create enough chaos to get the Caudex to the Beacon.

As the countdown reaches the end, the AirGliders are the first to respond, swooping in from the trees and barreling towards Landry.

The liberated Salamanders move next, forming a semi-circle around Landry, and Trae. Their feet glow brightly and the orange lightening breaks in large arcs, connecting them as a group. A true force to reckon with.

Landry spins in a circle, taking it all in.

The people in the field behind also move closer. Those with powers at the front—the others still willing to fight, just behind them. They hold their ground, waiting until an opportune moment to do their work.

Landry sends a signal and Trae's body springs into action. Jumping forward to protect him, he slams onto one of the vultures as it swoops in. Grabbing it by its wings, he promptly snaps them off and discards the body to flop about on the ground. Trae then returns to an alert, but oddly disconnected version of himself. Landry hovers just behind him, speaking something under his breath.

My eyes flit to the Caudex.

Before I make the conscious decision, my feet are already propelling me forward. I race to the Caudex, sliding across the snow and ice to reach it.

Trae moves quickly, springing into action and thrusting me back. Sliding backward in the snow, I hit a tree trunk with force—much more force than any man should be able to provide. Electrical energy from his action shocks my system, leaving my muscles stunned and useless.

Tethys springs into action, slamming herself against Trae's body. He spirals up, recoiling against the pain in midair. The conductive energy between the two of them ignites, sending a shockwave that extends through the entire

243

scene. Tethys wails in pain, surprised Traeton could carry this kind of energy. She spins around, grabbing Trae by the leg, then slamming him against the ground.

My stomach rolls and I feel like lurching at the sight.

Nothing Tethys does works though; Trae simply flops about and keeps coming for her. With a swift, sudden movement, Trae releases some sort of electrical blade, slicing open Tethys' side. Blood swells outward, coloring the snow and all around it.

Even if no one could see her before, they certainly see her blood as it sprays them.

"Tethys—" I scream, unable to move.

The TerraDwellers spring into action, walking over my body to stand as a wall between Tethys and the Salamander. They push her body aside, one spinning her gently in its long legs as it uses its web to bind her wound.

Videus laughs.

"Even with all of this, the Daughter of Five is no match for me," he says. "Some savior. You can't even save yourself. Pathetic."

Commanding the energy from the snow around me, I tap into the gifts from the Waterbears to aid my healing. The ground begins to shake and the snow hovers a couple inches off the ground. Suddenly, it melds itself into one large liquid ball and forces it's way into my body. As it moves through, the grounded water soothes out any of the electrical charge. My muscles begin to relax and I'm able to get up on my hands and knees.

Taking a deep, centering breath, I rise to stand.

Those who Landry had kept trapped at the vassalage move in, surrounding him and Trae. He clutches Trae's body closer to him, acting as a shield while their power builds. The energy in this space, in the snowy field, is enough to make hair and goosebumps rise.

"Just end this, Landry. There's no where else to go. You can't stop the inevitable. It was foreseen, for godsake," I say. "You don't have the upper hand here."

I allow my mind to travel, extending itself to Landry for the first time. I don't know if it will work, but I have to at least try to defuse this situation so I can finish the job.

Landry's mind at first is like a steel trap; cold and empty. Unlike the AirGliders and Salamanders who wanted liberation, Landry holds his secrets in tight.

Watching me closely, Landry takes a step forward, dragging Trae along with him.

"I can't believe that —" Landry says.

"Believe what?" I ask, momentarily pausing my assault.

"That this is all inevitable. Whatever happened to freewill? What happened to the opportunity to change things? Isn't that what this is all about?"

"I'm trying to change things right now. You just have to step aside," I spit.

"Do you even know what this will do? What happens when you throw the gigantic book into the Tree? What then?" he says.

"Time is reset," I say simply.

He waves a hand dismissively, "Sure, sure. But to *when*? To what end?"

I stare at him blankly, blinking slowly as I consider. I honestly have no idea to *when*. Or how the book will decide what to do in order to restore Pendomus and all its creatures. Most likely, it will wipe him out before he's even born. I simply know that's what it's meant to do. I have faith in its ability to set things right.

"When doesn't matter. What matters is setting the planet back on course before you interfered. Did it ever occur to you how much damage you'd do tidally locking Pendomus? Our planet is a wasteland because of you. We're all dependent on the Helix's stupid RationCaps, your guidance and acceptance. We think it's all our destiny, but it's just you pulling strings behind the scenes while we're none the wiser."

"Silly stupid girl," Landry says, ducking an incoming dive from three vultures. "You think that's the worst of your problems? I'm ready to die, my dear Everblossom. I don't care about the planet, about me, about *you*. The only thing I care about now is smiting the powers that be who turned their backs on me. The rest is all cupcakes and sparkles."

Behind him, Ammon steps forward, his eyebrows scrunched together. His lips are tugging down and he raises his hands as though he's commanding an orchestra. A large boulder covered in snow sails through the air, smashing into Landry's side. With a look of surprise on his face, his body sails through the air. The rock narrowly misses Trae, and I know Ammon did it specifically.

Landry hits the ground hard, snow flying in the air as he lands. It flitters about in the air, carefree and sparkling in the sunlight.

Others take Ammon's lead, stepping forward to add their gifts into the mix.

The energy swells and I hold up my hands, "Wait, wait."

All eyes turn toward me, the blood lust evident in all of them. They've been through so much, and I know this is more than I should ask of them, but I have to.

"Stop," I say, "Don't *become* him. Don't you dare let Landry destroy the humanity you have left just because he lost his. He's down, we can take things from here."

Landry chuckles. His eyes flick away for a moment; an insignificant look, really. But with damaging consequences.

Without hesitation, the rogue Salamander huffs forward, clutching the Caudex in his large paws. Blue flames ignite at its feet, and instantly, the Caudex is consumed in a plume of fire.

RUNA

*A*MANIACAL, GIDDY LAUGHTER fills the field while everyone else stares in horror.

With the Caudex smoldering in ashes at the Salamander's feet, Trae being controlled by Videus again, and Tethys bleeding out in the snow—I blink back my own horror and surprise.

How can we get this far—to the very end, only to fail now? It's not possible. Is it?

The scene feels like everything has been put on hold. No one dares move—we all know what was at stake. Some of the people behind Landry hold their fingers over their agape mouths. The Pillars by my side stand in stunned silence.

"You know, when I first learned of the prophecy, I knew it was the one thing I could overcome. Don't ask me why. I may not have been able to save Fenton from his fate, but I knew I would have control over this," Landry says, getting up and wiping snow from his robes. "The Beacon will die out. The Acropolis will be mine—a fitting place for a ruler, don't you think?"

He looks over at me and cocks his head. The smug look of

pleasure cast across his lips makes me ball my fists.

"Okay, maybe you don't find this as ironically pleasing as I do," he shrugs.

I think about the Acropolis becoming his, and bile builds at the back of my throat. There's no way I could allow this beautiful remnant of the past—the structure meant to signify peace, tranquility, and the unity of the Pillars to fall into his hands. Not after all that he's destroyed. Nothing is sacred to him anymore—nothing.

How could I have been so stupid? I practically handed everything over to him as a present. My eyes flick to Trae, who stands stiff at Landry's side. His face blank and devoid of his normal intense expressions.

It's all come full circle in a way. As I stand here now, a changed woman, but still the same trusting, naïve girl. I should have been wiser by now. I already knew Landry wasn't to be underestimated, yet here we are.

I shake my head in disgust.

"You know, Runa—I can call you Runa now, can't I?" Landry says, holding a hand to his chest in a false gesture of sincerity. "Just to really drive this situation home for you, I want you to know how really screwed you are. See, this guy here—he's always been a go-to guy for me, but Caelum, he's had to manage himself between inhabiting Trae and being in his own body, too. It's taken a toll on the poor thing. I think it's time to put an end to his back and forth suffering."

Pursing his lips, a high-pitched whistle pierces the battle-field. From high up in one of the trees, as if keeping surveillance, a little gray junco flies to Landry's shoulder. It's white beak opens and closes of its own accord, but no sound escapes it. The bird rests motionless, devoid of any sign of sentience—in a weird way, much like Traeton.

Landry pats Trae's shoulder and stands a little taller.

"Since the chances of completing the Beacon's mojo have

been flushed down the allay—I think it's time to remind you —and everyone standing here—I'm the one in control. Not you. I decide who lives and who doesn't. Who controls whom."

His hand lifts up, gently taking the junco with a white beak onto his outstretched finger.

"See, this here is an empty vessel. Sure, he flies like a bird, acts like a bird. But the essence of this bird—it's stuck in here," Landry taps the side of Trae's head. "Remember all the way back to when you entered my Helix and stole from me? Well, let's see if you like me stealing from you."

With his right hand, Videus snaps the neck of the junco and tosses the limp body at me. I step back, horrified.

"Why would you—?" I say, aghast.

"Fun fact," Landry says, holding up his pointer finger, "Now that you're trapped here like the rest of us, I won't kill you. No, I have a much worse fate in mind. You'll get to live every day knowing I took your love from you. You'll get to see him, talk to him, interact with him every day—but Trae's gone. Instead, I have full control of loverboy's body and that's the way it will stay. And if you think I can't do the same to each and every one of you, you're sorrily mistaken."

My eyes flit to the limp gray body of the junco with a white beak. The one I'd connected with early on—the one I thought was trying to help me. Rowan was the name I gave him before I knew better. Perceptions, they can be so deceiving. Maybe Caelum won't ever be able to leave Trae's body, but he hasn't always been the second in command Landry thinks he is. He's loyal to his ancestry—and he's even been loyal to me. I hope he still is.

"Traeton—please, you can fight this. You *have* to fight this," I say to him, wanting a reaction. Any reaction. Something that lets me know they're both in there, fighting.

When he doesn't even blink, Landry chuckles.

"I told you, he's not in there anymore. Well, nowhere he'll ever escape from. He's kinda in his own personal hell right now, thanks to my White Elephants. Right, Caelum?" Videus says, smiling in Trae's direction.

Trae tips his head in acknowledgement. The movement is odd for him, certainly more mechanical than Traeton.

"The boy is bound," Trae's voice says.

My heart slams against my ribcage. I can't let this be the end of things. I can't let Landry win. Maybe it's not the end I'd envisioned, not the result I'd wanted—but I refuse to simply sit by and allow him to do what he's saying.

The Beacon's energy behind me begins to waft outward in waves. I feel its dense, demanding call as if it's a part of my body. It tugs at me, beckoning for me to come closer. To touch the light.

I look around, but no one else seems to notice the shift.

As if a string were pulling me from the center of my body, it takes all of my strength to fight it and stand still. A few yards away, Tethys cries, her blood soaking the ground, despite the TerraDweller's best efforts to contain her wound.

She also pushes me toward the Beacon's call. She doesn't want things to end this way—the others will protect me, she says. They'll give their support.

~*The Caudex, it's destroyed. There's nothing left to throw into the Beacon.*

Suddenly, flashes of insight take over my vision. It's like seeing a few moments into the future. I witness myself running away, toward the enormous tunnel of light, and throwing myself inside. The rest of the Pillars guard me from any attack, ensuring I do what I came here to do. Their own bloody and battered bodies, shielding mine.

Then, Tethys' energy falters and her life force wanes from her body. The vision is pulled back and I'm still standing in the field in front of Landry.

Of course —it's all so clear. As soon as the mark was transferred to me, I became the Caudex. The Burden became mine and mine alone. I'm meant to deliver my *life's Burden* to the Beacon—

How did I not realize, it's meant to be me. It's *always* been meant to be me.

I cast my gaze over the scene, realizing for the first time the meaning behind this all. Blood and sacrifice.

It's my life the Beacon needs. My sacrifice.

Swallowing hard, I stand up straighter, preparing to make a run for it. Through my mind, I alert the others of my intentions. I need them to be ready.

Their energy instantly perks up. Many questions are thrown my direction, but I can't take the time to answer any of them. I need to finish this once and for all.

"—so the question really is, where shall I relocate you to?" Landry says, finishing whatever tirade he was on.

In an instant, two men tied to me in blood jump Landry, grabbing him around the neck and subduing him to the ground.

I turn on my heel and run— racing for the Beacon like I've never run in all my life.

"Really? *Really?* You're that much of a coward you're going to run away? There's nowhere to hide, *Everblossom*. This is mine—*all mine*," Landry yells.

I scramble over the large boulders and rocks of the caved in cavern system, making my way to the top of the crater so I can get to the Beacon.

Behind me, I hear screaming and commotion as the battle to protect me begins. Even from here, my hair rises and I feel the electrical energy of the Salamanders as they take up rank. I don't stop to worry about it, or see what's happening. I know they'll do whatever it takes to ensure I make it safely to the Beacon—it's their job. *Their* birthright.

This is mine.

As I get closer to the Beacon, every cell in my body vibrates, and feels as though it separates from the whole of who I am. Even if I wanted to stop, to change my mind and go back—the energy wouldn't allow it. It knows I'm near and it wants my blood, my sacrifice. I feel it like it's alive.

The wind whips at my face, and my fingers are frozen as I climb up through the debris. Cold air billows out of my mouth—my last few breaths. Everything I am is about to end.

I can only hope it's enough to set everything right. I hope Trae and the others will live a long, happy life. That the planet will be saved and the Pillars free to do what they please again. I wish for peace for everyone.

Near the mouth of the crater, the wind cyclones around the Beacon of light. As I reach the point of no return before making my descent into the center, I widen my stance, digging into the snow so I can turn to look back. One final goodbye.

The scene is a mess of people and remaining Pillars. Trae still stands guard over Landry. I don't know what's being said to Landry or what's happened since I ran, but I take a moment to reflect on everything that's transpired. All I had. I'll be gone soon.

"I love you, Trae. I wish you so much love and joy. Take care of everyone for me," I whisper.

I swallow hard, fighting back tears.

"Okay, Runa—let's do this," I say, shaking off the emotions welling up.

Sliding into the crater, I climb down to the lowest point where I can get inside the Beacon. Racing forward, I stop a meter or so away, gathering my nerves. The pull is intense, and I take a step forward.

"Took you long enough," someone says from behind me.

I spin around, coming face to face with Landry. *Our*

Landry. After all the devastation inside the Lateral, he must have found his way back.

Glancing around, I search for signs of accomplices. As far as I can tell, he's completely alone.

"What are you doing here, Landry?" I ask, playing the naïve one again. "You shouldn't be here. It's too dangerous —"

He chuckles, the same exact chuckle Videus did moments before. It gives me goosebumps. My heartbeat thrums rapidly in my chest, as I prepare to either fight or run. I look at the Beacon, knowing I could easily make the leap, but for some reason, I stall. There's something in his face that makes me question why he's really here.

"I know what you're doing," he begins, taking a step forward.

I watch the conflict in his face as he gets closer.

"And what's that, Landry?" I say, watching his every move.

"You're meant to fix time somehow. This thing—" he points at the Beacon, "it's meant to correct all the damage I've done," he says.

I stand motionless, not sure what to say. Instead, I nod.

"If you do this—please do something for me. I need you to do the one thing I've never been able to do. *Please*. Save Fenton. From what little the other me has shared, this guy— Videus—whatever you want to call him—he's been chasing you for years, maybe even jumping back and forth over centuries trying to find a way to you. From what I've pieced together, his time travel is spotty at best. It never puts him where he really wants to go, but he still manipulates stuff in the hopes it will change things. He wipes memories, changes them. He manipulates people to his end goals, in whatever means necessary. The only thing he's never been able to change is Fenton's death. But one thing's for sure—he always felt you'd be the one element that could change that."

"I don't understand. Why focus on me and chase me through the timelines? If I was the one who could change things, why not just let me?" I ask.

"No, it's more complicated that that. He didn't want *you* to change things. He wanted to *use you* to change things. You were the missing piece he thought he needed to harness. Videus believes this planet has magic. It's what he harnesses to travel back and forth, but it works against him—us. Every move he makes, the planet seems to counteract him. For some reason, he's connected you with the magic and energy of Pendomus. Since he can't control the way he time travels, he waits—watching to see what will happen, what changes. But every time Fenton dies; again and again. Then he goes back, trying to change something again, and every time—I think—losing a piece of himself. I mean, he has to watch Fenton die over and over and in different ways, different times. It's no wonder he's—I've—gone insane. If you can do this—if you can set time right, please, please find a way to save Fenton. I don't care if you have to take me out, do it."

"Landry, I don't think that's how this works. I don't know if I have any more control than Videus once I go in there," I say, pointing to the Beacon's light.

He takes a moment, considering.

"Okay. Then you need to kill me here, now. I need assurances I won't become—" his voice drops and he casts his eyes to the ground. "You need to stop me in this timeline."

"But what if it doesn't —"

"I don't care, Runa. Don't you see, everything I've ever loved is gone. Fenton—my daughter—*Alina*. She died in the flood. There's nothing left to tether me to anything good. I can't live with this anymore. End it."

He raises his arm, and in his hand is the same blade Kani used on Fenton.

I raise my eyes to his.

"Please, Runa. *Please*."

I shake my head, "Landry, I can't—"

"You know, I originally came here to kill you. To stop you from going in. That's what the other me wants. When he's in our timeline, he's always in my head. Telling me things. Constantly whispering. But, I don't know, when I saw you walk in, I knew it needed to go down differently this time. This can't keep spiraling out of control. I have to acknowledge that; take responsibility for it," he says, holding the hilt out for me.

I take the knife from Landry, holding it in the palm of my right hand. It's heavier than I thought it would be. It's sad to think this one small piece of metal extinguished the life of my dear friend.

"Landry," I sigh, "I know you're in pain, but killing you won't help. Not me, not you. Not when I'm this close to resetting time. And if I make it through the Beacon, something like that will stick with me. You're not Videus, and you don't have to be. I know right now it doesn't seem like it, but you have a choice. You *always* have a choice. The only one you have control over is you, and that's how it should always be. Don't you see? That's what the universe is telling you. Don't worry about the others. Focus on your inner state without trying to control everything else."

I fling the knife into the snow and rubble behind us. It clatters as it hits the ground, the sound reverberating around us as it disappears.

Landry blinks away his surprise, as anger and tears well in his eyes.

"I don't know how to live anymore," Landry admits, cupping his face with his hands.

"If this changes nothing with Fenton, you need to take things one day at a time. Stop expecting so much from yourself. Life isn't going to go back to normal. You'll need to find your way again. Fenton would want you to be happy," I say, reaching for his arm, "*I* want you to be happy."

Landry drops his hands, looking at me with surprise.

"After all of this? After all the pain I've done as Videus, you actually want me to be happy?" he says, his eyebrows pulling in.

"I do. Landry, you're a good man who was led astray. You have a chance at a redo. I know you'll make the right choice next time," I say, smiling.

"I just—I'm surprised," he says shifting his gaze from me to the Beacon. "I thought you'd happily kill me—that you'd want me to suffer. In fact, I banked on it."

"That's the difference between the two of us," I say.

He shakes his head, and I turn to face the Beacon.

For what it's worth, I'm no longer afraid to make this final leap. This resolution with Landry—the revelation that I don't want him dead, I never really did—it's enough to give me peace.

"You have to go inside it?" he asks, standing beside me.

As we stand shoulder to shoulder, the irony washes over me. Who would have thought I'd be standing here at the edge of the abyss and at my side would be the man who started it all?

"Yes," I say taking a deep breath.

"Is there anything you need from me? Anything I can do to help?" he asks.

I shake my head, "No, it's up to me now. But I do want your promise that you'll do better. That you'll push through the pain to see the other side."

"I'll do my best, Runa," he says. "I really will."

"Good," I say, patting his shoulder. "Goodbye, Landry. Take care of yourself. You're not alone."

Before he can respond, I leave his side and run into the beam of light.

23

RUNA

HE LIGHT SURROUNDS ME, blinding disorientation from every angle. I've felt like this before—as though I'm no longer me, but instead, part of the light. My consciousness is still oddly separate, though. It's a strange sensation.

After a moment, the searing white light subsides, and I feel myself pulled from the abyss as pieces of me slowly meld back together. No longer completely shattered, or disman-tled—instead, I'm becoming whole again.

The wind whips and howls loudly. My hair dangles, occa-sionally splashing up against my face. It's odd how I can feel my body, but am still slightly removed from it. Unable to move, unable to open my eyes—it's as though my soul is pouring back inside this vessel one drop at a time.

For a moment, it's nice to remain in this space—calm and waiting. My body sways from side to side in a movement very familiar, though I'm not sure why.

I never expected to feel myself again. I expected to enter the abyss and never come back. To allow the nothingness to wash over me and swallow up everything I was in order to make Pendomus whole again.

Suddenly, as if flicking on a light, memories of all I've done—what my friends and I have accomplished—our newly found comrades—the chance we have to heal Landry and prevent him from becoming Videus—each memory comes flooding back in rapid succession.

I open my eyes and lurch forward. The white light around me is as blinding, if not more so, than before. My physical eyes and body feel drained—tired beyond measure and I sink back into my cocoon. The air rushes up to meet me as I plunge downward, suddenly aware I'm not alone. I'm in someone else's arms. Once we've dropped, I feel a hand along the side of my face.

"I'm taking you to get help. Hang on for me, okay?" the man says.

I reopen my eyes, following his attempts to guide my gaze toward him. I take in all of his beautiful glory. His blue hair, his dark, concerned eyes.

My heartbeat quickens and elation washes over me.

I never thought I'd see him again.

And yet…things are still not fully righted.

The timelines are trying to repair themselves, to set things right. Flashes of the past, the present, and the future begin to jumble in an odd juxtaposition. It suddenly becomes hard to stay focused, as I try to sense which version I'm really in. Where I need to attend. Who I need to be.

"Runa, are you with me?" old Traeton from the future asks, blood running down the side of his head. His face is smattered in blood, ash, and dirt. Behind him, the forest burns. Everything burns.

"I'm so sorry, Runa. I'm sorry we couldn't stop this," he says, holding onto my limp body. "I need you to know that. And I need you to know how much I love you. I know things have always been difficult for us. Everything has gotten in the way. But I do. With all of my heart."

As the timelines flit back and forth, repairing and restoring themselves, I oscillate between the future and my past as they shift and realign. Trae's face changes each time I blink between bloody and damaged, to the man I first met in the woods.

I reach out, placing my hand along his jaw and running my finger across his lip. He doesn't know it yet, but when the timelines heal the way they should, he'll never experience this pain. This future will cease to exist. I can already feel it.

"You don't need to be sorry," I say, my voice barely a whisper. "I understand."

Searching his eyes, there's so much pain and angst hidden there. He has to know there's nothing to be sorry for. He wasn't in control of Caelum. Caelum wasn't even in control of Caelum. They tried—they tried until the end.

The one thing in all this world I know to be true is how much his presence means to me. How much I need him to be okay. How much his words send shockwaves through my soul because I know we can change everything and make a difference.

His dark eyes watch my every move, and I concentrate on them as the surroundings begin to flash between a fiery backdrop and the frozen wasteland. I try to hang on, needing him to know in his core how much I need him.

"I love you too," I say as the timelines seal together, resting on the day Traeton found me in the woods for a second.

My body feels so heavy, so disoriented, but I hope he understands.

Instead, he looks so confused—but I can't worry about that now. One day, maybe he'll understand.

Then this moment, too, slips away. The light consumes

me and I'm thrust back further, beyond anything I've seen in my own lifetime. I flash forward and back, bouncing from one event to another. As I do, the landscape and scenery on Pendomus shifts slightly—becoming just a little less civilized —a little less built up.

I watch the Helix go from the fully formed building, to slightly smaller, to being under construction. Then, completely missing.

The power in the bloodlines sends a message we're heading to one final stop. One mission I need to complete before stepping aside and letting it all go.

As the light pulls back, I'm laying on my back in the snow. It looks like the same old Pendomus, with a small exception; the sun is held higher in the sky. Not by much, but still noticeable.

I wipe the cold dampness from my face and sit up. The trees surrounding me look the same, but in the snow are inklings of white flowers buds. They're everywhere.

"It's over here. Ya gotta see it," a voice says nearby.

I search for the source and see two young men walk in the direction of the Tree of Burden. They're dressed differently, in bulkier clothing and hats on their heads. It's hard to tell anything else from here, but I get the distinct impression they're my mission.

I pull myself up to a stand and follow them. Surprisingly, there are others outside. In the distance, a group of children are building a snowman. Not far to my right is a couple kissing. The woman's back is against the tree, as the man leans in —both consumed by each other and oblivious to the rest of the world.

The younger man stops, surveying the area.

"Please tell me you aren't lost," the older one says.

"No, uh—just need to orient myself here," the younger says.

I shake my head and smile. Kneeling down, I pluck one of the little flowers from the ground. Twirling it between my fingertips, I'm mesmerized by its five white petals. They glimmer in the sunlight, giving off a subtle, but noticeable energy.

"What is it you want to show me?" the taller man says. "You could just tell me."

"You'll see," the other laughs. "Ah yeah, this way."

I hold the flower between my fingers and continue after them. My feet crunch loudly in the snow. I'm surprised it hasn't alerted them to my presence, but they continue on undeterred.

"It's the craziest thing. Every time I go out adventuring, I'm always finding new, amazing things. You really gotta get outside more often," the younger one says.

"Sure, I'll keep that in mind. There's a lot to do with getting this new technology I've been working on developed, but yeah—I'll get out and play in the snow with my little brother," the older one laughs, grabbing the other's hat and wrapping his arm around his neck. He pulls him in close and runs his knuckles across the top of his head.

"Hey, quit it, man," the younger one says, grabbing the other's arm and breaking free.

He stands tall, straightening out his jacket—his golden hair shining in the sunlight.

"C'mon Landry, I'm not twelve anymore, for phugsake," Fenton says.

"You sure? Ya kinda look—"

"Do not finish that sentence if you want to keep your toes," Fenton says, pushing Landry aside.

The two of them laugh. The sound is so carefree, and it's oddly unsettling, considering.

"Alright, we're almost there," Fenton says, his signature accent clearly missing.

I shake my head, not totally surprised. He always said it was just to impress the girls. Maybe he was telling the truth.

"God, I hope so. My feet are frozen," Landry chuckles.

"You're such a baby," Fenton says, leading the way.

We walk past the Tree of Burden, to wherever we're going. I stop to run my hands along its bark, then turn a full circle around its trunk. The gaping hole is missing. Instead, the enormous tree is completely solid.

"Hello old friend," I whisper, patting its trunk and continuing on.

The two of them walk all the way to the entrance of the Safe Haven's cavern system. No longer sunk in or destroyed, it looks almost the same as it had before. The only change is the entrance is closed off by two large boulders, rather than being open wide. A narrow walkway, barely wide enough to squeeze through is all that exists.

Hiding behind a tree, I pause, getting as close as I dare.

"Whaa-la," Fenton says, flourishing his hands.

Landry stops and makes a face. His eyebrow quirks up and he says, "Really? You brought me all this way for a cave?"

"Yeah. How cool would it be to build our home away from home in this? The temps would remain consistent, it's got great protection, plus, I like the darkness," Fenton says.

Landry stands still, a stoic look of almost boredom spreading across his features.

"C'mon, ya gotta come inside. Give i' a try, bro. Ya won' beyes dissapoin'ed," he says, a hint of his accent bleeding through.

"You're ridiculous," Landry laughs.

"I learned from the best," Fenton says, patting Landry's shoulder and heading inside.

"Don't ever do that accent again, and I'll check it out," Landry laughs.

"Deal," Fenton says, a gigantic grin spreading across his face.

With that, Fenton turns on his heel, clamoring over the boulders and through the tight squeeze.

Landry follows him in, shooting one final glance around the snow covered woods before ducking inside completely.

Torn, I wait for a moment, debating whether or not to follow them further. Surely they'd notice me if I did? The question is, would it matter?

Finally, I take the risk, acting on the hunch I'm meant to be here. To see something, or do something.

The darkness as I enter the cave is consuming the moment I walk in. Far in the distance, the ambient light from their handheld microLights are all I can see as they explore further on. Reaching into my pocket, I find it empty of my own.

"Looks like I'll be sticking to the shadows," I mutter under my breath.

The two of them explore the cavern, but it's far more rough than I've seen it. The tunnels lack their moulded shape, and all of the built in lighting is absent.

As we reach the area of the Haven, Fenton stops.

"Check this out, Landry. I could see this being a mainframe room," he says, holding his hands out and creating a square with his fingers.

Then he turns and looks in another offshoot.

"And over here, this could be a kitchen or something. Oh, wonder if there's another offshoot for a bedroom or two. I could get Trae in here with me. I'd need my own space, though. You know, for when I've got the ladies back at the locale," he laughs, jabbing Landry with his elbow. "We all know Trae'll be celibate until he's an old man. So I'm sure he'll need some book shelves or something for his virginity to collect dust."

Landry snorts, "Look, Fenton, this is great and all. But I really don't think it's necessary to have another home. I mean, c'mon, the Helix is nearly finished after all these years. We can finally get outta the Lateral and into someplace above ground. Why would we want to develop another cavern?"

My eyebrows shift downward—as confusion consumes me.

Helix is nearly finished?

I thought we'd been on Pendomus for centuries?

Then it occurs to me—that was the story of my timeline. One of the tangents Landry had taken us on.

"Why do you always gotta do that?" Fenton says, frowning. "I just want something to look forward to for once. Besides, maybe it connects to the Lateral. How awesome would that be?"

"I'm not meaning to disappoint you. But you have to know it's just a pipe dream. We need to get out of this planet's natural habitat in into our own. The locals could be hostile. Did you see those gigantic spiders the other day? They came outta nowhere, and tried to, I don't know what. They were damn scary. Not to mention the rumors floating around about an invisible beast. Pendomus isn't safe," Landry says, heading my direction.

I lean back, pressing my body against the cold stone, trying to remain hidden.

Fenton follows, his head hung in disappointment.

"It would be really cool, you know."

"I know," Landry agrees.

Not wanting to draw attention to myself, I hold as still as possible. I even hold my breath as they walk past me. Neither of them notice I'm here, both probably lost in their own thoughts.

When I feel there's a safe enough distance, I leave my

current location and follow them, sure to hang back in the shadows as we exit.

"Maybe I'll just go ahead and develop it on my own," Fenton mutters.

"It's up to you, I suppose," Landry says. "Lane likes it here, too. She keeps talking about how she'd like to remain in the Lateral," Landry says as they exit the cave.

"Well, I hope they do. It's not that there's anything wrong with the Helix—it's just, I dunno. Too sterile," Fenton says.

"I know it's not for everyone," he says, "but trust me, it will be great."

As I reach the cavern exit, in the distance is a herd of Waterbears. An actual *herd*.

My mouth drops open and I stare in awe. They're absolutely beautiful.

"You say that, but—c'mon Landry, look around you. This place is practically paradise," Fenton says, opening his arms out wide.

"Shhh—did you hear that?" Landry says, suddenly serious. He draws a finger to his lips, signaling to be quiet.

Fenton looks around, trying to see the source of Landry's concern—but it appears he doesn't see what he's looking for.

"What is it?" Fenton says, leaning in toward his brother.

"There's something here with us. It's those invisible monsters—I know it is," he says.

My eyes flit to the herd of Waterbears, not far from where they both stand. None of them are giving a second thought to the two men, crouched nearby. They lazily munch on the grass and sip water from the stream. Off to the side, two cubs wrestle playfully.

"You're hearing things, Landry—honestly, there's nothing here but us. I'll prove it," Fenton says, standing up and heading out into the clearing where the cubs play.

He swings in circles, "Hey—hey, anybody out here? Monsters? Are ya here to eat us both?"

As he makes another full circle, he trips over a rock, falling back on top of the two cubs, who cry out in surprise. Instantly, two of the Waterbears, probably the mother and father, come charging from the stream. Fenton scrambles to his feet, his face white and eyes wide.

"I just landed on something," Fenton says, putting his hands out in front of him. "Animals or something—they were soft."

"I told you," Landry cries, "I told you they were out here."

He whirls around, wildly trying to locate what he can't see. The two of them gather together, back-to-back, surveying the scene.

The mother and father charge—one veering off to help the cubs, the other butting in between the cubs and the two men. The howl the father releases is terrifying—and believe me, I know what it's like being on the brunt end of that, not knowing how gentle they really are.

Landry is the first to lunge forward, his fist connecting squarely on the male's muzzle. He recoils his hand, shaking out the shock.

"Holy hell—whatever it is, it's huge," Landry says.

The male takes offense, roaring again, and leaping forward. His front paws pin Landry to the ground—ripping open his trouser leg, and splattering blood in the snow. Instantly, Landry screams out in pain as he arcs back from the weight.

This is why the Waterbears were all but wiped out in my reality.

The realization hits almost too slowly as I watch Fenton clamber over his brother to attack the Waterbear. He swings wildly, trying to find the source of the attack.

The Waterbear rears up, its claws engaging for a fatal swipe.

In an instant, I know if I don't do something—if I don't act immediately—this will be the beginning all over again.

Racing forward, I reach out mentally to the Waterbears—letting them know to stand down. I use whatever form of persuasion I can, sending memories of Tethys, myself, and my friends. At the same time, I push out my gifts as far as I can—doing for Landry and Fenton what I did to Trae before. Only this time, I have to do it from meters away.

I gift them the sight.

The men recoil, blinking away the surprise of being able to see the Waterbear herd in all their glory. The shock is enough to stop the entanglement, as they scramble backward.

The male snorts, glancing briefly toward me, before leaving the men to check on the cubs. No longer interested in a fight.

"Who are—" Fenton begins. "What are—"

Before he can say the rest, I'm consumed again by the intense white light—I'm back in the mix of it all and no longer a part of history. I meld with the restructuring of time, allowing it to do it's magic on me as well—changing whatever necessary—and allowing me to keep the rest.

As the light pulls back again, I open my eyes and find myself sitting against the Tree of Burden.

With one simple, phenomenal change.

No longer are the trees completely barren. Or the woods filled with mountains of snow. Tiny buds unfurl from the branches—little bursts of green and gold.

At the base of the trees, large circles of brown grass is matted to the ground, with tiny green shoots making their way to the surface. From everywhere the eyes can see, unfurling from beneath the snowy blankets are thousands of white flowers. Their five petals tilt up toward the sunlight. The beautiful sun no longer locked in the sky, but currently located high up in the distance on the opposite side from where it had always been.

We did it. I did it.

Whatever may come now, whatever may be—it could only be made possible through these acts of rebellion and ... *revolutions*.

24

TRAETON

*W*ALKING THE GROUNDS OF the Acropolis, I'm still amazed at the sheer number of flowers blooming here. I've seen so many seasons come and go, but these hardy little white petals refuse to fade. Something about them has always impressed me. Maybe it's their hardiness. Or maybe even their iridescent colors. They just have a special kinda power rolling off of them.

I bend down, plucking one from the ground. I'm not sure why, but they've always seemed oddly familiar to me. I've lived here for the past five years, so you'd think it would be that. Hell, maybe it is—but it doesn't feel like it.

Keeping the flower pinched between my fingers, I continue to walk the grounds. The enormous trees sway in the breeze, their leaves gently tossing aside to allow the midday sunlight to stream through the branches.

Who would have thought humans would ever have been so lucky to find this place? Pendomus is like a heavenly variation of what Earth had become. I'm still so grateful, every single day my family decided to take the risk of coming here.

Who knows what would have happened to the four of us if we woulda stayed. We'd probably all be dead.

Among the trees, birds flit in and out. Little gray things we call Juncos because they remind us of the birds we had back home. But they call themselves AirGliders.

The grass out here is so green and the little white flowers definitely contrast against it.

"Though' I migh' find ya ou' here," Fenton says, coming up from behind me.

"You know me. There's something about being out here. It's not something I'm able to take for granted," I say.

"True dat," Fenton nods, then takes his yellow glasses off to clean them.

"Where have you been, anyway?" I ask, pushing him in the shoulder. "I thought you said we were going to go exploring again today. Did you and Kani get lost in your bedroom again?"

I laugh, knowing it's probably true. The two of them are practically inseparable. I'd never have pictured the two of them as a couple, but yet, here they are. Honestly, they're a good match until you have to listen to one of them going on about their prospective professions. If I have to hear one more talk about the sterilization of scalpels or how to tie in a mainframe to the planet's soul—I think I might puke.

"Well, as a matter o' fact, there mighta been some of tha' going on. When are you gonna put yerself ou' there an' find someone to smooch up to?" Fenton laughs, making a kissy face.

I roll my eyes.

"Not all of us are as obsessed as you are with the opposite sex," I say, chuckling.

"Sure, sure. Yer jus' repressed. Wha' ya need is a good romp wit—"

"Gentlemen," Delaney says as she approaches.

Fenton clams up, knowing his jab at my non-existent sex life was just ruined by the appearance of Delaney. Internally, I've never been more thankful to see her. Knowing Fenton, our entire conversation would deteriorate into a lesson on dating.

"Hi Lane, what's up?" I ask, turning from Fenton's disappointed face.

"Beautiful day, isn't it?" she says, deflecting.

"Lane," I warn.

"Alright, I need your help, Trae. Do you have a moment?" she says, eyeing Fenton.

Both she and I like to keep my arrangements with her separate from my ordinary life. While it's sorta a job, it's not at the same time. So it's nice to keep it all in separate baskets.

Fenton gives her a once over, raising an eyebrow and pursing his lips.

Lane's dark skin contrasts the cream colored top she has on today. It gives her a regal appearance, especially with the way she piles her dark curls on her head. The air about her is all business and I know better than to turn her away.

"Sure, whatcha need?" I finally respond.

I shoot Fenton an *'I'll come find you'* glance and continue to walk with her. Fenton takes the hint and turns stiffly on his heels. He raises a hand in the air, flicking me off as he heads back toward the Acropolis.

I can't help but grin.

"Yep, tha's fine. Wan'ed more SEX, anyway," he mumbles as he heads off.

Delaney watches him depart and waits until he's out of earshot before she smirks at me and shakes her head.

"He's never going to let you live alone, you know. He might be right. Get out and date once in a while," Lane says.

"Not you, too. C'mon Lane. Get to why you came out here to find me," I say, rolling my eyes.

"Alight," she nods, "Traeton, I know you've been at a bit of a loss lately. The Pillars and I need some help and I'm wondering if you'd be interested in an adventure," she begins. "Humans have been here for a while now and we're ready to expand our reach. We're interested in scouting out more of Pendomus and I think you'd be a good fit for this type of mission," she says. "You've never shied away from getting involved in the larger picture. I'm hoping I'll be able to count on you now."

I consider her words for a moment. This could be the exact change of pace, I need. Leaving the confines of our encampment here could be amazing. As much as I love it here—who knows what's out there. Exploring our boundaries has been an interest of mine, that's for sure.

"How long are you thinking the mission would last?" I ask, considering my sisters. I've never been away longer than a few days at a time. Though I'm no longer living with them, we're still so close.

Delaney shrugs.

"However long it takes. Could be days, or months. Honestly, it's really up to you. We're just wanting to learn more about what's beyond this place. We need topographical maps created and I can get you the equipment you need. Of course, Ash could go with you. Or perhaps I could find a lady friend?" she says, smiling.

I lower my eyebrows.

"Think about it. I'll get back to you in a couple of days. Sound good?" she says.

I nod, "Sure, Lane. I'll think about it. Might be fun."

"Excellent," she says, nodding back.

With that, she pats me on the back and continues on her way.

I walk away, my thoughts swirling around my new choice.

Who wouldn't love to explore more of Pendomus?

I'd be a fool if I said the thought wasn't utterly enticing. I've been hanging around Fenton on and off for nearly three years now and he'll manage just fine without me. Besides, he and Kani have their thing going now. They need a third wheel about as much as I need to be one. That's probably why he's been trying so hard to hook me up with random women. He wants the flat all to himself.

Maybe this could be for the best? It's not like I'd be gone forever.

Then again, my sisters won't like it—but they'll have to learn to live with it. Especially Ava. They're both getting older now and with my parents working with the Council, it's not like they don't have plenty of people to talk to.

I continue my walk, taking in the sights and enjoying the way the AirGliders flitter back and forth through the trees. Their chirping is cheerful as they follow me on my path. Fenton would never have let me take in the sights and sounds this way. He would have been talking the entire time, so I guess it's kinda a godsend that Lane interrupted.

Twirling the flower between my fingertips, I catch myself smiling. This day has turned out far better than I anticipated. New adventures on the horizon and all that.

Maybe this is the very reason I haven't found someone for me. Going on this mission, traveling the world. Who could do that sorta thing with someone left behind? I know for damn sure, I couldn't keep my mind in the game if that was the case. It would be too much.

I pass a large tree with wide, open branches that look like they could wrap around you with a massive embrace. Many of the trees here are ancient—far older than most of the trees that existed back on Earth. From what I hear, they're millennia old.

Walking up to the edge of the large stream that runs the

circumference of the Acropolis, I take a seat on the grass and cross my legs. I unfold the small snack I'd packed and look out over the water. There's something calming in the effect—watching the sunlight glitter across its moving surface.

"Alright, Trae—so what do you think? Should I go, or should I stay?" I say out loud.

A small junco flitters down from one of the trees, and begins to scritch in the dirt beside me. Its white beak pecking for something I can't see.

"Hunting for the unknown," I say, "Good idea, little guy. Head out on the trip it is."

Of course it was going to go that way.

"Hey, mind if I join you?" Landry says, walking up beside me.

His bald head reflects the sunlight and I shield my eyes.

"Suit yourself," I say, motioning to the spot next to me.

"Alright, so Lane just told me she let you in on the adventure. Whatcha thinking? You haven't told Fenton yet, have you?" he asks.

I shake my head, "No, just talked with her thirty seconds ago. Why?"

"Well, I don't want to spoil anything, but I think Fenton might take it kinda hard. He considers you to be like a brother, Trae. You know that," he says.

I snicker, "Sure, but it's not like I won't be back. He's not gonna care. He and Kani—"

"Are pregnant," Landry finishes.

"Say—say that again?" I say, my mouth dropping open.

"Yeah, he doesn't know yet. Kani asked me to keep it quiet for a few days while she figures out the best way to break the news. But, I thought you better know before you make a decision. He's gonna want someone to lean on, I think."

I blink my eyes, my mind suddenly flooded with images

of Fenton changing nappies and running after kids. It's scary, and oddly appropriate. He's like a gigantic kid himself.

"Wow," I say.

"I know. Crazy, right? I'm going to be an uncle," Landry nods, a satisfied sort of sigh escaping his lips.

"You're actually happy about this, aren't you?" I say.

"Well, yeah. Then Liana will have someone in the family to play with. I mean, unless Alina and I end up having another. I suppose that could happen. She's already hinting at it," Landry says, shrugging.

"What? Lia's only a year old. How can Alina already want another? Doesn't she realize all the kid does is eat, poo, and sleep?" I say, chuckling.

"Women, man. Who knows? Something about how she misses the 'baby phase' now that Lia's walking and chucking her food at the walls. I don't see it," he says, grinning.

"Sure. Whatever, man. I see it in your face. You're totally on board," I snicker, shaking my head.

"Seriously, though. I never knew how awesome being a parent was going to be. How fulfilling and amazing. I hope one day you'll know what that feels like, Trae."

My eyebrows raise, and I shake my head. I can't say I've given it any thought whatsoever. Kids? Me? I've got enough on my plate just keeping Fenton out of trouble. And now—with a miniature Fenton on the way, things are about to get far more interesting.

"I don't know. Not ruling it out, but I just don't see it happening. At least, not any time soon," I say. "But I'm more than happy to support all of you. Just call me uncle Trae."

"Speaking of which—think you could babysit tonight?" Landry asks, a big cheshire grin spreading across his lips.

"Yeah, sure," I say, my eyes attempting to roll around in their sockets. "You Tabet men think you're so clever. Don't think I don't know the manipulation techniques you're applying here."

Landry holds a hand to his chest in mock surprise.

"Why, Traeton Revasco, I have no idea what you're talking about.Whatever do you mean?" he says, blinking his eyes innocently.

"Yeah, yeah. Get outta here before I change my mind. I wanna spend a few hours in solace before getting covered in baby food and juice—while you and Alina have a nice night out," I say, smiling.

Landry stands up and pats my shoulder.

"Thanks, man. See ya at seven."

He walks away, knowing better than to say anything else. Just in case I change my mind.

I inhale deeply, taking a bite of my apple.

Wow. Fenton and Kani are pregnant, too. It's happening all around me. There must be something in the air. In my left hand, I twirl the everblossom again, watching it spin.

Circle of life, I guess. Good for them.

This doesn't change anything though, if anything, it makes more sense than before to take Delaney up on her offer. They'll want to use my room as a nursery. I'll go, explore, and find another place to stay when I get back. Simple.

With my mind made up, I finish my apple and chuck the core into the stream. One of the animals will enjoy the rest of it.

Pushing up to a stand, I walk the stream, straying further from the Acropolis. Out this way, it's usually so peaceful because only a handful of others will venture this far. Human curiosity only goes so far for some people, I suppose.

The light filters in just right, bouncing up from the floor of the stream, allowing me to see a small herd of Waterbears walking slowly, along the water's edge. Because of their iridescence, they can be hard to spot. They've got a tendency to blend into their surroundings with a natural camouflage, but they never travel far from water. Thus their name, I suppose. They're beautiful creatures and so unique. Nothing like them ever existed on Earth. Well, not that I know of, anyway.

Smiling, I follow the stream, watching the sunlight sparkle on the moving water. The stream itself weaves gently in and out of trees, meandering its way through the forest before looping back around to the base of the Acropolis.

As I continue walking, I notice a shoulder poking out from behind a tree. A young woman is sitting at the base of one of the more enormous trees. Surprised to see another person this far out, I walk toward her. I'm curious to know who she is and why she's willing to travel so far from the beauty of the Acropolis' courtyard.

"I'm going to head back. See you at home?"

A young man, roughly the same age as the woman stands up and begins to walk away. His hair is the same color as the woman's and their features are extremely similar as well—clearly siblings.

"Okay, Ammon. See you at home," she says. "Tell Dad I'll be there in time for dinner."

The young man nods, and then spots me. He tilts his head, and quirks an eyebrow, but continues walking, clearly unfazed. Guess I'm not too threatening holding my lunch sack.

The young woman sits still, her head down as she flips pages of a large book in her lap. The tree behind her has an aura all its own. The massive branches extend outward in all directions, with beautiful leaves of green, gold, and red. The dark trunk enhances the contrast of her light hair. It's so light it's practically white. Woven into the braids on the side of her head are bright purple strands of hair.

Nice.

I thought I was the only one these days who liked the more unusual colors for hair. Instinctively, I run my hand through the darn brown tuft at the top of my head.

I continue to follow the stream, throwing glances toward the girl. I don't know what it is about her that keeps drawing my attention. She's completely engrossed in her book—not once has she even looked up. The girl also has an aura around her, not at all unlike the regal stature of Delaney, or the subtle energy of the Waterbears. It's a gentle power, if such a thing exists.

Unable to help myself, I deviate from my course along the stream and make my way to her. As I get closer, I catch the iridescent light of a lone Waterbear sitting by her side.

The mysterious girl looks up at me, setting the book down in her lap. She gasps and her mouth drops open with a sense of surprise. She recovers quickly, though, setting the book aside and standing up.

Something in my core shifts, and it makes me feel uneasy. There's something about this girl. Something I can't quite put my finger on. Have I seen her before? Do I know her? No —I don't think so. I'd remember a girl with hair as white as snow.

I'd remember her.

"Hello, Trae," she says. "I've—I've actually been waiting for you."

Brushing aside her long white hair, she tucks a strand behind her ear and smiles the most beautiful smile I've ever seen. For a moment, I can't stop staring at her beautiful, flawless face. My heart skips beats and I take a step back.

Who is this girl? How did she know my name? Why was she waiting for me? Do I know her? Because I feel like I do— or I should.

All of these mysteries circle in my mind, but I can't take

my eyes off her unwavering gaze. She stares at me with the most intense, scrutinizing eyes.

One amber, one blue. *Both incredible.*

THE END.

NEXT UP—
The Final Five
An 8th Dimension Novelette

AFTERWORD

Thank you so much for joining me on this wild ride known as the Pendomus Chronicles!

Did you love **Revolutions**?
If so, please kindly leave a review for it or the entire Pendomus Chronicles Trilogy wherever you love to find books. It helps others like you stumble on this crazy, beautiful series.
You Rock!
Carissa

ALSO BY CARISSA ANDREWS

THE PENDOMUS CHRONICLES

Pendomus: *Book 1 of the Pendomus Chronicles*
Polarities: *Book 2 of the Pendomus Chronicles*
Revolutions: *Book 3 of the Pendomus Chronicles*

THE 8TH DIMENSION NOVELS

The Final Five
Oracle: *A Diana Hawthorne Supernatural Thriller*
Awakening: *Rise as the Fall Unfolds*
Love is a Merciless God

THE WINDHAVEN WITCHES

Secret Legacy *(Sept 8, 2020)*
Soul Legacy *(Oct 6, 2020)*
Haunted Legacy *(Nov 3, 2020)*
Cursed Legacy *(Dec 1, 2020)*

ABOUT THE AUTHOR

Carissa Andrews
Sci-fi/Fantasy is my pen of choice.

 Carissa Andrews is an international bestselling indie author from central Minnesota who writes a combination of science fiction, fantasy, and dystopia. Her plans for 2020 include publication of her highly anticipated **_Windhaven Witches_** series. As a publishing power-house, she keeps sane by chilling with her husband, five kids, and their two insane husky puppies Aztec and Pharaoh.

To find out what Carissa's up to, head over to her website and sign up for her newsletter:
www.carissaandrews.com

facebook.com/authorcarissaandrews

twitter.com/CarissaAndrews

instagram.com/carissa_andrews_mn

amazon.com/author/carissaandrews

bookbub.com/authors/carissa-andrews

goodreads.com/Carissa_Andrews